"We got company!"

Automatic fire erupted from the boulders, ringing against the metal shack and tearing geysers of dirt from the ground. McCarter crawled to the rear as a column of gunshots ripped at the earth near his legs. Encizo was next to him.

"I figure at least four opponents," Encizo declared as he peered up at the rocks.

"That's enough," McCarter replied. "They have rifles. I'm gonna try to flush them out."

But the enemy had a definite advantage. They had the high ground and were positioned about a hundred yards away—beyond accurate range of submachine guns or pistols, but well within effective rifle range.

"That does it," McCarter muttered, then suddenly rose to his feet and charged toward the boulders. "Cover me, mates!" he shouted as he ran, spraying 9 mm messengers before him.

Mack Bolan's

PHOENIX FORCE.

PHOENIX FORCE®

GAR WILSON

AFRICAN BURN

A GOLD EAGLE BOOK FROM
WORLDWIDE®

TORONTO • NEW YORK • LONDON • PARIS
AMSTERDAM • STOCKHOLM • HAMBURG
ATHENS • MILAN • TOKYO • SYDNEY

First edition January 1990

ISBN 0-373-61345-8

Special thanks and acknowledgment to
William Fieldhouse for his contribution to this work.

Printed in U.S.A.

1

"I think I could learn to hate Africa," Ken Forest complained as he swatted at his neck.

He looked at the red smear of the crushed insect in his palm and muttered, "Disgusting six-legged vampire," as he wiped his hand on his khaki shorts.

"He bit you, huh?" Dr. Saul Ebstein inquired with a wry grin. "Well, you killed him, so you more than settled the score. Not to worry, Ken. I saw it was justifiable homicide."

"Homicide only applies to killing human beings," Forest said sourly. "These bugs are eating me alive."

"They're attracted by the salt in your sweat," Ebstein told him as they trudged through the heavy ground cover of elephant grass, tall ferns and the occasional aboveground root.

"I can't help sweating in this god-awful weather," Forest replied, his voice dripping with misery.

"It's only eighty degrees," Ebstein stated. "That's not terribly hot. Rwanda actually has a very pleasant climate—one of the most agreeable in all of Africa."

Seko, their guide and translator, smiled at the Americans. His white, even teeth flashing in dazzling display against his dark brown skin. Seko walked to some oil palms and selected a young tree, barely as tall as himself. He tore several leaves from the tree and carried them to the Americans.

"Rub these on your skin," he advised, handing a couple of leaves to Forest. "Rub it on real good, and it makes the sweat less salty. Bugs don't bother you as much."

"What does it?" Forest asked as he wiped his neck and face with a leaf. "Is it the oil from the leaf?"

"I don't know why it works, but it works," Seko replied, amused that the Americans always wanted to know exactly why things worked. To Seko, nature was simply present. It was real and what it offered man was good. No explanations were necessary.

"Thank you, Seko," Ebstein said, accepting a leaf from the African. "Is it much farther to the lake, Seko?"

"Not much, Doctor," the guide assured him. "We would have been there by now if you had taken the usual route."

"True," Ebstein agreed, "but this way we can observe the streams and rivers that flow down from the north."

"Oh, yes," Seko said, tilting his head toward the north. "The volcanoes. I don't understand why we didn't go to the Kagera National Park or Karismibi Mountain. They are to the north. Near the volcanoes."

"What we need to determine is the likelihood that there are heated ground waters from sources flowing to Lake Kivu," Ebstein explained. "It doesn't matter if the water near the volcanoes are hot. Lake Kivu is what we're concerned with."

"I don't understand, but I suppose I don't have to," Seko said with a smile.

Ebstein shrugged. Seko did not see any reason to question the forces of nature, but Ebstein was a scientist and had a very different point of view. Seko didn't care that Lake Kivu was potentially dangerous. He did not worry that the largest body of water in his small country was probably the most gaseous lake of considerable size in the entire world.

People who lived near Lake Nios had not been terribly concerned either, until August 21, 1986. On that date, seventeen hundred villagers near the lake were killed by carbon dioxide gas. The world had been stunned when that story broke. For a brief time, the "Cameroon Tragedy" made major headlines throughout the world.

Most people had all but forgotten the incident, but Ebstein still remembered. He had been in Cameroon three days after the tragedy occurred. Ebstein had seen the rows of corpses in the village of Nios and nearby Cha and Subum. He and dozens of other toxicologists and limnologists had investigated the incident. They tested the air, water, soil and plant life. They exchanged information, theories and horrors. Eventually they understood why seventeen hundred people had died.

Ebstein also knew it could happen again, in Cameroon or Rwanda or anywhere else with the conditions that trapped the lethal pockets of carbon dioxide under Lake Nios. Nowhere was the potential for a similar disaster greater than Lake Kivu. The carbon dioxide level in Kivu was always high, but so far Rwanda had been spared the fate of its neighbor.

The toxicologist believed such a disaster could be avoided if the danger could be detected in time to prevent the series of events that led to the Cameroon incident. He also believed the summer months were the most likely for such a deadly natural phenomenon to occur. A less-publicized disaster had occurred near Lake Monoun, Cameroon in 1984. As in the Nios case two years later, the Monoun carbon dioxide deaths—which claimed thirty-seven lives—had occurred in the month of August.

Sometimes the understanding of nature could save lives. Ebstein intended to do so if possible. Ken Forest had never been to Africa before and he complained about minor hardships, yet Ebstein had worked with the young toxicology lab technician in the States and respected his ability for accurate analysis with simple field equipment. Forest knew what they were looking for, and Ebstein was confident his assistant would stop bitching and do his job when the time came.

"So this is life in the African jungle," Forest muttered as he followed Ebstein and Seko.

The comment forced Dr. Ebstein to suppress a grin. The area was a rain forest, but hardly deserved to be called a jungle. In fact, very little of Africa was actually jungle. The closest thing to a real jungle in Rwanda was the national park, where the majority of the exotic animal life lived, protected by law. For one with Ken's last name, Ebstein considered it amusing that Ken found a rather tame rain forest so formidable.

Maybe Ken was exaggerating the "hardships" of the trek because he was already fabricating a colorful story about his adventures in "darkest Africa." By the time he returned to America, Forest would probably add man-eating lions and nests of poisonous snakes. The truth would probably bore all his family and friends, so a bit of poetic license was understandable if necessary.

Ebstein felt that Africa did not need any exaggerations. It was poetry in nature and native customs. The beauty of the rain forest and the savannas, the snow-capped majesty of Mount Kilimanjaro and the vast sea of sand in the Sahara. The remarkable variety of Africa was a constant fascination to him. The wildlife, animals native to a world unlike any other on the face of the earth, never failed to impress the American. Africa was the home of many animals unique to it, and they had come to symbolize worldwide the vast continent teeming with color and life.

Perhaps most remarkable of all were the people of this great land. Many Africans lived in modern cities, with nine-to-five jobs and a life-style not unlike that of most Americans. Others lived in the same manner as their ancestors. They made their own clothes, built their homes, hunted or grew crops or fished in traditional ways. Generally they were friendly and relatively content with their simple way of life and tribal customs. More than three thousand ethnic groups are found in Africa. Christianity, Islam, Buddhism, Hinduism and hundreds of other religions, including numerous forms of animism and other local religions, saturated African beliefs. Marxism, too, as a belief, had made respectable inroads on the continent. Numerous African nations were Communist or socialist states.

Ebstein was always glad to return to Africa. He had visited five countries in the so-called "dark continent" and hoped to eventually see all the nations of Africa. Though that was unlikely, he still intended to try.

"The lake is not far, now," Seko announced as he pointed at a line of trees surrounded by a carpet of ground vines with large heart-shaped leaves. "See? Those plants only grow near water."

Ebstein gestured for Forest and the two Rwandian carriers who hauled extra packs with supplies to remain still. He strained his ears, but the forty-nine-year-old toxicologist's hearing was not as keen as Seko's.

The guide heard the sound and smiled. "Water," Seko declared. "Running water."

Forest also heard the musical trickle of running water. He approached the tangle of vines and stared down at the narrow stream. Forest removed his Australian-style hat and slipped out of his backpack harness. He knelt by the bank as the others stepped closer.

"It's running downstream from the north," Forest stated with a happy look. "From the volcanoes."

"We don't know that for certain," Ebstein corrected. "Not yet. We need to take temperature readings, water, soil samples and test the bed. Well, you know what to do."

"No sweat," Forest confirmed. "Seko? Will you tell the other guys to unload the rest of our gear?"

Seko addressed the porters in crisp Kinyarwanda, the most common Bantu language in Rwanda. They lowered the packs to the ground while the two Americans scooped out test tubes of water. They both examined the contents as if they expected the clear liquid to give them some sort of clue.

"No bubbles," Ebstein declared with a trace of relief in his voice, "but the water does seem warm. Too soon to say if it's from the volcanoes."

"If it is, there'll be traces of volcanic rock," Forest assured him. "Maybe even lava."

"The volcanoes have not been active for more than a year," Seko told them. "I doubt you will find anything."

"Active or not," Ebstein began, "volcanoes always generate some degree of heat and transfer particles into the water that passes through them. Considering the high level of carbon dioxide and methane gas in Lake Kivu, this can be very serious."

Suddenly from behind them came a man's grave voice. "Nothing is more serious than death, monsieur."

Ebstein and his group whirled toward the voice, startled to discover they were not alone. A large black man, dressed in green fatigues with brown camouflage markings, frowned as he looked at the investigative team through the dark lenses of gold-framed sunglasses. A brown beret was tilted rakishly on his head, and his brawny arms were folded on his wide, muscular chest. A button-flap holster hung on his belt.

Three other men stood behind the big African. Two were also black and were dressed in a similar manner. One held a machete in his fist, and the other pointed a compact machine pistol at the two Americans and their Rwandan allies. The fourth intruder was a slender white man with a lean face and a sour expression. He, too, was in uniform. Although barely more than five and a half feet tall and of a slender build, the white man had a pistol in his hand that made him as formidable as his comrades. A nine-inch metal cylinder was attached to the barrel of his weapon.

Ebstein had seen a few spy movies and police shows on TV. He had never seen a real silencer on a gun before, but he realized that's what he was looking at. In the films, silencers were short, stubby objects jammed on to gun barrels. The real thing was longer, a bit clumsy in appearance, but the black hole at the end of the silencer seemed serious enough.

"Massamba!" Seko exclaimed with surprise, his eyes fixed on the big man.

"Do you know this person?" Ebstein inquired, wondering whether they had somehow trespassed on private property.

"Massamba is fairly well-known in Kigali," Seko explained. He did not raise his hands, although the white gunman was pointing his silenced pistol at Seko's chest. "A rabble-rouser, you might say. He likes to start trouble, but he is all talk and no one takes him very seriously."

"You'd be surprised who takes me seriously, monsieur," Massamba declared with a smile as cold as a crack in an iceberg. "Henri knows I am serious. *Oui*, Henri?"

"Oui," the white gunman replied with a nod.

The silenced pistol barked, and a burst of flame appeared at the muzzle of the sound suppressor. Seko staggered backward, a bullet hole in his shirtfront. He gasped, more surprise than pain in his voice. Henri fired another silenced shot and got Seko in the center of the chest. The guide sank to his knees, fingers trembling as they groped at the bloodied holes in his upper torso. His eyes bulged in amazement and terror, and his mouth hung open in a scream that stayed unborn as he slumped across the bank and slid into the stream.

"My God!" Forest cried, tearing his eyes from Seko's still form to stare in shock at Massamba and Henri. "You killed him!"

"May I assume that means you take me seriously now?" the big African inquired calmly.

The man with the machete suddenly stepped forward and swung the big jungle knife at the nearest porter. The poor fellow was so stunned by Seko's death that he failed to notice the attack until it was too late. The heavy blade of the machete chopped into the front of his skull and split open

African Burn

his forehead with a single stroke. The porter fell backward, his life oozing slowly from the fatal wound.

The other porter hurled himself at the man with the machete. The knife man slashed a quick cross-body stroke, and the blade cleaved through muscle and bone. The porter screamed and stumbled away from his attacker, clasping his right arm near the wrist. Blood spurted from the stump where his right hand had been.

"Bastards!" Forest cried, his anger suddenly stronger than his fear. He sprang toward Massamba, his hands going for the big ringleader's throat.

Henri's pistol barked, and the muffled report was loud in Forest's ears as he lunged for Massamba. The American thought for an instant that he was hearing the shot that would kill him. But Forest had not been Henri's target. Instead, a bullet hole appeared in the forehead of the wounded porter, and the man collapsed beside his severed hand.

Massamba allowed Forest to close in and suddenly unfolded his arms to sweep them against Forest's wrists. The blow knocked the American's arms aside and nearly spun him off balance. Massamba stepped forward and grabbed a fistful of Forest's hair. The big African moved behind his opponent and snaked his powerful forearm around Forest's throat.

"Stop it!" Ebstein cried, baffled and terrified. "For God's sake, stop!"

"In a moment," Massamba replied through clenched teeth as he held on to Forest's neck and head.

The powerful black man's shoulders turned as he delivered a vicious twist. There was a cracking of bone, and Forest went limp in Massamba's grasp. The big man dropped the lifeless body onto the ground. The American's head rolled uselessly on the stem of a broken neck.

"Why?" Ebstein demanded, quivering in rage and fear. "Why are you doing this? We're trying to help..."

"I know why you're here, Dr. Ebstein," Massamba assured him as he stepped over Ken Forest's corpse calmly. "I know you have Rwanda's best interests at heart. You're an American toxicologist and, unfortunately for you, that's exactly what I've been waiting for in order to carry out a plan of my own that isn't quite as noble as your reasons."

"What are you talking about?" Ebstein asked. "What do you want me for?"

"Nothing personal, Doctor," Massamba began as he stepped forward, followed by Henri. The white gunman had stuck his pistol in his belt and removed a leather packet from a hip pocket as he approached. "I just need you to carry out a small but vital role in a sort of real-life drama. Now, don't make us chase you. That would really be pointless, Doctor."

"I don't know what you want from me," Ebstein said as he turned his eyes fearfully toward Henri and saw him unzip the packet to remove a syringe filled with amber fluid, "but I have no intentions of helping murderers like you carry out any sort of twisted plan."

"But you don't have any choice," Massamba replied with a sigh, as if bored by Ebstein's protests.

The American swiveled around and began to run. He splashed across the shallow stream to the far bank, his heart racing and legs pumping as hard as he could manage. Then two bodies hurtled on him from behind, bringing him down before he could flee farther. Ebstein struggled, but his opponents were younger and stronger than he. They easily pinned him to the ground.

There was a sharp jab on the side of his neck. The drug acted swiftly, and Ebstein could no longer try to fight. His consciousness rapidly slipped away as fear and confusion slowly melted into a black velvet pool of oblivion.

2

Calvin James stared up at the circlet of bone mounted on the wall above the bar. The yellow-tinted bone was nearly two feet in diameter, and the inner area was lined with triangular teeth. James shook his head and shuddered theatrically.

"What's the matter?" Rafael Encizo inquired as he sat on the bar stool next to James.

"You know what that thing is?" James replied, tilting his head toward the object. "That's a set of shark jaws. You remember what sharks are, man? We damn near got eaten by one last time I let you talk me into going diving off the coast of Florida."

"You know how rare it is to be attacked by a shark?" Encizo asked with a sigh. He raised a glass of beer to his lips and sipped a few drops before he continued. "About one chance in fifty million. It already happened to us once, so the odds must be even higher."

"That's crap," James insisted. "Sharks are like muggers. They can sense when you're from outta town. They'll get one whiff of me in the water and say, 'Chicago ghetto kid headed this way.' You know how everybody likes beef from the Midwest."

"How do they feel about chicken?" Encizo inquired mildly.

"You can kiss my ass, hombre," James told him. "How the hell did you ever talk me into coming here again?"

"I seem to recall it had something to do with some women I know," Encizo reminded him. "Speaking of which, I ought'a call them and see if they're interested in a night on the town.''

"Half the women you know are like sharks in high heels," James muttered, looking at a glass of scotch and water on the counter as if he forgot that he had ordered the drink.

"Nobody's perfect," Encizo said with a shrug.

The conversation did not sound as if either the tall black man from Chicago or the muscular Cuban was accustomed to risking his life in extremely dangerous missions that made swimming in shark-infested waters seem like a stroll in the park on a sunny afternoon. Yet Encizo and James were members of Phoenix Force, a top secret special operations commando team.

The five men of Phoenix Force had been selected from candidates throughout the entire world. Originally they had been a special antiterrorist unit, but their scope of operations had gradually increased to include missions against criminal syndicates and espionage conspiracies as well as other situations that required a small group of highly trained professionals to accomplish what armies and conventional intelligence networks could not.

The hubbub increased in the tavern, and Calvin James glanced around with some interest. Being aware of one's surroundings was a fundamental character trait of men in a profession such as James's. The tavern was similar to dozens of other small watering holes along the Florida Bay. The bar was a simple wooden counter with a polished, smooth top and a rather limited selection of drinks. A plastic replica of a swordfish was mounted on one wall, along with an amateurish watercolor painting of a sailboat at sea with gulls that resembled Vs in the sky.

Several men and three women were in the tavern, seated at the tables or on the bar stools. Most were Hispanic, and the others were black. James and Encizo fit in perfectly, except the other patrons seemed to follow a type of voluntary segregation. Hispanics sat with Hispanics and blacks with blacks. A couple of the men looked at the two Phoenix Force commandos with contempt, as if they had violated some unwritten code of social behavior.

The separation of the two ethnic groups had more to do with differences in culture and language barriers than racial prejudice, though a degree of distrust and resentment existed between them. The Spanish-speaking patrons had various origins. Some were natives of Florida, but most came from Central America, Cuba, Colombia or Bolivia. The black customers were Jamaicans.

Two of the women watched Encizo and James with professional interest. The men were strangers, new faces in the tavern. The ladies of the evening recognized the regulars at the bar, and they guessed the Phoenix pair were out-of-towners. Both men wore casual but good quality clothes. The hookers had developed a second sense for "reading" men, which was a necessary talent for women in their line of work; they didn't want to pick up a vice cop or a sadist who enjoys getting his kicks from beating up women—or worse.

Despite their aptitude, they did not find James and Encizo easy to read. The tall black man glanced in their direction but didn't seem particularly interested. He was a nice-looking guy, late twenties or early thirties with a lean athletic build. Ramona, the younger hooker, tended to associate people with movie stars. Calvin James reminded her of a cross between Billy Dee Williams and Richard Roundtree. Maybe he was less handsome than either actor, but James had that curious animal magnetism or charisma or whatever that makes some men very appealing to women.

Although the well-defined cheekbones, clipped mustache and intelligent dark eyes seemed pleasant enough, James also had a dangerous quality Ramona could not quite put a handle on. She figured he might be a cop, but he didn't seem to follow the usual behavior of plainclothes police—up tight or too-nonchalant-to-be-real.

Rafael Encizo was slightly shorter and more heavyset than James. He was also fifteen years older, although Encizo did not appear to be older than thirty-five. Ramona thought

Encizo looked like a Cuban version of Burt Reynolds. Handsome, prone to smile and generally in good humor, Encizo could be very charming and had little trouble attracting the opposite sex. The aura of danger was even more pronounced in the Cuban than in James, which of course made the pull stronger. Yet there was also a trace of sadness in Encizo's eyes, and the lines etched around his full mouth suggested he had known great grief and suffering.

The two women were partly correct. Calvin James had been a member of the Special Weapons and Tactics team of the San Francisco Police Department before he joined Phoenix Force. James had actually been recruited during a SWAT operation for his first mission and remained with Phoenix Force ever since. Rafael Encizo had indeed known grief and suffering. He'd been a youth when Fidel Castro seized power in Cuba, and his family had been accused of "crimes against the state." Exactly what these "crimes" were supposed to have been remained a mystery to Rafael Encizo, since his family had never been involved in politics. Young Rafael's parents and older brother were killed, his younger siblings taken away for reeducation. Captured during the Bay if Pigs invasion, Rafael had been a political prisoner, half-starved, beaten and tortured, until he managed to escape.

They had also guessed correctly about a sense of danger associated with both men. James and Encizo had faced death hundreds of times, survived a thousand battlefields and lost count of how many men they had killed. Of course, the two prostitutes were in no danger from the Phoenix pros. Their enemies were fanatics, conspirators and terrorists who threatened human lives and entire nations.

James noticed Ramona and Maria as he glanced about the room. The ex-cop guessed their occupation. Both women wore a lot of eye makeup and lipstick. Maria's outfit consisted of something resembling leather tights with a plunging V neckline, and Ramona wore a tight red sweater and a miniskirt short enough to reveal the garter straps to her fishnet stockings. James found them neither appealing nor repulsive. He thought hookers were sad. They sold sex because they didn't have a legal job skill. Most had such low self-esteem they wouldn't consider themselves good enough to deserve a better life than hustling tricks.

He had seen women like these all his life, from the ghettos in Chicago to the streets of Saigon and a dozen other cities in almost as many countries. James thought that everybody might be better off if they legalized and regulated prostitution as he had seen in other countries. Busting hookers used up time and man power the police could better use against more serious crimes, and the working girls would be subject to medical checks and legal age requirements. Presently nobody came out ahead except vicious pimps who didn't mind getting girls hooked on drugs to control them, used teenagers to get customers, and didn't give a damn what venereal disease the girls might pass on to their johns.

However, the subject was not a major concern for James one way or the other. The men in the bar did not seem even vaguely interested in James and his partner. A couple of Jamaicans argued about where they were going to go after they left the tavern. Three Hispanics, dressed in overalls and boots, discussed their jobs with the city and whether or not their union would go on strike.

Another group of Spanish-speaking customers made James a bit uncomfortable. Eight men had gathered around two tables shoved together. They were well dressed in expensive sports coats, genuine leather jackets, silk shirts and gold jewelry. A number of them wore sunglasses or hats, and the eyes of the men without dark lenses seemed hard, reptilian. James noticed more than one bulge in jackets that suggested some of them, if not all, were armed.

"I saw them, too," Enzico whispered, gazing at the mirror behind the bar.

James raised his drink, sipped a little scotch and glanced at the bartender. The man was wiping shot glasses with a stained towel. He didn't seem to care who his customers were, and maybe he didn't want to know.

"Those suckers are hoods," James muttered, his voice barely loud enough for Encizo to hear him. "I can just smell it."

"They don't seem interested in us," Encizo replied. "Local problem. We'd better not get involved. Got our own security to think of, and we're not equipped to get mixed up with anything while we're here."

James shrugged. He knew the Cuban was right, but he didn't like the idea of a bunch of low-life hoods, probably dope dealers, sitting less than a dozen feet away and being unable to do anything about it. Still, he wasn't sure they were criminals, and he knew that a lot of people who look respectable enough are utter slime. James had a personal reason to hate drugs and anybody who dealt in narcotics, but his gut feelings had been wrong before and he was not about to start busting heads unless he knew he had the right person.

Besides, trying to bust the head of somebody who is probably packing heat is an invitation to a fast and violent death for somebody unarmed. James and Encizo were not armed. That was a rare condition for any member of Phoenix Force, but they had flown to Florida on a commercial flight just to brush up on their frogman skills and get in a little scuba diving for pleasure. There had been no reason to expect they would need weapons, and smuggling guns through airline security was a greater risk than there seemed to be reason for.

Encizo placed a hand on James's shoulder and slightly inclined his head toward the door. The best thing they could do was to leave and find somewhere else to spend their time. James nodded, and both men started to rise from the bar stools.

But before they could head for the door, three men entered the tavern. Two wore baggy suits, white shirts and striped ties. Their haggard features identified them as police officers as surely as the gold badges clipped to the breast pocket of each man's jacket. The third man was in full uniform.

"Guerrera?" one of the plainclothes officers began in a hard, authoritative voice. "I'm Detective Barton. This is Detective Rodriguez and Officer Gonzales."

"Hey, man," a heavyset guy in a pink sports coat, scarlet shirt and several gold chains began as he slowly rose from the group clustered around the two tables. "I'm all impressed. You even got a couple spic pigs to visit me."

"Who you calling a spic?" Gonzales, the uniformed officer, growled. "You Colombian piece of—"

"Don't waste your breath on this guy," Barton told the uniformed cop. "Come on, Guerrera. We want to have a few words with you at the station."

"Am I under arrest?" Guerrera demanded, hands held out with palms upturned in a display of innocence. "What's the charge?"

"Just want some questions answered," Barton explained. He glanced at the faces of Guerrera's companions and looked over his shoulder at James and Encizo. "You guys goin' somewhere?"

"We were about to leave," Encizo replied. "We're not with that group your friend Guerrera is part of, so I don't know why you'd object if we go now."

"Just hang around until I tell you otherwise," Barton ordered. He turned to face Guerrera. "You'll probably want to call your lawyer. Guys like you always do."

"Constitutional right, man," Guerrera stated.

"You're not under arrest, sleaze bag," Detective Rodriguez reminded him. "You don't need your lawyer."

"He has a right to have his lawyer present during questioning," Barton told the other cop. "There's nothing incriminating about a fellow wanting to have his legal rights, so don't get on his ass, Rodriguez. We don't want to give this guy anything to bitch about."

"Well, I bet Guerrera's amigos here are breaking a few laws even if he isn't," Rodriguez declared. "Parole violations? Associating with known criminals and fellow ex-convicts? Maybe some weapons or drugs. I'd say we have ample cause for search and seizure considering the criminal records some of these lice have. I busted Santiago once myself and I know Morales and Trujillo have served time for a couple felonies each."

"Fuck you, pig!" one of Guerrera's companions snarled as he jumped from his chair and yanked a snub-nosed .38 from his belt.

The police were caught off guard, startled by the action. Rodriguez had made the comment about searching the henchmen with Guerrera as a warning, but the hood had taken the threat seriously. Obviously he was committing enough parole violations to go back to the joint for a long time or he was unstable and a little crazy or, most likely, a combination of both.

"Santiago!" Guerrera cried, as surprised by his comrade's reaction as the police were. "No, Santiago!"

Guerrera's voice was all but lost in the roar of the .38 revolver. Santiago fired two shots point-blank into Detective Barton's chest. The plainclothes officer staggered backward, his mouth open, eyes wide as if astonished that he had been shot. Barton turned to stare at Rodriguez with an expression of accusation plastered across his features. Rodriguez gazed back at his partner, horrified, aware that his actions had triggered Santiago's violence.

"Dumb b-ba-s..." Barton rasped as his knees buckled and he fell to the floor.

The detective's white shirt was drenched with blood as he attempted his final act on earth. Barton pawed at the Smith & Wesson snubnose holstered on his belt. He managed to draw the revolver from leather, but a boot slammed into his forearm and sent the gun skidding across the floor. Barton uttered a sound that could have been a sigh of disappointment. It was the last sound he would ever make.

Ramona and Maria gasped and pushed their table over as they hit the floor. The prostitutes were survivors. They had been in tough places before and reacted with speed and efficiency that would have done justice to a combat veteran. They ducked behind the cover of the tabletop and stayed low while other customers panicked and bolted for the door.

Santiago, the trigger-happy killer, swung his .38 toward Rodriguez. The detective was still stunned by the death of his partner and didn't even look up from Barton's corpse until the gunman's weapon was pointed at his face. However, another member of Guerrera's group suddenly slapped a backhand stroke under Santiago's wrist to knock the gun toward the ceiling. The .38 discharged and drilled a hole in the plaster and wood overhead.

Rodriguez snapped out of his daze and reached for his service revolver. A short, ratlike hood quickly closed in and swung a fistful of blue-black steel made by Colt. The slide of the .45 autoloader smashed into Rodriguez's face and knocked him to the floor before he could draw his pistol.

Officer Gonzales yanked his revolver from leather, but another goon had already drawn a 9 mm Star autoloader from a shoulder holster and pointed it at the uniformed man. A bar stool suddenly crashed into his skull before he could squeeze the trigger. He collapsed across the table, blood oozing from a smashed temple.

"¡Madre de Dios!" a Colombian low-life near the man exclaimed as he stared into the face of Rafael Encizo less than two feet away.

The Cuban Phoenix Force warrior turned sharply with the bar stool still in his fists. The startled hoodlum reached for a .380 Astra Constable at the small of his back, but the stool slammed into his face before he could draw the gun. The blow lifted him off his feet and dumped him unconscious on the floor.

Santiago tried to point his snubnose at Encizo. In a pure reflex action, Gonzales had opened fire and pumped two .38 slugs into the man who had shot Detective Barton. Santiago fell backward, triggered his weapon and blasted a useless bullet through a plate glass window. Gonzales shot the gunman once more and drilled a .38 round through his abdomen. Santiago screamed and thrashed about on the floor, then soon shock and loss of blood overpowered him.

Encizo ducked low as two Colombians swung their weapons toward him. They held their fire as the Cuban vanished under the table. Suddenly another bar stool hurtled across the room and crashed into the pair. Struck in the face and chest, the two gunmen fell backward and tripped over their own chairs to tumble to the floor. Calvin James had thrown the stool as he rushed forward, then the black commando dove to the floor. He shoulder-rolled next to the Smith & Wesson snubnose that had been kicked out of Barton's grasp. An enemy bullet plowed into the floorboards near James's hurtling figure, but the warrior hardly noticed as he landed in a kneeling stance and grabbed the dead policeman's revolver.

Guerrera dumped himself out of his chair and landed near Santiago's corpse to grope for his handgun while two of his men scrambled to point weapons at James and Officer Gonzales. Rafael Encizo suddenly rose up from under the table and flipped it over, smashing the top into the two gunmen. The Cuban ducked low once more and scooped up a dropped Star autoloader.

James triggered the .38 snubnose and fired two rounds into the upper torso of a confused Colombian who was unsure who his targets were. A 125-grain bullet shattered the man's breastbone and drove him back three steps. James rose from the floor and pumped another round into his opponent. The second bullet punched through the Colombian's heart, and he toppled lifeless to the floor.

Another would-be assassin swung his pistol toward James. Encizo triggered the confiscated Star pistol and blasted a 9 mm parabellum slug into the gunman's shoulder. The man screamed as the high-velocity projectile severed nerves and tore into bone and cartilage. The gun popped out of the man's hand, and his arm spun in a wild backstroke action. Encizo fired two more 9 mm rounds and saw the gunman fall to the floor.

James rushed the Colombians, firing the borrowed S&W revolver as he ran. The enemy was still confused and disoriented, and they were not accustomed to such demanding situations, especially fighting on equal terms. James realized that if they continued to hit the hoods with a strong offensive from different directions, the odds were in their favor.

Another member of Guerrera's thugs swung his stainless steel Magnum toward James, but the black warrior fired first. A .38 slug burrowed into the man's right biceps, making him cry out and drop his Magnum just as another triggerman pointed his pistol at James. James fired the snub gun, and Encizo did likewise at virtually the same instant.

The man went down, blood spurting from the mortal wounds. The one that James had shot in the arm reached for something in his pocket with his other hand. Calvin James didn't figure the man was looking for a cigarette. The Phoenix pro stepped closer and launched a high roundhouse kick to his opponent's head. The Colombian's skull snapped back from the blow, his knees folded and he dropped like a stone.

Guerrera remained in a kneeling position, using the capsized table for cover from the Phoenix pair. He held Santiago's revolver in unsteady hands and pulled the trigger. A bullet struck Officer Gonzales in the right thigh. The uniformed cop screamed and his leg swung out from under him. Guerrera tracked Gonzales's fall with the barrel of the snubnosed weapon and pulled the trigger again.

The hammer clicked and the firing pin struck a spent cartridge. Guerrera had fired the last round from the 5-shot .38 revolver. He cursed under his breath and stared at Gonzales, who was thrashing about on the floor, with both hands clutched to his thigh. Gonzales was helpless, Guerrera realized. The policeman had dropped his gun when he fell. The hood discarded the empty firearm and, when he spotted another .45 autoloader, he crawled up to it. As Guerrera reached for the pistol, a tense smile stretched across his broad face.

"Guerrera!" a voice cautioned in a hoarse whisper.

He glanced up and saw Detective Rodriguez less than two feet away. Rodriguez had sat up, and there was a dark bruise on his cheek and a trickle of blood at the corner of his mouth. Rodriguez held his Colt snubnose in one hand and pointed the gun at Guerrera's face. The smile vanished from Guerrera's features as the Colt roared and a .38 bullet smashed through the bridge of his nose to pierce the brain.

The last hoodlum cried out as a spray of Guerrera's brains splattered his face and shirt, then he thrust his empty hands overhead in surrender. He slowly stood in full view of Encizo and James. The Phoenix pair trained their pistols on him.

"That's it, man!" the man announced, his accent more Tampa Bay than Bogota. "I give up! You win!"

"Step away from the table," James ordered. "Walk backward and keep your hands up. You even breathe suspiciously and they'll be cleaning pieces of you off the ceiling."

The hood obeyed and slowly stepped away from the table. Encizo approached him, the Star autoloader pointed at the guy's chest. The Cuban smiled at the thug and raised the pistol as he stepped closer. The hoodlum's eyes, fixed on the black muzzle of the 9 mm weapon scant inches from his nose, widened with fear.

"Don't shoot me, for Crissake!" he begged. "You cops can't go round shootin' people after they give up . . ."

"I'm not a cop," Encizo replied.

Without warning, the Cuban lashed a boot between the man's legs. Gasping in agony, the man doubled up from the kick. Encizo grabbed his hair with one hand, yanked his head forward and slugged him behind the left ear with the butt of the Star pistol. The hoodlum collapsed unconscious at Encizo's feet.

The silence that followed was almost sinister. The ears of the survivors were ringing from the aftermath of the gun battle. Detective Rodriguez slowly rose from the floor, still dazed and not quite certain what had happened. He glanced about, stunned by the collection of bodies on the floor as James and Encizo calmly went about checking them for signs of life.

"Hey, fella," James began, gesturing at Rodriguez, "Three of these guys are still alive. One has a fractured skull and seems to be in a coma, but the other two ought to be cuffed."

"Uh..." Rodriguez nodded awkwardly. "Yeah. Gonzales is hurt..."

"I'll take care of him," James assured him. "You just snap the cuffs on. More cops are probably on their way, but you might want to call them after you take care of those two."

"Yeah," Rodriguez agreed with another mechanical nod. "Who are you guys?"

"Public-spirited citizens," Encizo replied as he walked to the bar.

The bartender carefully poked his head up from behind the bar. Encizo reached for the cloth on the counter, and the barman fearfully ducked out of view again. The Cuban sighed and moved along the bar to where their drinks were still sitting.

"It's okay," Encizo told the bartender. "I just need to borrow this rag for a minute or two."

Ramona and Maria glanced out from their cover behind a table and watched the Cuban wipe off the glasses with the bar cloth. The prostitutes decided the danger was over and the best thing to do was to leave before more of the law arrived. Encizo smiled at the pair as he held the Star autoloader in one hand and pressed the magazine catch. The clip rom the magazine well at the butt dropped out, with two parabellum cartridges still loaded in the mag.

"Why don't you two ladies hang around for a while and volunteer some information to the police?" he inquired as he guessed what the pair had in mind. "They might appreciate a witness or two."

"We got our own problems, mister," Maria replied. "Why don't you stay here and play witness for the cops?"

Encizo worked the slide and a 9 mm round hopped out of the breech. He locked the slide back and wiped the frame and trigger of the empty pistol. That done, he shrugged nonchalantly. "We have our reasons, too," he declared. "Okay. Take off. Watch who you associate with. It can be a dangerous world."

"Yeah," Ramona commented. "That's what they tell me."

As they headed out the door, there came the wailing of police sirens in the distance. The Phoenix Force commandos would have to hurry. They couldn't afford to be questioned by the police or, even worse, the newspaper and television reporters who would also swarm to the aftermath of a violent encounter.

"Hey!" Rodriguez exclaimed as he saw the women depart. "Why'd you let those two go?"

"Because they wouldn't be willing witnesses," Encizo replied. He placed the empty Star pistol on the counter and strolled across the room. "They'd say they didn't see or hear a thing. Besides, they figure the police would probably haul them in as well or use the information about where they live, phone numbers and even their names in order to go after them later. Sad thing is, they're probably right."

"Don't tell us the department wouldn't try to take advantage of a situation like that, either," James commented as he knelt beside Officer Gonzales and finished tying a tourniquet around the cop's wounded thigh. "Sorry I don't have anything for the pain."

"Me too," Gonzales said through clenched teeth.

"You lie still and try to stay calm," James instructed a he guided the man's hand to the broken chair leg that held the improvised tourniquet bandages in a pressure-on posi tion. "Just hold this thing. It's tight enough to keep the bleeding down. Don't twist too tight or you'll cut off cir culation entirely. The bullet missed the femoral artery You're not gonna bleed to death if you just stay put and don't get the blood pumping any faster."

James raised his head as Encizo approached. The Cuban held out a hand, and James offered him the borrowed Smith & Wesson. Encizo nodded, stepped back and pressed the cylinder catch. He dumped the spent shells from the cham bers. James had fired all five rounds during the battle. The Cuban wiped off the cylinder, frame, trigger and guard.

"That gun belonged to the dead officer," James an nounced as he placed a hand on Gonzales's shoulder. "You're gonna be okay, man. I was a corpsman in the Navy. Seen lots of dudes shot up in Nam. I'm sure your leg hurts like hell, but you won't die and you won't lose the leg, so try to relax."

"Thank you," Gonzales replied with a feeble nod.

Rodriguez watched Encizo place the revolver on Bar ton's chest, cylinder still open. The Cuban stepped away from the body and James rose to his feet.

"Did you cuff those two guys?" James inquired.

"Yes," Rodriguez answered. "I found a bag of white powder on one of them. I suppose some of the others were carrying cocaine, too. Probably why they reacted the way they did. God, I shouldn't have set them off..."

"What's over is over," James declared. "Call an ambu lance for your buddy. He needs more medical care that I can give him now."

"Okay." Rodriguez stared at the empty revolver on Bar ton's chest. "Why did you do that? Wipe off that gun and put it there?"

"It was his gun," Encizo said. "First I cleaned off my pal's fingerprints. Wiped off the pistol I used, too, as well as the glasses we had our drinks in."

"What?" Rodriguez looked at them with astonishment. "Why? You two are heroes..."

"We gotta go," James announced. "And we can't answer any questions. Sorry, man. We got our reasons."

"I can't let you leave," Rodriguez began, his tone reluctant. "You're witnesses to the shooting of a police officer..."

"The only way you can stop us is to shoot us," Encizo told him. "I don't think you'll do that."

"Dammit," Rodriguez muttered through clenched teeth.

"Go call that ambulance," James suggested. "You'll be busy, and you won't see us leave."

"I owe you guys," Rodriguez admitted. "I'm gonna make that call now."

He headed for the public pay phone at the opposite side of the room. Rodriguez kept his back to the tavern entrance as he reached inside a pocket and fished out some change. He took his time sorting through the coins until he selected a dime and two nickles. Rodriguez didn't want to waste too much time, because Gonzales needed medical attention.

The detective glanced over his shoulder. The two mysterious warriors were gone. Rodriguez sighed. He wondered who they were and what they were. Maybe they were criminals of some sort themselves or fugitives. But if they were, it was strange. They rescued policemen and took out armed hoodlums as easily as most men swat flies. If those two were crooks, Rodriguez wouldn't mind if half the population of west Florida was that type of crook.

Maybe they had some other reason, he reasoned, wondering if they were DEA agents working undercover, wanting to keep their identities secret. Why would they want to keep that a secret from the police? Were they worried about

crooked cops on the force? Rodriguez didn't know if his line
of thought made any sense. It was never general knowledge
what DEA, FBI or any of those intelligence outfits were up
to.

Whoever they are, Rodriguez told himself, they saved his
life, and he didn't really give a damn what they did when
they were not bailing out cops who were about to get their
butts shot off by goddamn dope dealers. The detective in-
serted the coins in the telephone and dialed the emergency
number.

"I'm gonna have to write up a report on this," Rodriguez muttered as he jammed the telephone receiver next to
his ear and listened to the muffled ringing on the line.
"They're never gonna believe what happened. I'm not so
sure I believe it myself."

3

akov Katzenelenbogen walked barefoot to the sink. He
urned the spigot with his left hand. Water flowed as he
icked up the bar of soap with the same hand and rubbed it
cross a washcloth. Katz returned the soap to the dish and
athered up the cloth again, then held it under the water and
orked the cloth with his thumb and fingers.

This was one of the inconveniences Katz had learned to
ccept since his right arm had been amputated at the elbow
lmost two and a half decades ago. Washing his hand was
n action that still seemed odd at times. The stump of his
ight arm often moved methodically with the rhythm of the
eft as if the ghost of his missing limb still tried to carry out
is fundamental act.

Katz glanced up at the mirror. His reflection was that of
man in his mid-fifties. Iron-gray hair, clipped short, blue
yes set in a face that seemed at least ten years younger than
is true age. Katz's lips often smiled, but the expression was
enerally fleeting and his eyes seldom reflected it. Not that
atz was without a sense of humor. Many things amused
im, but as often as not Katz smiled to reassure others or to
ask his true thoughts. Occasionally irony made him smile,
r some painful memory stirred and forced some sort of re-
ction. A smile was better than tears.

He had known tears and grief through the years. Knew
hese things better than most. Yakov Katzenelenbogen had
een born in France, the son of Russian Jews who had fled
heir homeland due to the oppression of the Communist re-

gime. But new and even more terrible things were to follow
as Adolf Hitler and the Third Reich swept across Europe
like a tide of destruction and madness. The Katzenelen-
bogens were regarded as upper-class Jewish intellectuals and
were accused of being Communist agents working for Stalin. The Nazis arrested Yakov's family and packed them off
to a concentration camp. Yakov would never see them
again.

Barely twelve years old, he joined the resistance and
started on a career in intelligence, espionage and covert
warfare that would continue for the rest of his life.

Katz later worked with the American OSS during World
War II. When the Nazis were defeated, Katz moved to Pal-
estine to join the battle for the creation of the state of Is-
rael. He soon became a top intelligence officer and
battlefield commander. Katz lost his arm and a son during
the Six Day War, but this disability didn't chain him to a
desk job.

He looked at his reflection again and thought that he was
not much for dwelling on the past, but occasionally life offered some compensations—among them the ability to act
on what he believed in. Katz recalled the early days that led
to his current position as unit commander of Phoenix Force.
He finished washing his hand, turned off the water and
reached for a towel. Katz dried his hand and pulled the right
lapel of his house robe across the left. The lapels were lined
with Velcro, which was a wonderful invention for somebody with only one hand. Velcro made some of these tasks
a little easier.

Katz opened the door and stepped from the bathroom.
He padded across the carpet toward the bed. The room was
dark, but slender slivers of pale light entered from the window, falling across the face of Julia Kyler. The gray streaks
in her reddish-brown hair appeared almost white in the half
light. She turned her head on the pillow to face Katz.

"I was afraid you might vanish from the bathroom," she
declared as he approached the bed. "The way you're al-

ways rushing off on another mysterious assignment, I never know when you'll be gone again."

"Well," Katz began as he took a pack of Camel cigarettes and a Ronson lighter from a robe pocket. "You've always known I have a top security job that I can't really talk about."

"You shouldn't smoke, Yakov," Julia said with a sigh. "I know I've told you about this before . . ."

"Just every time we get together," Katz confirmed as he sat on the edge of the bed, a cigarette between his lips. "But I appreciate your efforts to save me from myself."

"I see people at the hospital every day who are dying of cancer, heart disease, respiratory conditions," Julia continued. "Maybe you ought to take a look at some of the cases of lung cancer, or heart troubles to which smoking can seriously contribute. There are a host of health problems that are caused or aggravated by smoking."

"Sounds quite morbid—like a horror show," Katz said, lighting his cigarette. "Will I have to pay for tickets to get to look at this stuff, or can you get me in free?"

"That isn't funny, Yakov," she replied as she propped a pillow under her shoulders to sit up and pulled on the sheet to cover her breasts. "Smoking is a serious health hazard, but I suppose you already know that."

"I guess I do a lot of things, which are a health hazard," Katz stated. He puffed the cigarette and placed it in an ashtray on the nightstand.

"Yeah," Julia said dryly. "I know you do."

She didn't know exactly what Katz did for the government, but she knew it was extremely dangerous. Dr. Kyler had first met Katz when he was a patient at the St. Michael's Medical Institute in Arlington, Virginia. Katz had been injured by an explosion, temporarily blinded by the blast. She had gotten more involved with Katz than she'd intended. It hadn't been very professional, but she had never met anyone like Yakov Katzenelenbogen before.

Julia soon learned how treacherous and deadly Katz's world could be. Two neo-Nazi fanatics had tried to murder Katz in his hospital room. Yakov had made many enemies, Julia realized, and whatever he did for Uncle Sam meant he would make more. Katz did not talk about his missions, but she knew the assignments were very high risk. Every time Katz left for another mission, Julia knew, the odds were high that he wouldn't return.

However, they had seen each other whenever their busy schedules allowed them a few hours together. For two years their occasional romance had continued. Julia told herself many times that it was foolish to keep seeing Yakov. Their relationship would always be awkward and strained, scant hours scattered among long months.

Yet she hadn't met anyone who could replace Katz. She was highly motivated and dedicated to her profession and career, which was her first priority. Many men couldn't accept that. More women accept relationships with workaholic men, but rarely the other way around. But Katz always understood. He was career motivated, too, but one day his profession would get him killed and they both knew it.

"How long will you be in Arlington, Yakov?" she asked.

"I don't know," Katz answered. He took another puff from the cigarette and crushed it in the ashtray. "A couple days before I have to report in."

"Gotta check with M, huh?" she remarked.

"Something like that," Katz said with a nod. "Although I might have to leave immediately if something unexpected comes up."

"I know, I know," she said with a sigh.

He stretched out on the bed beside her, his bathrobe still in place. Katz had always been a modest man. Middle-aged and somewhat thickened around the waist, he was even more modest about his body, although he was in better physical condition than most men half his age.

"You also know I can't change the way things are, Julia," Katz stated. "Even if I wanted to quit, too many old enemies from the past would still be looking for me to settle old accounts. I have to be careful just meeting you like this.''

"We've been through this before," Julia said wearily. "For now, at least, I'll accept the way things have to be. I don't know how much longer I can put up with it."

"I understand that," Katz assured her. "And I'll understand when the time comes for you to say goodbye."

"I sort of always thought you'd be the one to break it off," Julia remarked.

"Don't count on that," he said with a half smile. "This arrangement works better for me than it does for you. And we do enjoy it, don't we?"

"I can't deny that," she admitted as she moved closer and pressed her lips to his.

The phone rang as they kissed. Katz held the embrace while it rang the third time and stopped. Julia was pleased that he hadn't disengaged and held him close. His arm snaked around her shoulders to draw her closer.

"It will ring again in five minutes," he whispered.

"Oh, God," she muttered. "One of your spy-guy signals?"

"Security is a big part of my business," Katz replied.

"So, you have to leave?" Julia asked.

"In another hour or so," he confirmed.

"So, let's make the most of that hour," Julia whispered as she pulled on the lapel of his bathrobe. The Velcro parted with a characteristic ripping sound.

GARY MANNING held the pistol in both hands, his right hand supported by the left in a firm Weaver's Grip. It was a handsome weapon with a satin-chrome finish. He had not fired it before, but the TZ-75 was similar in design to other handguns he had used in the past. He peered through the sights at the target and squeezed the trigger.

The first 9 mm parabellum round pierced the dark green, man-shaped silhouette twenty-five yards away. Manning adjusted his shooting glasses and examined the target with a pair of binoculars. The bullet had struck a bit high and to the right of center. He heard the sharp report of another 9 mm pistol at the next stall. The Apache ear protectors spared him the ringing headache of exposure to gunfire within a confined area. Manning raised the pistol, aimed and fired once more.

The next shot was better, almost dead center. He got off three rounds, rapid fire. The shot-group was clustered close, about two inches. He continued to squeeze off shots until he burned up the ten remaining rounds. Manning checked the target with the binoculars. At least three rounds were dead center and the rest were pretty close. He grunted with satisfaction.

Manning favored rifles to handguns. He could drive nails with his FAL assault rifle on semiauto and a good scope at two hundred yards. The pistol, however, was a primary defense weapon for close range and could be carried in circumstances that didn't allow him to use the long arm. Skill with handguns was necessary for a member of Phoenix Force.

A big Canadian, muscular and as strong as a bull moose, Manning had no trouble handling the recoil of the most powerful weapons, but every member of Phoenix Force carried a 9 mm handgun, because the caliber was international and parabellum ammunition could be found anywhere in the world. All team members also used a common cartridge in case they needed to share ammunition.

Manning pressed the catch and dropped the spent magazine from the TZ-75 autoloader. Following the basic firearm safety, he left the slide back the reveal the empty breech. Manning stepped back and watched David McCarter in the next stall.

The tall, lean Briton fired his Browning Hi-Power at another silhouette target. He exhausted his ammunition, removed the spent magazine and set down his pistol with the slide locked back, just as Manning had done. McCarter turned to face Manning. The Briton's foxlike features displayed a wry grin as he slipped the Apache earmuffs from his head and stepped forward.

"So how's that new nine mill?" McCarter inquired, taking a pack of Player's cigarettes from a shirt pocket. "Italian version of the Czech CZ-75, isn't it?"

"Yeah," the Canadian replied. "Handles pretty well. For now, I think I'll stick with the Walther P-5, but I might switch over to another piece if I can find one I like better. You want to try it?"

"I've used the Browning for years, mate," McCarter stated, lighting a cigarette. "Never found a better pistol, yet."

"Browning holds thirteen rounds," Manning remarked. "The TZ-75 has fifteen. So do a lot of the other double-action nine millimeters that you turn your nose up at."

"Not much difference between thirteen rounds and fifteen rounds," the Briton stated. "Not if you make your bullets count. Care to take a look at the targets now?"

"Hell," Manning muttered. "You're showing off again, aren't you?"

McCarter grinned as he walked to his stall and pressed the switch at the left side of the bench. His target rode forward on an overhead wire. It reached McCarter, and he tore it off the brackets. The Briton cheerfully handed the target to Manning. The center had been chewed out by so many rounds it was impossible to say how many hit dead center. The middle of the silhouette's head had also been punctured by a close set of bullet holes in the area that would have been between the eyes of a human being. Not a single bullet had missed one of these two shot groups.

"I hate it when you do this," Manning complained.

"Hell, you're better than I am with a rifle," McCarter said with a shrug. "And I don't mess about with explosives if I don't have to. You love to blow things up. Best demolitions man in the business. That ought to be enough to keep your ego intact when you witness a true master pistol shot like myself.''

"And you're modest, too," Manning muttered. "Still, you might try that TZ-75. The design is very similar to the Browning, and you'd have more ammunition.''

"It's a double-action auto," the Briton said, shaking his head. "I just don't care for that type of pistol. Too much gimmicks, if you ask me. Put the double-action in an automatic and you install something else to go wrong and make her jam. The Browning is a single-action auto.''

He tapped a finger on the bullet-torn head of the silhouette target and added, "That suits me just fine.''

The door of the firing range opened, and two familiar figures entered. When Calvin James and Rafael Encizo reached them, Manning and McCarter smiled and shook hands with their partners. All four men were close friends, bonded by the common experiences of battlefields and years of teamwork.

"I thought you blokes were in Florida," McCarter remarked.

"Something came up, and we decided we ought to cancel our plans," Encizo replied. "Good thing we did. Hal met us when we arrived and said we got another mission.''

"Why didn't he tell us?" Manning wondered aloud. "He knew we were down here at the range. There's an in-house phone here.''

"He just got off the phone with the President when we arrived," Calvin James explained. "We volunteered to deliver the message as sort of a surprise.''

"Don't you like surprises, Gary?" McCarter inquired, tapping the silhouette target again.

"Oh, shut up," Manning muttered. "Is Yakov here?''

"He's in Arlington, so it won't take him long to get here," Encizo answered. "Hal already gave him a call to signal him. If he's at the apartment, he'll know to make contact. If Hal can't get him that way, he'll use the beeper again.''

"Yakov didn't respond to the beeper?" Manning was surprised.

"Hal thinks Yakov is probably with Julia," James said with a smile. "Maybe he stuffed the beeper in a drawer and was somewhat distracted when it signaled. Easy to ignore a little 'beep-beep' in the company of a lovely woman, especially after time spent apart. At least, it's always been that way for me. By the way, Rafael, you never did get in touch with those women you were talking about."

"We'll try another part of Florida some other time," the Cuban promised.

"Next time I go with you, I'm taking along my Beretta and a bulletproof vest," James muttered. "Whenever I go someplace with you, I almost get killed."

"You ought to be used to that by now," Encizo said with a shrug.

"Yeah," James admitted, "But having people shoot at me is too much like work. I shouldn't have to do that when I'm off duty."

"Sounds like something interesting happened in Florida," McCarter commented as he gathered up his Browning pistol and shoved a fresh magazine into the well. He slid the Hi-Power into a shoulder holster rig under his wrinkled sports jacket.

"Knowing you, I think you would have enjoyed it," Encizo stated. "But for now I won't tell you because I can't wait to find out what Hal has in mind."

"Let's go," McCarter said in agreement, and clapped the Cuban on the shoulder.

4

"Hurry up," Hal Brognola growled from behind the cigar butt jammed between his teeth. "Your mission is on the eleven o'clock news."

"Oh, hell," Calvin James muttered as he hurried to the conference table in the Stony Man War Room. "It always makes me real uncomfortable when we have a top secret mission that everybody knows about."

Encizo, Manning and McCarter also settled themselves down. Brognola had switched on a wide-screen television set mounted on a wall. A local anchorman for a Virginia television station was saying something about a tragedy in Africa as a map appeared on the screen behind him with the small country of Rwanda colored red and surrounded by yellow countries labeled Zaire, Uganda and Tanzania.

The scene changed to a network television report from Rwanda. A village of adobe dwellings with tar rooftops, surrounded by green foliage, appeared on the screen. Several black Africans, dressed lightly in cotton clothing, lay in the dirt streets. They appeared to have fallen asleep, sprawled across the street, until a closer shot revealed wet mucus at their mouths and nostrils. A network reporter's voice accompanied the grim footage.

"It happened at dawn this morning," the voice began dramatically. "This quiet little village along Lake Kivu in Rwanda became the site of tragedy. One hundred and four people lived in this village. Now they are all dead. Men, women and children, slain by a cloud of carbon dioxide that blanketed an area of at least two square miles this morning."

The village vanished from the screen to be replaced by a scene of dozens of dead cattle strewn across a grassy meadow. The reporter explained that the animals had also died from the carbon dioxide fog. A couple of close-ups revealed that birds and small mammals had also been victims.

The reporter himself, with microphone in hand, finally appeared on screen. James thought he looked out of place a little at the scene of the tragedy with his styled hair and immaculate safari-styled clothes. He continued in a grim but monotone voice. Behind him was a hospital with two ambulances parked outside.

"People in neighboring villages along the Kivu became ill this morning," he explained. "Some passed out, a few are in a coma and doctors here say their odds of recovery are no better than fifty-fifty. However, these villages were lucky. As terrible as this tragedy is, it could have been far, far worse."

The scene changed once more to a lake set in a crater, surrounded by rock and tropical foliage. Beneath the lake yellow letters bore the legend: August 21, 1986.

"Cameroon," the reporter's voice began. "One thousand, seven hundred people died when a similar incident occurred at Lake Nios."

Yakov Katzenelenbogen entered the War Room. The others nodded and waved him forward. The Israeli joined them at the table. He wore a tweed suit, turtle neck and his favorite prosthesis. The artificial arm that filled his right sleeve was made of plastic and steel with three metal hooks for "fingers." The device could do almost anything a human can do and a few things flesh and bone fingers cannot. Katz took a seat at the table as the report concluded.

"The people who live near Lake Kivu are afraid that the terrible poison cloud of nature may return," the reporter said. "No one can predict when the volcanic gases will

combine with the lethal formula to once again spell death
for the innocent people of Rwanda.''

Brognola hit the remote control and switched off the
television. He turned to face the five men of Phoenix Force.
They had played out this scene many times in the past seven
years, ever since Stony Man was created. It seemed like a
lifetime ago to the highest placed federal agent in the United
States.

Stony Man had started as a top secret organization to
utilize the unique skills and combat experience of a single
man—Mack Bolan, also known as the Executioner. The incredible one-man army had successfully fought the criminal octopus of the Mafia for more than a decade. Though
Bolan was forced to operate outside the law, the President
still realized he was the best man to help America in a war
against a ruthless and evasive enemy that threatened civilization itself.

International terrorism was the new monster that worried the President. Conventional military and intelligence
organizations had had only limited success against terrorism. A new approach was needed to combat the barbarians
of the twentieth century. Bolan's success against the Mob
convinced the President that he was the right man to spear-
head the new war against terrorism.

But even the Executioner couldn't do that alone.

Hal Brognola became the chief of operations for Stony
Man. Due to his past association with Bolan and his high-
ranking position in federal law enforcement, Brognola was
the ideal choice for the job. He became the middleman for
the organization and the President. Two elite new commando units were established to help Bolan and Brognola
combat terrorism. Able Team consisted of veteran warriors
of Bolan's campaigns against the Mafia. Phoenix Force,
however, was assembled from the ranks of the best trained
and most experienced antiterrorist experts in the world.

Their role had changed since Stony Man was first established. The super-secret organization soon discovered ter-

orism was often connected with enemy espionage and
anatical conspiracies. Criminal syndicates and political
ealots were also associated with the minions of terror. The
:ommando squads, especially Phoenix Force, often had to
nvestigate and dig out the truth about who was responsible
or enemy actions. They had become experts at sorting
hrough the murky data to find the reality behind the threats
o American lives and American interests throughout the
vorld. At times intervention of a certain kind was needed,
ather than a confrontation with terrorism, and it required
a small unit of highly skilled professionals who could keep
absolute security and do whatever was necessary to get the
ob done.

"So our next mission concerns this incident in Rwanda?"
Katz inquired, taking out his cigarettes.

"Yeah," Brognola confirmed as he took a seat at the
ead of the table. "Did you catch enough of the broadcast
o know the details?"

"I heard about it on the car radio on my way here," Katz
answered. "Apparently the deaths of the villagers aren't the
esult of natural disaster as the news claimed. Correct?"

"We don't know for sure," the Fed began, "but what we
lo know is disturbing enough. A CIA source has reported
hat the Rwandian authorities discovered a small shed by a
iver leading into Lake Kivu, less than two hundred yards
rom the village. Two dead Americans were in the little
building. Carl Brandworth, a low-level employee with the
State Department attached to the American embassy in
Rwanda, and Dr. Saul Ebstein, a toxicologist who was in
Africa to study the effects of volcanic gases or whatever in
he lake. Supposedly he suspected the same thing could
appen at Lake Kivu as what occurred in Cameroon in '86."

"Looks like he was right," Manning commented.

"That's not the disturbing part," Brognola continued.
"Inside the hut were two large tanks with pipes that ex-
ended into the river and all the way to the lake. The tanks
ontained a combination of powdered magnesium and so-

dium and there were powerful pumps to feed the solution into the lake through the pipes.''

"Sodium is explosive in water, and magnesium will burn like a Roman candle,'' remarked Manning, drawing on his demolitions expertise. ''But I don't know if it would work well enough underwater to cause an explosion.''

"It would in Lake Kivu,'' Calvin James declared. ''I've read that it contains a high level of methane gas as well as enormous volumes of carbon dioxide.''

"That's right,'' Brognola said with surprise as he checked his printout sheets. ''How did you know that?''

"*National Geographic* had a detailed article about the Lake Nios incident in Cameroon that included information about Lake Kivu,'' James explained. ''A limnologist named Curt Stager, if I remember right, did a fine job investigating the lakes. As a chemist, I was interested in the Cameroon tragedy, so I remember the article fairly well.''

"You mean this disaster in Rwanda was caused on purpose, Hal?'' Encizo inquired. ''And they think Brandworth and Ebstein did it?''

"That's what some people think,'' the Fed answered. "There are some very hostile voices claiming it is some sort of CIA plot. Brandworth was a translator, not with the CIA, and Ebstein has no connection with the Company and never did. Poor bastard was apparently trying to help Rwanda protect itself from something like this. Of course, they both died from carbon dioxide fumes along with the villagers.''

"Jesus,'' McCarter growled, shaking his head. ''CIA wouldn't have anything to gain from butchering innocent people like this. Women and kids? Bloody hell! I don't know why anybody would do something like this.''

"Well,'' Brognola began. ''The President wants you to find out who is responsible. Somebody wants Rwanda to think the United States has gone into the genocide business in Africa. Needless to say, relations between our country and Africa could be ruined by something like this. I don't need to tell you guys that African politics can be pretty damn unstable at the best of times. The Soviets and the Cubans have been active in that part of the world for years, and a hell of a lot of African countries are already Marxist and linked to the Soviet Union."

"The Russians are supposed to be our buddies now," Encizo said, his voice filled with sarcasm. "Haven't you heard about *glasnost* and all that stuff?"

"Yeah," the Fed replied with a nod. "I remember SALT and détente and a bunch of other notions that were supposed to signal the end of the Cold War, too. They usually ended with Russian tanks rolling into Poland, Czechoslovakia or Afghanistan. I don't know if the Soviets are involved with this or not, but somebody is trying to set us up. Uncle Sam is still on good terms with Rwanda and most of its neighbors. We want to keep it that way."

"To say nothing about having two innocent Americans accused of mass murder," Katz added. "Or letting whoever did this atrocity get away with it. No one who slaughters more than a hundred innocent people should be allowed to walk free."

"They shouldn't be allowed to live," James stated, his ebony features as hard as stone.

"That's okay, too," Brognola replied with a firm nod. "You guys handle this any way you can. Any way you have to. Just remember, the mission isn't revenge. If you just kill whoever is responsible and you don't prove that the U.S. wasn't involved, then that means America, and probably most of Western Europe, will be on very bad terms with at least one African country and in all likelihood a few others as well. A small Third World nation like Rwanda needs foreign trade for the sake of its economy. If they quit dealing with us, they'll turn to somebody else. *Glasnost* or no *glasnost*, the Soviets have a long history of moving in on vulnerable African countries and enlightening them about Communism with the barrel of an AK-47."

"Yeah," Manning agreed. "The Portuguese had barely pulled out of Angola before the Russians and the Cubans moved in. Same thing happened in the Congo, Mozambique and a few others I can't recall offhand. A small country like Rwanda, it could happen overnight."

"Africa has the greatest natural resources of any continent in the world," Brognola said. "Right or wrong, that's the main reason both the Soviets and the United States have an interest in African politics. If Africa falls under Communist control, we lose and so does Africa. It's that simple."

"So let's get packed for our trip," Katz announced. "Obviously we need to get to Rwanda as quickly as possible."

"I'm getting your transportation and contacts in-country taken care of now," Brognola assured the commandos. "Now, I know you guys are the best and you don't need any advice from me about taking care of yourselves, but bear in mind this may be a very hostile environment. I don't know how much cooperation we can expect from the Rwandian government or how the people might react if they even suspect your connection with the U.S. government. There's also the problem of the media to consider. American television news is already there, and you can bet newspeople from about a hundred other countries will be present too. Trying to maintain security with TV cameras all over the place can be damn near impossible."

"As long as it's only 'damn near' and not totally impossible, we should be able to pull it off," McCarter said with a shrug. "We've always managed to do it before."

5

The French airliner landed at Kigali International Airport. The five men of Phoenix Force were among the passengers. They had taken a military flight to France and, thanks to Stony Man's connections with the Oval Office, immediately boarded a commercial plane to Africa. A phone call from the President of the United States to the president of France had arranged for the Paris authorities to wave the commando team through customs. The majority of the passengers deplaned at Kenya. Few had any desire to go on to Rwanda.

When Katz and his men disembarked, they saw that a large group of demonstrators formed a ring around Kigali airport. They brandished signs written in French and English that accused the United States and the CIA of murder. A dummy, made of old clothes stuffed with straw, hung from a T-shaped post. A sign with the American President's name hung around its neck, and protesters spat on the effigy and shook their fists at the crudely drawn paper face.

A small black man, dressed in a white shirt, khaki trousers and a straw hat, stood by the customs section. A pipe with a curved stem hung from the corner of his mouth. He drew the pipe from his lips and raised it to his eyebrow in a modified salute. Phoenix Force headed toward the man.

"Mr. Kagera?" Katz inquired. He shifted his briefcase to his right arm and clasped the trident hooks of the prosthesis around the handle.

"Yes," the black man replied in slightly nasal English. "I didn't have any trouble spotting your group. Welcome to Rwanda."

"I think we might have gotten a pretty nasty greeting if we arrived on an American plane," Gary Manning remarked. "We saw some of the demonstrators outside the fence. They seem to be all the way around the airport."

"Oh, yes," Kagera confirmed. "They're putting on a show for the media. News reporters from all over the world are here. My little country seldom gets much attention. I think perhaps I like it better that way. When your luggage comes through, I'll instruct customs to leave it unopened."

"We got some stuff in there that we wouldn't want to declare," Calvin James commented dryly. "How bad is the situation here?"

"Over a hundred Rwandian citizens were killed," Kagera answered. "All things considered, I wouldn't say the situation is any worse than there is reason for it to be."

"You sound as if you think the claims that the U.S. or CIA is responsible for those deaths are true," Rafael Encizo remarked.

"Let's say I have an open mind on the subject," Kagera replied with a shrug. "I believe your luggage has arrived."

They collected their gear. Most of their equipment was stored in large aluminum suitcases and duffel bags. Each man also carried a briefcase. Burdened with their luggage, Phoenix Force followed Kagera outside. The African led them to a Volkswagen minibus. Some of the demonstrators just watched the foreigners with suspicion, but two surly-looking men approached them.

"Où est la pharmacie la plus proche?" Katz asked Kagera. He glanced over his shoulder and looked at the demonstrators as if surprised to see them. *"Bonjour. Comment allez-vous?"*

"Très bien, merci," one of them replied with a nod as he gestured to his companion to withdraw.

The pair joined the others while one of the protesters set fire to the effigy of the President. A cheer went up as the dummy began to burn. Phoenix Force and Kagera calmly finished loading the luggage into the bus and climbed inside. Kagera sat behind the steering wheel and started the engine.

"Do you really want to go to the pharmacy?" he inquired.

"No," Katz replied. "I just thought it would be better if those fellows heard us converse in French instead of English."

"A wise decision," Kagera agreed as he drove toward the parking lot exit. "By the way, your French is excellent. It is one of our official languages, you know."

"Well, I don't speak French," Encizo admitted, "but the rest of team speak the language. Giraudeau also speaks some Swahili."

"Kinyarwanda is a Bantu language that is rather different from Swahili," Kagera stated. "I assume Giraudeau is the black member of your group?"

"That's the name I'm using," James answered with a sigh. "Gonna take me a while to get used to being called Giraudeau. We figured it wouldn't be a good idea to use U.S. passports, and I wound up with a Martinique cover identity to go along with a French passport."

"We figured Americans wouldn't be too popular right now," Encizo added.

"That is something of an understatement," Kagera said dryly as he steered the VW onto Kayibanda Avenue.

Considering that Kigali was the capital city, it didn't have much traffic. A bus rolled along the avenue, and a few cars, apparently more than a decade old, traveled the streets. A traffic cop, with white helmet and matching gloves, stood at an intersection and made rather elaborate hand signals to the drivers. That hardly seemed necessary. A traffic jam in Rwanda seemed about as likely as a snowstorm.

Many Rwandians pedaled bicycles along the street, but the majority traveled on foot. About one third of the pedestrians were barefoot. Most were in Western-style clothing, but some were dressed in colorful dashikis. Men and women wore dashikis and many of the women also wore bright head scarves. The majority of the men were bareheaded, but a few wore headgear similar to a skullcap or a flat-crowned fez.

Street merchants pushed carts piled high with merchandise along the sidewalks, while in the markets a variety of fresh foods were displayed. Rwanda is largely an agricultural country and grows crops that range from arabica coffee to sweet potatoes. Most of the surrounding buildings were not large, but construction of new buildings was in progress throughout the city.

"Yes," Kagera remarked as he drove past a pair of farmers with an ox-drawn cart. "We are a quiet little backward country, aren't we? You Americans must find Rwanda very quaint."

"Nobody said anything against your country, mate," McCarter told him. "Maybe no one explained this to you, but we're here to help you blokes."

"Of course," the African replied, his tone sarcastic. "Our president was contacted by your President. He, that is the president of Rwanda, agreed to let you people come here and promised that our government would cooperate with you in every manner possible to try to find the truth about the deaths at Lake Kivu. Since I happen to be the assistant director of the Rwandian National Security Services, I was ordered to see to your group personally. I also happen to speak English as well as French, Kinyarwanda and Swahili. I'm also semifluent in Kirundi and Lingala."

"And you think we're here to get the CIA off the hook," James said. "Right?"

"I don't understand that expression," Kagera admitted, "but if you ask me if I believe your only interest is protecting the reputation of the United States, the answer is yes. I doubt anyone cares much about the lives of some Rwandian villagers except Rwandians and perhaps other Africans who may fear they might face a similar fate."

"I'm sure you've already been told that Brandworth and Ebstein, the two Americans found in the shed near the lake, were not CIA," Katz began. "That happens to be the truth. You may not believe us, but I fail to understand what reason the CIA would have for murdering the villagers. By the way, we do care about the crime itself, although you probably don't believe that, either."

"We Africans have learned that Westerners don't always tell the truth," Kagera remarked. "Your people tend to regard us as backward and expendable. The CIA may have decided to poison the village simply to see if it could be done. Maybe they plan to do the same thing to some lake in the Soviet Union or Nicaragua."

"Well, sounds to me like you met a few bad apples, and now you can no longer tell the good guys from the bad ones," Calvin James said with a sigh. "Just don't screw us up, because we've got a job to do."

"That job would have been easier if they'd kept a lid on the story about those dead Americans and the shed with the tanks of sodium magnesium and pumps," Manning commented. "Of course, we knew that little secret couldn't stay that way for long. Not with the media swarming all over a country the size of Rwanda."

"I thought you Americans believed in freedom of speech," Kagera said with some irony.

"We believe in freedom of speech," Katz assured him, "but there are times when making certain facts—or apparent facts—public knowledge can endanger lives and make it difficult for people like us to find out who is responsible for atrocities such as the Kivu incident."

"The public may have a right to know," McCarter added, "but we'd rather they didn't know *right now*. Not until we get this mess sorted out."

"At least you fellows sound sincere," Kagera remarked, although he didn't sound convinced.

THE VOLKSWAGEN DREW CLOSER TO the American embassy. A large mob of demonstrators had gathered outside the building, waving signs and shouting angry curses. Rwandian soldiers formed a barrier to keep the protesters at bay. Members of the press shuffled about with cameras and microphones trying to get the best angles to cover the event. After taking stock of the situation, Kagera stopped the minibus about two blocks from the embassy.

"I don't think you want to get any closer," he remarked. "The crowd isn't violent, but that could change. Even Massamba may have trouble keeping them in control if we drive up and try to enter the building."

"Massamba?" James inquired as he craned his neck to get a better view of the demonstrators.

Then he spotted Massamba. The big African stood on an improvised platform of a large board placed across four crates. Massamba held up his arms for silence, and the mob obeyed instantly. Speaking French, he addressed them in a loud, clear voice, then quickly translated each sentence into English before he continued.

"The imperialism of the West has long been a curse to the people of Africa," Massamba began. "The Europeans came here for ivory and gold and slaves. They claimed Africa was their property. The French, the British, Portuguese, Belgians, Italians, Germans all said they owned our land. Said they owned *us*. The whites formed colonies with provisional governments that ruled over the rightful people of Africa. They said our religions were wrong, our customs were wrong and even our languages were inferior to theirs. They said we were inferior and ought to thank them, kneel down and worship them, for coming to save the savages from themselves."

Massamba turned to point at the embassy. "Now the Europeans are gone. The colonies are no longer here, but

he whites still try to control us. They still want our land and
all the great natural resources that Africans should be us-
ng for the sake of Africa instead of giving them away to the
Westerners who still regard us as ignorant little monkeys
without tails. Now the great white devil comes from the
worst imperialist empire of the lot. It comes from the United
States of America!''

Calvin James had to admire Massamba's charisma even
f he did not agree with what the man was saying. Massamba spoke with conviction and enunciated every word,
clearly and loud enough to be heard two blocks away without any need for mechanical amplification. He seemed to
truly believe in what he said, and he smoothly switched from
French to English and back again without any hesitation.
He addressed the Africans in French and turned to the TV
cameras when he repeated the sentence in English.

Massamba delivered his speech in a dramatic manner.
Passionately he gestured with his arms and hands to punc-
tuate his message. Even his height seemed to change as his
broad shoulders heaved and made it appear as though in
response to his emotions he grew taller or was deflated by
dejection. Throughout his speech, his expression changed
from a mask of outrage to exaggerated sorrow.

As he observed Massamba with the keen eye of an ex-
policeman, James thought it was a masterful performance.
He realized Massamba was a gifted speaker, an expert in
communication and certainly very well educated, probably
better than the average African. Physically, too, Massamba
cut an impressive figure, powerful-looking yet agile and
graceful. The smooth coordination of each move required
both physical and mental discipline.

Much of what Massamba said was true. James was proud
to be a black American, and he also fully appreciated his
African heritage and knew enough about the history of his
ancestors' homeland to appreciate the facts behind Massamba's claims. Much of Africa had been colonized by the

West, and in the process exploited and its peoples subjugated to become third-class citizens in their own land.

James admitted to himself that Massamba had also told the truth about American interests in Africa being largely motivated by selfish intentions centered on Africa's enormous natural resources and mineral wealth. But the accusation of U.S. "imperialism" was unfounded. The majority of African countries still traded more with Europe than with the U.S. Their governments were not particularly friendly toward America, and their ambassadors seldom backed the U.S. at the United Nations. America had not established anything vaguely similar to the colonial rule of the Europeans nor influenced puppet governments in the Communist nations of Africa in the style of the Soviet Union.

"The Americans have once again shown their contempt for the people of Africa," Massamba continued, thrusting an accusing finger at the embassy. "Everyone knows this so-called superpower experiments with chemical and biological warfare. Germ warfare, they used to call it. Their government poisons their own people with toxic waste and radioactive fallout. They created acid rain that destroys their crops and threatens the safety of their Canadian neighbors. There has been a price when their tests have gotten out of hand—flocks of sheep have been killed in America—" He paused to raise both fists overhead and seemed to swell into a great ebony mountain of anger. "But here, in Africa," he bellowed, "in Rwanda, *we* are the sheep! The Americans think so little of the African people they will use us for experiments! Guinea pigs to test their chemical weapons and biological plagues! They called Hitler a monster because the Nazis conducted human experiments on prisoners in concentration camps. What do you call someone who creates a cloud of carbon dioxide to slaughter innocent men, women and children?"

Massamba held out his hands with the palms up and uttered a mighty sigh as if the weight of the terrible truth was too great to bear. He appeared grieved and distressed by the story he was forced to tell his audience.

"Even the Americans admit the man Brandworth worked for their embassy here," he continued. "And it is no secret that the CIA operates through the American embassies in countries outside the United States. Even the Americans admit the man Ebstein was a toxicologist, an expert in poison of all sorts. They even admit Ebstein worked for the government, and he was in Cameroon in 1986. At Lake Nios in 1986!"

The mob responded with angry shouts and curses in several languages. More than one protester hurled a rock at the embassy. The Rwandian soldiers raised their rifles to port arms and seemed ready to charge on command. An army officer signaled for the troops to stay put as he stepped to the platform and said something to Massamba.

"This officer warns me that I may be arrested for inciting violence!" Massamba cried out. "Hear me, my brothers! I tell you do not cast those stones at the embassy building! Violence is *their* way! The way of the white dictators! The European stormtroopers and the CIA assassins use violence to murder innocent Africans. We will not stoop to the level of the savages of the West. They would like nothing better than to show black Africans carrying out a violent assault on an American embassy. Their television would like that. The Americans might even call that an attack on United States territory and use it for justification to invade our country and take it over just as they did in Grenada. Don't give them that satisfaction! Don't let them trick you into their deceptive traps!"

The crowd gave a roar of approval and began chanting, "Massamba! Massamba!" The big man lowered his head and modestly nodded, apparently embarrassed by their praise. He was a picture of humility as he stepped from the platform.

"That's one natural, born showman," James remarked, impressed by Massamba's performance.

"Bloody agitators usually are," McCarter added with a grunt.

"You don't believe Massamba is sincere?" Kagera inquired as he held a pocket-size transmitter in one hand and pressed the key-signal button repeatedly.

"I don't give a damn if he's sincere or not," McCarter replied. "He's stirring up more trouble for us, and that's about the only thing that concerns me right now. Hell, he might be right about some of the stuff he's said, but he's got a few other facts wrong. Ebstein never worked for the government. Sure, Ebstein was in Cameroon in 1986, but *after* the Lake Nios tragedy."

"Yeah," Manning added. "He was misleading with that business about CIA operating through U.S. embassies. There is a degree of truth to that, of course, but that doesn't mean Brandworth was CIA because he worked for the embassy. That business about CIA conducting experiments on humans in Africa is totally unfounded."

"Last week I would have agreed that Massamba was just an anti-American extremist, probably left-wing, possibly a secret Marxist," Kagera said with a shrug. "Now, I'm not certain he's been wrong about many of the things he's said."

"That doesn't make us feel terribly comfortable with your company, Kagera," Katz told him in a flat, hard voice. "Who did you signal with that code-key transmitter?"

"Some of your people," Kagera answered. He pointed at two figures on the sidewalk. A beefy black man in a dashiki and fez and a white guy clad in khaki shirt, matching shorts and a brown beret approached the van. Kagera gestured for Phoenix Force to make room for the pair as they reached for the sliding door.

"Hi, I'm Carson," the black man in the dashiki announced as he took a seat in the back, next to Encizo and Manning. "I'm with the embassy, but I don't think it's a good idea for us to meet there right now. You saw Massamba's rally?"

"Kind'a hard to miss it," Manning replied.

"This is Monsieur Lebrun from the French embassy," Carson explained as he introduced his companion. "He's going to help us with this mess."

"Oui," Lebrun declared with a nod. *"Enchanté*, gentlemen. We shall discuss business at my embassy. It is a more relaxed setting for conversation. No?"

"That wouldn't be too hard to do right now," David McCarter commented. "You're with Sûreté?"

"Of course," Lebrun confirmed. "French intelligence."

"Some might call that a contradictory term," McCarter muttered. Like many Britons, he was less than fond of the French people.

"What was that, monsieur?" Lebrun inquired.

"I said some call this contact a fortunate turn," the Briton replied quickly. "Turn of events, you understand. We didn't know the French were involved in this business."

"Actually my country and others in Western Europe have considerably more trade with Rwanda than the United States," the Frenchman explained. "However, it might be wise to wait until we arrive at the embassy before we discuss things in detail."

"One thing we need to know right now," Katz began as he turned to face Carson. "Did the Company have anything to do with Dr. Ebstein or Brandworth? We know neither man belonged to the CIA, but sometimes branches of your organization enlist individuals for missions Washington knows nothing about."

"Absolutely not," Carson answered, slightly offended by the question. "Brandworth was hired as a translator. He was an African studies major, expert in Bantu languages, spoke about five fluently. I had him translate some propaganda pamphlets once, but that's the closest he ever came to working for the Company. Ebstein had absolutely no connection. Oh, we knew he was in Rwanda. He brought an assistant with him from the States, a guy named Forest who, by the way, has apparently disappeared."

"The information we have suggests Ebstein and Forest were in the area of Lake Kivu with some local fellows hired to help them locate rivers flowing into the lake," Kagera added. "None of them have been heard of since."

"Well, we know what happened to Ebstein and Brandworth," James remarked. "You know if autopsies have been performed on the bodies yet?"

"Autopsies are being performed on almost everyone who died at the village and on several cattle," Kagera answered. "Of course they'll do an autopsy on the men who seemed to have assassinated more than a hundred Rwandians. I don't know what you hope to gain from such an autopsy. Cause of death was clearly the same as the murdered villagers."

"There isn't definite proof of murder," Carson declared.

"You have every type of proof except a signed confession by the persons responsible for the incident," Katz corrected. "The chemical solution, pumps and pipes for transferring the stuff into the river so it would affect the lake—it's all pretty clear evidence that the carbon dioxide clouds were caused by intentional sabotage."

"Nobody better get any ideas about claiming this was an accident of nature or an act of God," Encizo added. "This mess isn't going to just go away. If we don't come up with some answers, men like Massamba will twist things to their advantage."

"That rabble-rousing loudmouth is wrong," Carson snorted.

"Well," Manning said with a sigh. "I sure hope we can prove that. Otherwise someone is going to get away with mass murder, and Americans in Africa will be walking targets. God knows what else it might lead to."

6

"I hope you people can come up with something that's more use to us than Carson or the rest of these so-called intelligence personnel have managed so far," the U.S. Ambassador to Rwanda commented as he puffed on a cigarette stub, then used the burning tip to light another one.

"Giraudeau is assisting with the autopsies," Katz began. The Israeli sat at the conference table and scanned file reports in French and English. "There isn't much here concerning activity by the KGB or agents from Communist African countries. Do they really have so little interest in Rwanda, or am I wasting my time looking at confidential files instead of top secret material?"

Carson and Lebrun exchanged glances. They had gathered at the soundproof conference room of the French embassy's S-2 section. The Sûreté officer and his CIA counterpart were professionally paranoid and reluctant to share any information with anyone, even people on their own side. The United States and France were still allies, although their relationship had been a bit strained in recent years.

"There really hasn't been much Communist espionage in Rwanda," Lebrun announced. "Oh, we know that some listening posts have been set up by the Soviets, usually operated by Congolese agents. However, their interest has been to gather intelligence about Zaire more than Rwanda. The Communists have been less active in the past two years. The Soviets have had quite a few problems of their own. Economic woes, social unrest in East European countries and even within the USSR itself. The Afghanistan war, the civil conflicts in Southeast Asia and the Soviet-backed forces in Angola have all been expensive and less than successful ventures.''

''CIA doesn't have much to add to the Sûreté evaluation,'' Carson added. ''To be honest, there have probably been more listening posts and intelligence operations carried out in Rwanda by American and West European intelligence outfits than by the Soviets. Not that we've had any great concerns about the future of this country. Hell, Rwanda is a republic. A one-party republic, so the elections might be more show than substance, but at least they have elections for the president and National Assembly members. The government here is pretty stable. The last time there was a coup was in 1973, and it was bloodless. Rwanda has stayed on friendly terms with the West. There are no serious concerns about how this country is developing.''

''So, why have the Company and other Western intel outfits been fairly active here?'' Rafael Encizo inquired.

''The Communists are trying to keep tabs on Zaire,'' Carson began, ''and we're concerned with two other neighboring countries. Tanzania is a socialist country to the east, and Uganda is to the north. Now, the Company doesn't worry about Tanzania as much as we used to. Their brand of socialism is about half capitalism. They do more trade with the U.S. and Japan than with Communist countries, and the only time the Tanzanians invaded another African country in recent history was when Idi Amin declared war on Tanzania and attacked them back in 1978. The Ugandans actually invaded Tanzania first, but the Tanzanians counterattacked and kicked the hell out of Amin's forces. After they won, and Amin fled the country, the Tanzanians withdrew from Uganda. You can't get too worried about Tanzania becoming a puppet of Soviet aggression in Africa when they have a track record like that.''

"We Rwandians don't worry about Tanzania," Kagera remarked. He sat at the conference table and stuffed tobacco into his pipe as he spoke. "Uganda is another story."

"I understand that," Carson said with a nod. "The present government in Uganda hasn't given anyone much reason to stay up nights worrying, but it's questionable how long it will remain in power. Politics in Uganda are unstable at the best of times and downright terrifying in the worse times. People in the U.S. have tended to forget about Uganda since Idi Amin was forced into exile. Fact is, Milton Obote wasn't any better than Amin."

"At least Obote didn't invade Tanzania or protect terrorist hijackers at the Entebee Airport," the American ambassador remarked, still chain-smoking and pacing the floor like a nervous father in an O.B. waiting room.

"Amin butchered about three hundred thousand of his own countrymen during his seven years in power," Carson stated. "It is estimated that Obote's regime was responsible for one hundred thousand deaths in Uganda during the four years after he took over. I'd say Obote doesn't deserve any cheers. Anyway, a military coup bounced Obote out of office. Since 1985, different leaders have been taking over Uganda about every other year. They had an election a while back. There were elections when Obote was president, too. Maybe we're a little paranoid about Uganda and sort of pessimistic about its ability to govern itself, but considering recent history, those feelings aren't without reason."

"They may not be justified, either," Gary Manning remarked as he poured himself a cup of black coffee, sniffing appreciatively at the aroma of the rich arabica. "I don't think Uganda is responsible for the incident that brought us here."

"I'm not convinced the Soviets are, either," Kagera declared. He held a match to the bowl of his pipe and puffed gently. A second later a ring of blue-gray smoke surrounded his head, and he continued, "None of you want to consider this, but there is the possibility Dr. Ebstein was involved in some sort of mad scientist operation on his own.''

"Bullshit!'' the ambassador snapped. ''How did Brandworth get involved in something like that?''

"There isn't any evidence to suggest Ebstein was insane or a fanatic of any kind,'' Katz stated as he placed his elbows on the table. ''He had a fine reputation as a humanitarian as well as an accomplished toxicologist. From what we've been able to learn about the man, he loved Africa and admired its people. Ebstein was in Rwanda to study the rivers and streams flowing from the volcanic areas to Lake Kivu. I don't pretend to know about such things, but apparently Ebstein supported a theory by French limnologists that the tragedy in Cameroon was caused by an input of volcanic lava or magma or whatever. Ebstein believed a similar tragedy in Kivu could be avoided if this was detected in advance and the volcanic influence cut off from the lake.''

"Instead, someone used the same general idea to create a massacre that occurred at the village,'' Manning said with a frown. He sipped his coffee and gazed thoughtfully at Katz, then went on. ''Actually the incident at Kivu could have been much worse. The sodium magnesium compound triggered a pocket or two of methane, and the explosions drove up carbon dioxide from the bottom of the lake. Had a chain reaction taken place, then dozens of methane gas pockets might have gone off, and the clouds of gas would have been a hundred times larger.''

"I'm curious about this Massamba fellow,'' Katz declared. ''He certainly took advantage of the tragedy to use it for anti-American propaganda. You said he was formerly regarded as something of a rabble-rouser, Kagera. Does your organization have a file on the man?''

"I'm sure we do,'' Kagera confirmed. ''I must remind you, however, that Massamba hasn't done anything illegal judging by the assembly we witnessed today. He even kept the crowd from getting violent.''

"Yes," Katz agreed. "Massamba put on a very nice show or the television cameras. Sorry if I'm not terribly impressed by that. See what you can find out about him. He's obviously educated, very comfortable with public speaking and outspoken. When a man states his opinions as if they were ironclad facts, he aims to gain something from it. I'm not accusing him of anything, but still want to know more about him. If nothing else, his actions may possibly cause problems during our investigation."

"I think that's a waste of time," the American ambassador snorted as he crushed out a cigarette butt and reached or the pack in his breast pocket. "Look, I can't even go back to my own embassy. What the hell are you people doing to do about the security of the American embassy and its personnel? Brandworth was one of our people, and he's already dead. We could have a repeat of the Tehran situation if things get any worse."

"Your problems will be solved when we take care of ours, Mr. Ambassador," Encizo told him. "I think we should check the scene of the crime—the lake and the area where the shed was found with Ebstein and Brandworth inside."

"There isn't much there," Kagera stated, "and it may not be entirely safe to go there. Carbon dioxide levels are still dangerously high."

"It's still one of the few leads available, and I say that makes it worth some risk," Encizo insisted.

"I think I should make it clear that the French embassy granting you fellows asylum," Lebrun began, "but we can't afford to get too closely associated with any investigations you Americans may carry out. After all, our relations with Rwanda are still solid, and we don't want to risk a turn for the worse."

"Guilt by association, huh?" the American ambassador muttered. "You know, I seem to recall that France had a little problem with a bunch of goose-stepping Germans during World War II. You guys sure didn't object to America getting involved to bail you out of that mess, but your country has been a pretty poor excuse for an ally ever since. You pulled out of NATO in 1967, and then criticized American involvement in Vietnam—when the French had fought there for years before we went to Southeast Asia. Then in 1980 you ignore America's boycott of the Olympics and go to the Soviet Union to participate in the games, anyway. You moralized when we invaded Grenada, flew over French airspace to retaliate in Libya . . ."

"I think this will only be counterproductive, Mr. Ambassador," Katz said. "Mr. Lebrun isn't responsible for the policies of his country, and it is hardly fair to criticize France for being more concerned with its national interests than pleasing the U.S. The French embassy is granting us sanctuary and assisting us to the extent that they feel comfortable doing under these circumstances."

"Okay, Bidault, or whatever your real name is," the ambassador began, pointing the glowing tip of a cigarette at Katz. "I don't need a lesson on diplomacy. That's my job, remember?"

"I think it's hard to remember the job at hand, because it is a threatening kind of situation with a lot at stake," Katz replied with a shrug. "Don't be offended. You have a right to be frightened. Being the ambassador to Rwanda was probably a pleasant, safe assignment until now. You've suddenly found yourself in the eye of a political hurricane. There's a threat of violence, fear of failure, new concerns about problems that seemed a world away before now. I understand you're not accustomed to this, but please try to bear in mind that a lot is at stake, and we don't need any problems with those who are willing to help us."

The ambassador looked at "Mr. Bidault" as if the mysterious one-armed man had just explained the riddle of how the universe had been created. No doubt the man was more than just a sneaky-pete troubleshooter on the government payroll. More than a hired gun with a bankbook for a conscience.

"Have you found yourself in circumstances like these very often in the past, Mr. Bidault?" he inquired.

"From time to time," Katz replied. "I'm in a better position to move about the streets than you are, Mr. Ambassador. According to my passport, I'm a French Canadian from Quebec, not a U.S. citizen. My friends have similar identification. Two of them are posing as Canadian journalists who work for the same magazine, along with me as an editor. Of course, Mr. Giraudeau and Mr. Cordero have different passports because they wouldn't pass easily as Canadian citizens. Actually there are black and Hispanic Canadians, but that isn't common knowledge to anyone who lives outside Canada or the United States."

"I think the possibility just wouldn't occur to some Canadians," Manning commented with a slight grin. He thought it ironic that he was a Canadian claiming to be a U.S. citizen who was pretending to be a Canadian.

"Nonetheless," Katz continued, "we can poke about and ask questions without seeming too suspicious. For now, Mr. Ambassador, I suggest you keep a low profile. Mr. Carson can probably help us with anything we'll need from the Company, and he can also keep you informed of how our mission is going. You'll also be able to contact us through him if the need occurs."

A knock on the door interrupted the conversation. Lebrun answered it and opened the door to admit Calvin James. The tall black man headed straight for the coffee maker and poured himself a cup.

"The four medical examiners I was working with only drank tea," he commented. "Really weak, lousy tea that was, aside from a few bits of something floating around in it, hardly more than hot water."

"Some of the hardships we endure is beyond the realm of human imagination," Encizo said with a grin. "Learn anything from the autopsy?"

"Autopsies," James corrected, "of five people and two cows. All died the same way—asphyxiation caused by an excess of carbon dioxide in the respiratory and circulatory systems. No surprises there. Of course, two of the guys we did autopsies on were Ebstein and Brandworth. I found something in a chemical analysis of their blood that wasn't present in any of the other bodies."

"Do we have to guess?" Manning inquired.

"Traces of pentobarbital," James explained.

"That's like knockout drops, isn't it?" the ambassador asked, probably recalling something he had heard in a detective movie.

"Let's put it this way," James answered, "if somebody gave you a dose of pentobarbital, he wouldn't have much trouble gettin' you to take a trip with him and leaving you at a little shed somewhere to take a nap."

"So Ebstein and Brandworth were drugged," Carson remarked. "That proves they were set up. Whoever killed those people at Lake Kivu killed them, too."

"I'm afraid you're going to need more evidence than that, gentlemen," Kagera insisted. "My countrymen are outraged by what happened at Lake Kivu. They want someone's head for this. I can't honestly say I blame them."

"You don't really believe the autopsy report," James began, as he looked curiously at Kagera. "Do you?"

"I don't know if I should," Kagera replied, tapping his lower teeth with the stem of his pipe. "Wouldn't you fabricate evidence if it could spare your country embarrassment?"

"Maybe," James admitted, "but I didn't. What should concern you is the fact that whoever killed those Rwandian villagers is still at large. Maybe we should check out the lake. Could be some evidence there."

"Mr. Cordero already suggested that," Katz commented. "You two want to go to Lake Kivu in the morning?"

"Sure," James agreed. "Can you get us a guide, Kagera?"

"Of course," the African said with a nod. "But I'll do better than that. I'll come along myself."

"We need you here," Katz insisted. He glanced at the wall clock. "It's getting late, and we could all use some sleep. Kagera, you choose someone to accompany my friends. Someone you trust who can assist them and keep an eye on them at the same time. Since you don't fully trust us, I'm sure you'd do that, anyway."

"You're a clever man, Mr. Bidault," Kagera replied. "I don't imagine much gets past you unnoticed."

"If it's unnoticed, I wouldn't know about it," Katz told him.

Another knock on the door drew Lebrun's attention, and the Sûreté agent got up to open the door to admit David McCarter.

As the Briton approached the table, he took a pack of Player's from his pocket, but before he could even fish out a cigarette, Encizo spoke up.

"Please don't light one of those," he urged, waving a cloud of blue-gray smoke from his face. The Cuban was a nonsmoker who found the habit difficult to tolerate in a closed area with no ventilation. "Kagera's pipe has been going like a smokestack, and the ambassador has been smoking cigarette after cigarette as if he's determined to get lung cancer before the night's over and he wants all the rest of us to inhale enough to join him at the cancer ward."

"All right," McCarter agreed and stuck the Player's back into his pocket. "I can make a small sacrifice for you, amigo. A couple of Lebrun's mates showed me the helicopters they've got for the French embassy. The one I picked is a Deschanel H-4, similar to the Bell choppers we've used in the past. A little smaller than the Bell. You can only carry about ten blokes in it, but it's in excellent condition and all fueled and ready to go first thing in the morning."

"I'm glad you approve, Monsieur Miller," Lebrun remarked, calling McCarter by his cover name. "Especially

since we French don't have any intelligence. I believe that'
what you said, monsieur?''

"I didn't think you caught that," McCarter said withou
attempting to deny the previous remark. "Actually I be
lieve I said French intelligence was a contradictory term
You must admit Sûreté hasn't got a terribly impressive trac
record as intelligence outfits go."

"You must be British," Lebrun replied with a grin. "I'v
always suspected the English climate does something to th
disposition. As for Sûreté, I wish to remind you that Brit
ish MI-5 allowed Sir Anthony Blunt to rise to a very hig
position of authority and failed to realize the man was
Soviet agent until a considerable amount of damage wa
done. Then there was Kim Philby and McClean and severa
others who turned out to be traitors who defected to th
Soviet Union."

"Are you two going to be able to work together?" Car
son asked nervously.

"Oh, hell yes," McCarter assured him. "Just the usua
sort of sibling rivalry between sister nations of Western Eu
rope. It's been going on for centuries, and we'd disregar
tradition if we didn't express a bit of contempt for eac
other's country. I doubt if you'd understand."

"Oui," Lebrun agreed. "You see, it is acceptable for
Frenchman and a Briton to respect each other as individu
als and assist each other to accomplish common goals, bu
for a Frenchman to like England, or a Briton to like France
that's a bit unpatriotic. I suppose it is because we fought s
many wars with one another before the twentieth century
took turns occupying each other's country at different time
in history. Besides, the French and the English are the grea
snobs of Europe. We expect people everywhere to speak ou
language, respect our values, adopt our culture and believ
in the same religion and government that we do."

"That's why we didn't do so well when England an
France were empires," McCarter said with a shrug. "O
course, the French were a lot worse than the British..."

"Thank you for the lesson on European relations, Miller," Katz declared, eager to cut off the sharp-tongued Briton. "You need to be briefed about the matters we discussed while you were checking the helicopters. We'll fill you in on the way to the hotel. We need to get some sleep, because tomorrow promises to be a rather long day."

7

The streets of Kigali were relatively deserted at night. Calvin James and Rafael Encizo strolled along the poorly lit sidewalk on Urundi Avenue. A tour bus rolled by, the seats empty, the driver weary from a long day behind the wheel. Stores and shops were closed, with most of the windows protected by iron bars or heavy metal shutters. A few derelicts roamed the streets, but they were a timid lot. They avoided the Phoenix pair as if they feared James and Encizo might gun them down just for entertainment.

There did not seem to be much nightlife in Rwanda's capital. The taverns closed by midnight, and there was little reason for anyone with a roof over his or her head to be on the streets at one-thirty in the morning. The surrounding buildings were somber, bulky shapes in the meager light provided by the few street lights as the Phoenix pair walked toward the Mwami Hotel.

"Nice quiet little town," Encizo commented. A dog howled in the distance as if to contradict him.

"If this is what the capital city is like, I wonder what the small towns and villages do at night," James wondered aloud. "Put the one horse in its stall and turn off the kerosene lamp?"

"Have you seen this hotel yet?" Encizo asked. "Doesn't look too bad from the outside, but I'm afraid we might find hordes of insect life when we get in our room."

"Kagera's people took care of the reservations," James reminded the Cuban. He glanced at an alley. Two shapes oved among the shadows within. "The rest of our luggage is with the other guys. I'm glad it's not sitting up in the ooms or with some bell captain."

"Yeah," Encizo began as he unbuttoned his jacket to allow quick access to the H&K P9S pistol in a shoulder holster under his arm.

James realized Encizo had also noticed the movement in the alley. Still holding his briefcase in one hand, James reached up with the other to the lapel of his sports jacket, ready to draw his Beretta 92-F from shoulder leather. However, the figures in the alley did not venture forth from the shadows as the Phoenix pair strolled by.

"More derelicts," James muttered. "I sort of wish we hadn't decided to walk to the hotel."

"You wanted to get a feel for the city," Encizo reminded him.

"I've felt enough," James replied as he noticed three figures appear at the corner of a building. They stood on the sidewalk in the path of the two Phoenix commandos. "Oh, hell."

"Ditto," Encizo replied tensely through clenched teeth.

The trio looked tough enough to start trouble. All were young black men, although one was at least five years older than his companions. He wore a dashiki and fez. A machete in a leather sheath was thrust into his belt. An oval-shaped ring of polished wood hung from his left earlobe, and a multicolored necklace of beads decorated his neck.

The two younger men—each about twenty-one years old—wore short-sleeved white shirts and blue shorts. Their eyes seemed to burn with unreasonable anger, but the senior member of the trio appeared more calm, his emotions coolly held in check. The only weapon in view was the dashiki-clad man's jungle knife.

Encizo and James came to a halt. The black warrior released his briefcase and let it drop to the pavement by his feet. He folded his arms on his chest while he surreptitiously slipped a hand inside his jacket. Encizo held on to his

briefcase, not wanting to risk letting it fall into the hands o
potential enemies. The Cuban's free hand remained near th
gap in his jacket in case he needed to draw his pistol.

"Bonsoir," James greeted. He continued to address th
trio in French. "Do you want something?"

"This is our country," one of the younger Africans be
gan. "We will ask the questions. You Americans have n
right to demand anything of my people. Damned nation o
butchers!"

"I'm not an American, monsieur," James replied. "M
friend here is from Venezuela. He doesn't speak French
Now, what the hell do you want?"

The man with the machete raised his hands as if to bloc
the other two before they could rush at James and Enciz
He smiled at the Phoenix pair, but it was a sickly smile tha
was clearly meant to indicate hostility held in check.

"You say you are not Americans," the man began i
broken French. His accent suggested it was not a languag
he was particularly comfortable with. "Why are you here i
Rwanda?"

"Why should I tell you?" James replied curtly. "Yo
three are just some rude idiots who seem to think they ca
intimidate us for some reason."

"It is foolish to make us angry," the man with the ma
chete began as he lowered a hand to the handle of his jur
gle knife. "A true idiot is one who invites death."

"Draw that blade and you'll be sorry," James warnec
secretly gripping the Beretta in his concealed hand.

"Juvénal!" a voice called sharply. *"Non, Juvénal!"*

At the command the man with the knife suddenly move
his hands away from the machete. James and Encizo turne
toward the voice that had warned Juvénal. The large, pow
erful figure of Massamba approached, hands open an
palms turned up in a gesture that suggested he intended n
harm. He smiled broadly and tilted his head to one side.

"I must apologize for Juvénal," Massamba began. Hi
manner seemed sincere, or at least it looked like a convinc

ing act. "He's an old friend of mine, and I assure you he meant no harm, but he is very offended and outraged by what the Americans have done at Lake Kivu."

James again noticed how impressive Massamba could be. The African was huge, taller than James, and probably heavier by at least fifty pounds. None of it looked like fat. The man was built like a human bulldozer, yet despite a voice that could match his size, he was capable of speaking softly and in an articulate and precise manner. Massamba's gestures exaggerated his emotional reactions, but he seemed so big that large gestures and flamboyant behavior fitted his passionate and powerful personality.

At least, James thought as he glanced around for television cameras, it suited the personality Massamba was showing the public. He half expected to see more news reporters and cameramen, but apparently Massamba was offering a performance solely for their sake.

"Why are you so sure the Americans are responsible?" James inquired. He relaxed his posture slightly. If Massamba wanted to attack them, he would have done it already. For some reason, he clearly wanted to talk. "Some say the evidence against the Americans and the CIA is circumstantial."

"Perhaps I should introduce myself," Massamba began. "I am the spokesman of Rwandians who feel this slaughter by the CIA must not be ignored or accepted. My name is Massamba, but I am just a messenger. The people have given me the message. As for the Americans, I have no doubt they are responsible. You are aware the two men found in the shack were Americans? Oh, but I don't even know your name or where you're from, monsieur."

"I'm Giraudeau from Martinique," James explained. "It's a French dependency in the West Indies. I met Monsieur Cordero on the flight from Caracas. We're both journalists, in your country to cover this terrible news story."

"There are many other Frenchmen here," Massamba remarked. He looked at James with a curious expression.

"Paris sent a television news team here and several report ers."

"White reporters," James replied with a wry grin. "They seemed to think I'd have a different point of view. There may be some political reasons. Maybe it's for appearances but I'm good at my job and I've been to Africa before Kenya and South Africa, but this is my first visit to Rwanda."

"You're not getting a true picture of our country right now, Monsieur Giraudeau," Massamba declared. "It i usually a very peaceful, fairly quiet and pleasant little country. The CIA has ruined that for us."

"So you claim," James said. He glanced at Juvénal and the other two Africans. The trio had backed off and no longer seemed to offer any threat.

"Your friend doesn't speak French," Massamba mused "Does he speak English?"

"Oui," James confirmed. "That's how Monsieur Cordero and I communicate. Although I speak a little Spanish as well. I assume you guessed I speak English because it is a language widely spoken in both Kenya and South Africa You may also know that English is a common second language in Martinique. Much of our tourist trade comes from Americans."

"Do you like Americans?" Massamba asked in English.

"In Martinique we like American dollars in our casinos," James replied in the same language. "I'd like to interview you in detail. Maybe we can talk in the hotel?"

"Perhaps later," Massamba said. He turned to face Encizo. "Sorry to detain you, Mr. Cordero. I hope you have a pleasant visit in Rwanda. I've enjoyed meeting both of you."

"Maybe next time we can rely more on English during our conversation, so I understand what you're talking about," Encizo replied.

"That was rude of me," Massamba admitted with a nod. "I apologize for that and for any discomfort caused by Juvénal and his young friends. I must say I was impressed by how you stood up to them. I believe you refer to such courage as *cajones*?''

''Boxes?'' Encizo asked, apparently confused. ''You mean *huevos*?''

''I might be mistaken,'' Massamba said with a shrug. ''Perhaps we'll meet again, gentlemen.''

''I wouldn't be surprised,'' James replied with a nod. *''Au revoir, monsieur.''*

THE PHOENIX PAIR didn't discuss the encounter until they reached the hotel. The desk clerk, sound asleep at his post in the lobby, awoke with a start when James slapped the bell on the counter. Since they were already registered at the hotel, the clerk timidly handed them the keys to their room. The two commandos walked to an old elevator and pressed the button for the second floor.

''Any ideas about what sort of game Massamba was playing?'' James inquired as they rode the elevator up the dusty shaft. The ancient cable and gears creaked enough to make the trip less than reassuring.

''Well, I don't figure he and his pals were merely strolling along the streets at one-thirty in the morning and just happened to see us and wanted to have a friendly chat,'' Encizo answered as the elevator began to tremble. ''I hope this elevator doesn't come apart before we reach the next floor. You talked to Massamba more than I did.''

''You ought to learn to speak French.''

''Why?'' Encizo said with a shrug. ''The rest of you guys speak, and I'm always hanging out with at least one of you. So, what did he say?''

''Not much, really. I figure he was fishing for information. Trying to decide if we're what we claim to be. I don't think the son of a bitch is convinced we're a couple of innocent journalists. Probably thinks we're CIA, but he still isn't sure about that. Maybe if we were, those dudes would have tried to jump us.''

"He tried to trick me with that *cajones* remark," Encizo commented, and sighed with relief as the elevator reached the next floor without snapping loose from the cables.

"Now, I thought my Spanish was pretty good," James began as he shoved back the doors to the lift. "*Cajones* and *huevos* are both slang expressions for testicles, right? Like saying a guy's got balls?"

"Yeah, but *cajones* is used almost exclusively by Mexican-Americans in the United States. The expression is hardly ever used in South American countries."

"Gee, you learn something new every day," James remarked as they stepped into the hallway. "Massamba must have done some interesting research to come up with something like that. The guy's got more than a passing interest in the Western Hemisphere. I noticed something else. His French isn't quite the same as the Rwandians who speak the language that I've heard so far. The accent is different. Massamba either came from another country, or the dialect he was raised with was a lot different."

"Rwanda is about the size of the state of Maryland or New Jersey," Encizo commented. "How many different dialects could they have here?"

"People in different parts of Maryland and New Jersey have different accents," James reminded his Cuban companion. "Besides, Rwanda has two official languages and probably several other African languages are spoken here as well. It's not uncommon in African countries to find many tribal languages, each with various dialects, spoken in a single nation."

"Well, Massamba is certainly a curious character, and I have a hunch there's more to him than he's revealing with his public appearances," Encizo added as they walked toward number twenty-three. "That fellow Juvenile or whatever his name is sure didn't seem like Massamba's social director."

"Juvénal," Calvin James corrected. "And I agree—that dude wasn't packing that *panga* because he expected to chop bread with it."

Encizo unlocked the door. The pair entered cautiously, accustomed to expecting danger in virtually any new place. James kept one hand on the butt of his Beretta as he flicked on the light switch. An overhead bulb illuminated the room. There was not much to see. The two beds with lumpy mattresses, faded sheets and thin blankets took up half the space in the small quarters. The walls were drab with cracked plaster, and a single chest of drawers was positioned near an ancient sink.

"Well," Encizo remarked. "I've seen worse."

"So have I," James agreed, "but not lately." He carried his briefcase to the nearest bed and placed it on the mattress. Encizo put his valise on the sink, unlatched it and opened the lid. He made certain it blocked most of the mirror above the sink. It was unlikely the mirror was made of two-way glass, but it was still possible. Someone might be observing them from another room by using the "mirror" in such a manner.

James pulled the drapes shut and quickly checked under the beds and inside the small closet in one corner. He found nothing suspicious. There was no bathroom. That was probably located down the hall or possibly on the first floor.

"This room is not so bad, I guess," James declared, affecting a slight French accent to suit his cover identity. "No large furry vermin, at any rate."

Encizo reached inside his briefcase. It contained a compact H&K MP-5 machine pistol, its stock folded and two magazines loaded with 9 mm parabellum ammunition stored in a felt compartment next to the weapon. A small transistor radio was also in the case. Encizo picked it up and pulled out the antenna to full length.

"Maybe I can find some music or something on this thing," he remarked as he switched on the radio.

"There are two radio stations in Kigali," James answered. "I don't know if they are AM or FM and they may not broadcast at night. Also you might be able to receive a radio program from Tanzania or Zaire."

"Nothing but static so far," Encizo complained as the electrical crackle buzzed from the radio.

He glanced down at the dial. A small orange light had flashed on in the center. Encizo moved the radio along the pipes of the sink. The light began to blink. Encizo examined the pipes and found a small metal disc, no larger than his thumbnail, attached to the underside of the sink.

"That sounded like something," Encizo remarked, as he pointed at the sink. James nodded in response.

"Maybe you'll get better reception by the window," the black man suggested.

Encizo moved to the window and scanned the drapes with the radio. He ran the device along the first bed, and the light blinked when he stuck the radio under the bedsprings. The Cuban found another tiny disc identical to the one he discovered at the sink. He reached into the top of his boot and drew a Gerber Mark 1 dagger from an ankle sheath. The Phoenix pro pried loose the disc and held it up for James to see.

"That static is annoying," James said with a sigh.

"I'm sorry," Encizo replied, moving to the next bed, "but I almost had something here. Maybe if I adjust the antenna."

He found another device under the second bed and a fourth behind the chest of drawers. Calvin James continued to chat away with meaningless comments about their trip from South America, the crowd outside the American embassy, the encounter with Massamba and the tragedy at Lake Kivu. While he was speaking, the black commando used a screwdriver to remove the plates to the electrical outlets in the room. He found a tiny disc inside one outlet.

Encizo left the disc in place under the sink, but collected the others and placed them on a mattress. James used his screwdriver to probe along the edge of the mirror. Satisfied that it was mounted to the wall and not linked to the next room, he signaled to Encizo that the mirror was okay.

"Does this sink work?" James inquired and turned a faucet. Water poured into the sink and down the drain.

The Cuban turned up the volume button of his "radio" and set it next to the collection of discs. The static would block any sounds that might be detected by the small wireless microphones. Running water in the sink pipes would do the same to the bug installed there. James opened his briefcase and removed a radio similar to Encizo's and placed it on the windowsill with the setting on a different frequency. That created static vibrations against the glass of the window pane. The Phoenix Force veterans knew enough about surveillance methods to realize voices create vibrations that can be detected and interpreted by a "rifle microphone," or similar laser device trained on a window from outside. Now any eavesdroppers would only get an earful of static.

"Somebody went to a lot of trouble," James commented in a whisper.

"Short frequency wireless mikes," Encizo replied. "Probably means the people who did it have a surveillance team in the hotel or right outside the building."

There was a rapping at the door. Encizo hurried to the valise on the sink and slapped the lid shut to conceal the MP-5 subgun. James moved to the door, but waited for Encizo to position himself by the hinges. The Cuban pushed back his jacket and placed a hand on the grips of his H&K pistol as James pushed back the latch.

"Qui est-ce?" he inquired as he stepped away from the door.

"Bidault," Katz's voice replied from the opposite side of the door. "Remember me? We met on the plane."

James opened the door and Katz entered the room. He held his hand up and placed a finger to his lips. Calvin James pointed at the radio on the bed next to the pile of microphones. The Phoenix Force commander nodded with approval.

"I see you found the bugs already," the Israeli remarked. "We swept in our room and found the same thing. Someone is already interested, and it hasn't taken them long to start moving in on us."

"Any idea of who they are?" James asked, just as Manning and McCarter appeared in the hallway behind Katz. The Canadian and the Briton carried in two large aluminum cases that belonged to James and Encizo. Manning reached into his pocket and handed a small gray metal disc to James. It had been pried open. The insides consisted of minute circuits and transistors. The tiny battery had been removed, so the mini-mike was useless. James hummed with surprise when he noticed the shiny yellow wiring among the circuits.

"Looks like gold wires," James commented. "Best conductor circuit wires are made of gold, but it's expensive so most would use copper or some other metal."

"Someone cares enough to use the very best," McCarter said dryly. The Briton stepped back into the hallway. "I'm gonna keep an eye on our room. See you two blokes in the morning."

"It's already morning," Encizo replied as he examined the gutted mike.

McCarter snorted and closed the door. Katz walked to the bed and examined the collection of electrical eavesdropping devices to confirm that these were the same as the mikes the rest of them had found in their room. The Israeli nodded at Manning.

"It's interesting that these are fairly standard mikes by design," the Canadian remarked, "except for the material used. Gold wiring, nickel-alloy battery and a zinc casing."

"Not cheap junk," James agreed. "If CIA used simple bugs like these, half the materials used would be plastic. And probably just zinc batteries."

"I doubt they'd use gold wiring," Encizo added. "I don't think the Rwandians did this, either. Not Kagera's people, anyway."

"Well," Manning began, "just based on what we have so far, my first choice would be KGB. The Soviets are the second largest producers of gold in the world, and I seem to recall that zinc and nickel are very abundant in Russia. Since the KGB likes to rely on gadgets more than most other intelligence outfits, they tend to spend a lot more money on the materials for fundamental surveillance stuff like this. I wouldn't be surprised if they've got a stakeout truck somewhere outside or a team at a building across the street."

"Got a static vibrator at the window in case they train a laser mike on the glass," James stated. "If KGB is on to us, that means our cover is pretty shaky already."

"They might be routinely bugging all the alleged journalists who they suspect might be intelligence personnel from Western nations," Katz stated. "Let's not jump to any conclusions from this. We can't be certain these mikes are KGB or that this means the Soviets are responsible for the incident at Lake Kivu."

"I don't have any idea what's going on here," Calvin James admitted. "All I know so far is that we've only been in Rwanda for about eight hours, and already I feel like every one of us is walking around with a bull's-eye painted on his chest."

8

The Deschanel H-4 cruised across the morning sky above the tops of the trees. David McCarter expertly handled the controls as he piloted the helicopter over the forest near Lake Kivu. A Rwandian intel agent named Teisko sat in the copilot seat. He scanned the ground below with a visible degree of anxiety. Teisko was familiar with the Lake Kivu area, and he was apparently concerned because of what had happened to the village they were approaching.

"We are getting closer, monsieur," the Rwandian announced as he reached for the oxygen mask by his seat. "I suggest we use the air tanks now."

"Don't have to worry about it at this elevation," McCarter assured him. "Even if the carbon dioxide is still at a dangerous level, the concentrated gas is heavier than air. After more than forty-eight hours, you don't have to worry about lethal mists being this high above the lake."

"I hope you are right, monsieur," Teisko said, shaking his head in grim doubt.

"We're safe enough," Calvin James assured the African from the cabin of the helicopter. "Carbon dioxide isn't like cyanide gas, you know. We breathe it in and out all the time. Actually the air usually contains more carbon dioxide than oxygen."

"Well, I took some science in school, but it was a long time ago. I don't understand just what happened here and why we are safe now."

"You probably recall that we inhale air that consists of several kinds of gases. Oxygen is the most important. Anyway, what we exhale is pretty close to being pure carbon dioxide. The people at Kivu died because there wasn't enough oxygen. They suffocated."

"Oh, I see," Teisko replied, although his tone suggested he still wasn't too clear on the subject.

James shrugged. He had not come to Rwanda to give crash courses in basic science. The black commando checked his gear for the fourth time that morning. James had brought a gas analysis-detector. About the size of a standard suitcase, the GAD was a sophisticated contraption with several vents that filtered air to be analyzed by the compact computer within the miniature portable laboratory.

Rafael Encizo watched James with mild interest. The machine fascinated Encizo, but he had no intention of trying to use it. The device was fairly complex and registered information in chemical formulas that were meaningless to Encizo. James was a chemist by training, but Encizo didn't share this knowledge. The Cuban figured he would do better to stick with things he already knew about.

The oxygen tanks, however, were very familiar to the veteran scuba diver and frogman. Encizo checked the hoses, masks and valves to the tanks while the chopper headed for Lake Kivu. They might not even need the oxygen tanks if the carbon dioxide level had tapered off. But it was better to be prepared with unnecessary gear than not have it and discover they needed it to survive. That was the sort of golden rule that allowed Phoenix Force to win and survive.

It was also why the three Phoenix pros were armed to the teeth. There was no reason to expect danger from living opponents at Lake Kivu, but they weren't prepared to take any chances. Dressed in green fatigue uniforms, the commandos carried their weapons of choice.

Encizo had his H&K P9S pistol holstered on a hip and a .380-caliber Walther PPK in a shoulder holster rig. In addition to the handguns, Encizo carried a Cold Steel Tanto fighting knife in a cross-draw position on his belt and the Gerber dagger in a boot sheath. The Cuban's Heckler & Koch MP-5 completed his personal arsenal.

Calvin James wore a Jackass leather shoulder holster rig with his Beretta 92-F under his left arm and a G96 Jet-Aer fighting dagger in a sheath under the right. He was further provided with an M-16 assault rifle with a 30-round magazine in its well.

McCarter carried his trusted Browning Hi-Power in shoulder leather as he piloted the helicopter. The British ace also had a KG-99 machine pistol in a case near his seat and a stainless steel Smith & Wesson snubnose .38 Special was holstered at the small of his back. Teisko had been surprised by the amount of firepower the strange foreigners brought for a situation that did not seem to require weapons. The African had felt it was unnecessary to bring his French MAB pistol under the circumstances, but he had the 9 mm autoloader in a button-flap holster on a Sam Browne belt next to a pack of emergency supplies in the cabin.

The terrain below changed dramatically as the helicopter hovered above craterous Lake Kivu, which was surrounded by towering dark mountains of volcanic rock. Most of the water still seemed blue-green from the air, although a large rust-colored blotch at the surface revealed where the cloud of deadly concentrated gas had arisen. Calvin James peered through a pair of binoculars and gazed down at the reddish muck. Dozens of dead fish floated on the surface.

"That's the spot," James announced. "It doesn't look good, but it's still a hell of a lot better than the photographs of Lake Nios in 1986."

"Yeah," Encizo commented, "but we didn't have to land there two days after all those people died from carbon dioxide fumes. Have you found a place to land yet, Miller?"

"Bloody rocks all around," McCarter responded to his cover name. "The best clearing is probably in the middle of the village itself."

"Are you certain it is safe to land there?" Teisko asked nervously.

"Safer than trying to balance this whirlybird on the peaks of these rocks," McCarter replied. "It's a fishing village, right? Must be fairly close to the banks of the lake."

"Uh, yes," Teisko answered. "Shouldn't we put on the oxygen masks now?"

"Not a bad idea," the Briton agreed. "You blokes in the back? Get the air tanks ready. We're going down just as soon as I can find the village. Might have to circle around a bit, but you might want to put on the masks just in case."

"Just be careful you don't circle over to the opposite side of the lake," James warned. "That's Zaire over there. They might not care to have a French military aircraft fly across the border unannounced."

"That's all I need—a bleedin' back seat pilot," McCarter muttered sourly.

The sky was clear and very blue as the helicopter circled around the lake in a methodical surveillance of the area. Birds fluttered wildly as they rose from the rocks, frightened by the whirling roar of the rotor blades. The men noticed that no birds appeared near the rocks closest to the reddish-brown stain on the water. McCarter slipped the elastic band of his face mask over his head and fitted the clear plastic cup over his nose and mouth. The Briton had been a pilot for years and appreciated the warnings offered by the master fliers of nature. The birds sensed danger in the area, and McCarter was not about to ignore the signs.

The British commando soon found the village. It was little more than twin rows of thatched huts. Several lifeless human forms still littered the streets, covered by blankets and canvas tarps. About two dozen dead goats lay sprawled near the outskirts of the village. McCarter worked the throttle and rudders to bring the helicopter directly over the village.

A cloud of dust rose from the center of the hamlet of the dead as the chopper blades created a fierce gust of man-made wind. The copter descended smoothly and landed in the center of the dirt road that bisected the village. It touched down between two corpses. Encizo pushed back the sliding door and climbed from the chopper. He was wearing the mask, and the oxygen tank was strapped to his back in a harness rig. The MP-5 hung from a strap over his right shoulder.

Similarly equipped, James followed, toting the gas analysis-detector handle in his left fist. He maintained a close scrutiny of the digital screen of the GAD which displayed Formula numbers, atomic weight estimate and proportions of various gases.

"Everybody keep your masks on," James ordered, his voice muffled by the plastic cup over his nose and mouth. "Carbon dioxide reading is still dangerously high. Maybe it's just because so much dust was stirred up by the chopper. A lot of the gas would have seeped into the ground."

Encizo glanced about the village. It was even more grim from ground level than from the air. The current from the rotor blades had blown the cover from a dead body in the street. The Cuban glanced down and saw the corpse of an elderly woman. She lay on her side, her hands frozen in a clawlike position near her chest. Her mouth was open and coated with dried mucus. The eyes were glassy and seemed confused. Perhaps she had realized she was dying and didn't understand why.

The blades whirled at a gradually slower pace as James and Encizo ventured forward, ducking instinctively although the rotor blades were at least a foot and a half above James's head. Teisko emerged from the chopper and joined the Phoenix pair. James consulted the GAD as he continued to move away from the helicopter. The carbon dioxide evel gradually lessened the further he moved from the dust cloud.

Encizo walked to the nearest hut and pushed open the door. He glimpsed more bodies inside, but avoided looking too closely at the still forms. A single glance revealed at least one corpse had been a child. The angry buzz of flies inside the hut warned that the condition of these bodies was probably very unpleasant even with the oxygen masks to protect the men from the stench.

"Merde alors," Teisko gasped with repulsion as he looked over Encizo's shoulder and turned away just as fast. "The damn insects survived. There is no justice."

"Insects can live for days with very little oxygen," Encizo commented. "Little bastards can survive just about anything except a good stomp. We could wipe out the human race with a full-scale nuclear war, and there'd be cockroaches feeding on the radioactive remains the next day."

"S'il vous plaît, monsieur," Teisko urged, holding a hand to his stomach. "I already feel as if I may become ill..."

"You don't want to do that," Encizo said as he pulled the door shut. "If you throw up wearing that oxygen mask, you could choke to death on your own vomit."

Teisko groaned and hurried back to the helicopter. McCarter had stepped from the chopper as the African approached. The British commando also wore an air tank and mask. His KG-99 hung from a shoulder strap near his right hip within easy grasp if the need arrived.

"You want to stay with the bird?" McCarter inquired, and the Rwandian agent nodded in reply.

"Not a bad idea for somebody to watch it," the Briton stated. He guessed why Teisko had decided to head back to the craft. The man was not used to situations like the massacre at the village. McCarter figured he would help Teisko save face. "Keep an eye on things while we look around. Okay?"

"Oui," Teisko said with a nod. "I think maybe I will sit down for a while. Is this all right?"

"Sure, mate," McCarter assured him. "There's a walk ie-talkie radio in there. Keep it switched on in case we hav to contact you."

McCarter approached Encizo and James, and they movec on. There was little to be gained by examining the village i detail. Others had been there before, of course. About hal the bodies had been removed by the Rwandian teams tha had previously inspected the grisly site. The rest would b taken care of when they were sure the carbon dioxide leve was safe. The bodies that had been carted out earlier hac been subjected to autopsies, while those left behind were a the mercy of the insect scavengers. Corpses seem destinec to endure some sort of indignities, one way or the other.

The Phoenix trio moved to the edge of the village, glad to be farther from the clutter of dead bodies. None of the three men was squeamish, and they had seen human remains fa more ghastly than these. They were veterans of bloodiec battlefields where the ground was littered with dismem bered, charred and mutilated bodies. The difference wa that the village had not been a true battlefield, because the slain civilians had never had a chance to defend them selves.

The bloodless slaughter of the villagers was disturbing tc the Phoenix warriors, especially because the victims had been helpless and unaware when killed by whoever had in stigated the lethal chain of events. They had been mur dered simply because they were convenient for the purposes of the unknown assassins.

"Well, unless these people had a gold mine under their village, there wasn't anything to be gained by wiping them out if the killers did it for profit," Encizo mused.

"Let's find the stream that was used to pollute the lake with the lethal compound of sodium and magnesium that caused this atrocity," James suggested. "Maybe we'll find something more useful than a bunch of victims."

"At least it's bound to be less depressing than this place," McCarter remarked as he reached for a walkie-talkie on his belt. "I'll tell Teisko where we're going. Poor chap is about ready to lose his breakfast. Not that I blame him."

"This stuff is hard for us to take, so I hate to think of what it must be like for a guy who's basically a paper pusher back in Kigali," James added.

"If it's hard for us to look at, it must have been a lot harder on those people who asphyxiated in this village," Encizo said grimly. "Children with smaller lungs and old people probably died first. Parents had to watch their sons and daughters die in their arms, helpless to do anything to save them. They probably welcomed oblivion and death when their time came to join their loved ones..."

Encizo stopped abruptly. He realized he was relating to the tragedy because it reminded him of another village in Cuba long ago when he had seen his own family virtually destroyed by Castro's troops. James placed a hand on Encizo's shoulder.

"We'll find the bastards, man," James assured him. "Come on. Let's check out that shack."

THEY FOUND THE STREAM along a narrow pathway between the rocky formations that ringed the lake. The trio headed upstream, to the north, and spotted the small shack by the stream. James checked his GAD once more and slipped the plastic mask from his face.

"Oxygen level is higher and the carbon dioxide is down enough to be safe to breathe," the black warrior announced. "The wind has probably dispersed the concentration of the carbon dioxide gas clouds that reached this level, and more oxygen has reached the area thanks to the trees and other plants not far from here. In another day or two, the whole lake region will be pretty much back to normal."

"Not for the people of the village," Encizo commented as he pulled off his mask.

They approached the shack. It was slightly larger than a toolshed and appeared to be made of a flimsy tin alloy, held together by bolts at each corner. The roof had simply been fitted on top of the four walls by the use of slots and pegs. The door hung open to reveal the empty interior. The Rwandian authorities had already taken the tanks, pumps and pipes from the shack when they had removed the bodies of the two Americans.

"CIA experiment, my arse," McCarter muttered as he peered inside the shed. "I've seen outdoor latrines that are better built than this thing. Somebody just slapped it together for the occasion."

"Too bad we couldn't get here as soon as they discovered this thing," Encizo commented. The Cuban knelt on the ground and examined the dozens of bootprints that marked the area. "Any clues that were here have been trampled out of existence."

"Yeah," James agreed as he glanced around the rocky peaks. "Maybe the Rwandians have somethin'..."

He stopped in midsentence when he spotted movement along the craggy stone formations. James had a brief look at a young black man, dressed in green clothing with brown spots. The man also wore a metal oxygen tank on his back.

"We got company," James announced. He began to slowly lower the GAD to the ground.

"More than one," McCarter added as he tilted his head toward another cluster of jagged rocks to the south of where James saw the first man. "The one I glimpsed has a rifle."

"Hell," James rasped. "I wish I'd brought my M-16."

"Could be they're hiding because they looked down here and saw three armed strangers poking around this site," Encizo remarked. "That's reason to be nervous."

"Yeah," McCarter admitted, his hand dropping to the frame of his KG-99, "but I reckon we have call to feel the same way..."

Suddenly rifle barrels appeared around the edge of three different rock formations. The Phoenix pros immediately responded to the threat. James jumped back into the open doorway of the shed and ducked low. McCarter threw himself around the corner of the shack and Encizo hit the ground near the opposite side. They had barely managed to gain some cover when automatic fire erupted from the rocks. Bullets raked the metal structure and tore up geysers of dirt from the ground.

"Son of a bitch," James hissed through clenched teeth as a rifle slug pierced the metal wall less than an inch from his nose.

The warrior from Chicago sprawled on his belly as more bullets punched through the thin walls of the shed, making the metal ring and echo. James covered his head as the sound pounded into his ears. His head throbbed as he reached for the Beretta pistol.

McCarter crawled to the rear of the shack as a column of enemy gunshots ripped up the earth near his legs. The Briton reached the questionably secure shelter behind the shack and adopted a prone position with the KG-99 in both fists. Encizo low-crawled next to his British partner, his Heckler & Koch subgun in his grasp.

"Who you figure's more nervous now?" McCarter growled as he carefully peered around the corner.

The enemy had a definite advantage. They were positioned approximately a hundred yards from the Phoenix trio—beyond accurate range of submachine guns or pistols, but well within effective rifle range. And the mounds of volcanic rock certainly offered them good cover.

McCarter saw two figures bounding from rocky cover to rocky cover. Both appeared to be young Africans, clad in spotted camouflage fatigues and equipped with air tanks and face masks similar to those used by the Phoenix trio. One guy carried an assault rifle, a Soviet-made AK-47 or a weapon of similar design. The other was armed with a submachine gun with a short frame and a long barrel with a vented metal sleeve. McCarter recognized the weapon as a French MAT-49 with an extra-long barrel. He had seen such modified MAT choppers when he was a "special observer" in Vietnam. The French 9 mm subguns were converted to fire 7.62 mm ammo so the Kalashnikov cartridges could be used in the MAT-49s as well.

"I figure at least four opponents," Encizo declared as he peered up at the rocks. "Maybe more."

"That's enough," McCarter replied. He trained his KG-99 on the stony barrier where at least one gunman had ducked for cover. "I'm going to try to flush 'em out. Get ready to respond to however they react to this."

The Briton triggered his blaster. He aimed a bit high to compensate for distance and gravity. The 3-round burst sparked along the rock, sparks making two gunmen promptly pop up nearby and aim their weapons in McCarter's direction.

Encizo opened fire, and the trio of 9 mm slugs slammed into the face and throat of an African triggerman. The protective plastic cup over the man's mouth and nose split as the high-velocity round pierced the mask. Another parabellum burrowed into the hollow of the gunman's throat. He released his AK-47 and clawed at the wounds as he slumped along the rock wall and disappeared behind a jagged column of stone.

Calvin James aimed his Beretta 92-F as he lay on his belly. He gripped the pistol in both hands and squeezed off two shots. One parabellum round chipped stone just next to the second gunman, who immediately started to duck and managed to get his head directly in the path of James's second round. The 115-grain Silvertip 9 mm hollownose slug smashed into the man's forehead.

Another ambusher fired a frantic volley with his MAT-49 and tried to spray a burst of 7.62 mm rounds at James and Encizo. Even as he started to scramble for safety, the enemy gunman kept up his fire. He had forgotten about McCarter, but the Briton had not fallen asleep during the gunbattle. He aimed his KG-99 and triggered another 3-round message of destruction.

The parabellum hornets struck the fleeing figure in the left arm, tearing into the triceps muscles and shattering bone in the upper arm. The man was shoved by the force of the impact, and two 9 mm rounds slammed into the air tank on his back. At least one bullet punched through the metal container and sparked against the surface.

The tank exploded, tearing the gunman apart and scattering burning human debris across the rock wall. Another of the enemy cried out and tumbled from behind a boulder near the explosion. His left sleeve had caught fire, and he beat at it wildly as he rolled to the hard ground below.

Another panic-stricken rifleman bolted from cover. Perhaps he thought the Phoenix trio were armed with grenades or rocket launchers. As he desperately tried to crawl up the face of the rock wall, Encizo and James opened up.

Their bullets failed to fulfill their intent to wound, but a round struck the air tank on the man's back. The oxygen responded with the predictable results. It exploded like a Roman candle against the rocks and sent a shower of burning debris from the stony wall. Only a vague human shape revealed that the mangled, charred lump had formerly been a person.

James saw the body drop like a fiery meteor, then looked up at McCarter's shout.

"Cover me, mates!"

The British ace rose to his feet and suddenly charged toward the rocks. He fired his KG-99 as he ran and sprayed the area with 9 mm rounds. Encizo groaned and rolled his eyes as McCarter executed this high-risk tactic. The Briton was unashamed of his addiction to excitement. He liked putting his life on the line and thrilled at the chance to test his skills.

Nonetheless, McCarter's actions were not as foolhardy as they appeared. The Briton knew it was a dangerous move, but he also knew he could count on his partners to back his play. McCarter was not suicidal, but he was willing to take considerable risk in a situation that might ultimately help his teammates and himself survive.

He continued his dangerous run as a gun barrel poked from the edge of a boulder. Encizo instantly snap-aimed and fired at the enemy weapon. Bullets raked the position and ricochets whined all around the rocks. The hidden gunman yanked back his gun barrel in response.

McCarter glanced down at the fallen opponent who had taken a tumble after one of his comrades had exploded. The man was still dazed, his left arm badly burned. He had lost his weapon when he fell and presented no immediate threat. McCarter turned his attention back to the rocks above. The KG-99 was out of ammo and McCarter didn't want to spend time reloading. He reached under his arm and withdrew the Browning Hi-Power instead.

Calvin James scanned the rock walls in search of other opponents. Nothing indicated that more of the gunmen were in hiding, except for the one who had been forced to duck. The black commando took a deep breath and bolted forward. He raised his Beretta pistol and fired, while Encizo stayed by the shack to provide cover.

The man behind the rock formation leaned around the edge of his cover to point his MAT-49 at James. At the base of the rock wall, McCarter held his Browning pistol in a firm two-handed Weaver's Grip and raised it to line up the sights. He had the Hi-Power trained on the gunman's chest when he squeezed off two shots. Both 9 mm rounds punched into the opponent's chest.

The man's heart burst. Blood spurted across his shirt front and splashed the cloth. His eyes swelled with an expression of amazement as he realized he was a second from being dead. The gunman dropped his weapon and fell forward to tumble lifelessly down the rock wall to the ground. McCarter stepped back to make room for the corpse to land near his feet.

Then a blur of motion suddenly appeared in front of McCarter. He glimpsed a crimson stain along a charred shirt sleeve as two strong dark hands grabbed his wrist. A fierce black face bobbed inches from McCarter's as his opponent wrenched the Browning from his grasp. The Phoenix pro recognized the man as the formerly dazed figure whom he had discounted, but the man was obviously in better shape than he had appeared to be.

McCarter hooked his left fist into the angry ebony features. The man's head was jarred by the punch, and McCarter shoved his right arm forward to break free of the grip on his wrist. He pumped the heel of his palm under his opponent's jaw, making the head snap back from the blow.

The Briton's right leg lashed out to snap-kick the African between the legs. The boot slammed into the groin, and the man started to double up with a half-choked gasp. McCarter's left leg executed a roundhouse kick to his opponent's head. The African was hurled off balance from the kick and fell headfirst into the rock wall. The crunch of bone announced his contact with a boulder. The man's body slumped limply to the ground, the top of his head dripping blood.

"Oh, bugger," McCarter muttered as he knelt beside the still form and vainly searched for a pulse.

"Aw, man," Calvin James began as he approached. "Did you kill him?"

"I didn't mean to," the Briton said with a shrug. He stood and looked at the other bodies littering the ground. "Doesn't look like we managed to take any of these bleeders alive."

"Well," James began with a sigh, "it sure looks like somebody didn't want us poking around here. Wish we had some idea why."

"Be nice to know *who* they are while we're at it," McCarter added.

"Them," Encizo answered as he stepped closer and pointed at the dead man on the ground with his free hand. "But they won't be telling us any details now."

9

Massamba held a rock in each fist as he sat behind a small field desk and listened to Juvénal. He squeezed the stones harder as the henchman explained how he had sent half a dozen men to Lake Kivu, but none of them would be coming back. Juvénal saw the anger in Massamba's broad ebony features. He was tempted to move a hand toward the handle of the *panga* on his belt, but he realized that any sign of aggression would only make his situation worse. It might even get him killed.

Henri stood inside the tent, not far from Massamba's desk. The Belgian mercenary rested a hand on the 9 mm pistol in a cross-draw holster. His cold blue eyes remained fixed on Juvénal as if he was eager to draw his weapon and blast a bullet hole between Juvénal's eyes. The African didn't like white people of any sort, but he had a special dislike for Belgians, and Henri was the worst of the lot in Juvénal's opinion.

"I don't recall telling you to send anyone to kill those foreigners," Massamba began, squeezing the stones in his fists even harder. "I simply said I wanted your people to keep the Lake Kivu area under observation."

"I know," Juvénal began lamely, "but those two CIA bastards we confronted on the street last night were there with one of those other foreigners who claimed to be a Canadian journalist. They were together when they inspected the shed. They were well armed, too..."

"Obviously," Massamba said sharply. "They killed those fools you sent after them."

"The man in charge contacted me by radio and told me what had happened when the helicopter arrived at Lake Kivu," Juvénal explained. "He said the foreigners spoke English and they carried weapons, oxygen tanks and a machine of some sort, which he didn't recognize. He asked if these maggots should be terminated. I assumed that you would want them disposed of."

Massamba slapped both rocks on the desktop with enough force to startle Juvénal. The sound was not unlike a gunshot. Juvénal half expected to see the rocks crumble in Massamba's massive hands and the desk to collapse from the blow.

"You idiot!" Massamba snapped. "What did you think killing them would accomplish? All that would do is alert the CIA or whoever they work for that someone is willing to take drastic measures to discourage anyone from looking into the deaths at Lake Kivu."

"Well," Juvénal said lamely, "at least we know they're spies now."

"We already assumed that much," Massamba groaned. "We didn't have to confirm it. Six of our men are dead because of your bad judgment. I'm not very happy about that."

Henri yanked his pistol from its holster. Juvénal instinctively grabbed the handle of his *panga*, but the 9 mm pistol was already pointed at his face. The Belgian mercenary smiled at the African and flicked off the safety catch.

"Put it away, Henri," Massamba ordered. "If I wanted him dead I could have killed him myself."

"Oui, monsieur," the Belgian replied as he holstered his weapon.

Juvénal stared at Henri's grinning face. He hoped one day to get the Belgian without that damn gun. The scrawny little white man would not have a chance against Juvénal's big machete. He figured the Belgian bastard would soil his trousers if the contest consisted of cold steel instead of bullets.

"I like you, Juvénal," Massamba began as he tapped his fingertips together in a thoughtful gesture. "This time, and *only* this time, I forgive your trespass against me. Biblical mercy. The sort of thing the missionaries taught us when they wanted to convert all of Africa to Christianity. It was nonsense, of course. But no matter, even myths and parables have occasional pearls of wisdom. You agree?"

"Of course," Juvénal replied. He didn't see that he had much of a choice under the circumstances. "Whatever you say, Massamba."

"There was also some Old Testament business about an eye for an eye and all that," Massamba continued. "You've already caused six of our comrades to die. That means you already owe six lives. If anything happens like this again, I advise you to dig a grave and wait for Henri or one of the others to come along and shoot you in the head."

Massamba leaned forward and glared up at Juvénal as he added, "You see, if someone else has to dig your grave for you, you'll still be alive when they bury you in it."

"I understand," Juvénal agreed with a nervous nod.

"Good," Massamba replied. "This is a bad turn of events, but it could be far worse. I assume none of your people carried any sort of identification."

"Of course not, Massamba," Juvénal assured him. "They were well trained and always careful to obey our most fundamental rules."

"They were not as well trained as the enemy agents," Henri commented. "Two against one, with the advantage of surprise and long-range weapons, yet the three outsiders won. They must be something special. Members of an elite fighting unit, perhaps."

"They were lucky," Juvénal insisted.

"They were deadly," Massamba corrected. "Don't forget that and don't ever underestimate them again. Fortunately they still don't have any proof against us. Some overzealous locals discovered the three outsiders at Lake Kivu. Enraged by the CIA once again poking about, they confronted the American scum and the trigger-happy assassins killed them. That's the way our propaganda will read. We'll claim the CIA planted the weapons on the dead men to try to cover up their crime."

"The government may not even announce the incident," Henri remarked. "The Rwandians and the Americans may wish to keep the confrontation a secret for the time being."

"That's all right, too," Massamba stated as he gathered up the two stones and once again squeezed them in his fists. "However, this forces us to move on to the next phase immediately. It is time for us to leave the country. I don't want any of us here when the authorities start looking for associates of the dead men at Lake Kivu. Tell the others to strike camp and get ready to pull out."

"Oui," Henri replied. He cast a contemptuous glance at Juvénal and headed for the opening of the tent.

"I don't trust that Belgian pig," Juvénal said quietly when they were alone. "We cannot trust any whites. They have never brought Africans anything but misery..."

"When did you become a humanitarian?" Massamba asked with a bitter chuckle. "We have to remember the first rule of business and politics, my friend. You can't afford to worry about what happens to people, or you'll never be in a position to change things. You look after your own and your group's desires and needs, but everyone else can go to hell."

"Henri isn't one of us," Juvénal insisted.

"He does his job, and we need him if this operation is to succeed," Massamba stated. "His interests in this matter are the same as ours. You can always trust a man to remain loyal to his own self-interests. Don't worry about Henri or the other whites in our group. Have faith in them and their greed. Wonderful thing about greed is it is universal. Black, white or any other skin shade, greed is more reliable than patriotism and more durable than love. It is one of the greatest and certainly one of the most honest of all human emotions. Show me a man motivated by greed, and I'll show you a man I can do business with."

"I suppose we need the whites for now," Juvénal muttered.

"You and Henri never have gotten along very well," Massamba said with a sigh. He rose from his chair and stretched hugely. "I understand the hard feelings, of course. You're from Zaire and still recall the days of the Belgian Congo. The colonial rule is over, my friend. None of us are better off because of it."

"At least the Europeans have suffered, as well," Juvénal said with a smile.

"Just don't let your hatred for the whites get in the way of your mission," Massamba warned. "I meant what I said, Juvénal. I can't afford to have incompetents, especially among my top personnel. Henri hasn't made any serious mistakes. You have. Another major mistake will cost you your life. I can't expect to maintain strict discipline among my men unless the same rules apply to everyone, regardless of rank among my people."

"I understand, Massamba," Juvénal assured him.

"I hope so," Massamba said, his arms spread wide apart. "I really am angry about your behavior..."

Suddenly Massamba swung a brawny arm in a high arc. Juvénal jumped back in alarm and reached for the handle of his machete. Massamba's big fist slammed onto the desktop with bone-shattering force, and the folding legs under the field furniture snapped apart from the blow. The desk collapsed in a broken, splintered heap at Massamba's feet.

"You don't want to get me angry again," Massamba declared. "Do you?"

Juvénal bobbed his head in mute reply. He gazed down at the pile of junk that had formerly been Massamba's desk. It was a dramatic gesture that certainly spoke louder than words. Massamba could have broken his neck with a single blow before Juvénal could have drawn his machete.

"I don't want to get you angry again," Juvénal declared, enthusiastically shaking his head to make certain Massamba understood.

"I'm so glad," Massamba said dryly. "Clean up this mess and help bring down the tents. We have a great deal to do and little time to do it."

10

"We don't have a record of the fingerprints of any of the six men you killed near Lake Kivu this morning," Kagera declared as he entered the conference room at the French embassy. "That means none of them have ever been arrested and charged for any crimes here in Rwanda."

"You don't have a system of fingerprinting or printing the feet of infants for identification?" Gary Manning inquired.

"Only for children born in hospitals," Kagera explained, stuffing tobacco into his pipe. "Rwanda is still largely an agricultural country. More than half our population are farmers. Many children are born at home. Things are different here than in the United States or Europe."

"It's also possible they may have been from other countries," Carson, the CIA agent, suggested. "People go back and forth across the borders fairly freely here. Rwanda gets along pretty well with her neighbors. There hasn't been much reason to be suspicious of travelers from other African countries."

"Security never seems important in peaceful times," Yakov Katzenelenbogen commented as he leafed through a recent file of CIA intelligence materials. "Maybe if it did, peaceful times might last a bit longer. But I just found something of interest."

"That sounds more encouraging than most of what we've come up with so far," David McCarter said with a sigh. "What is it?"

"The CIA has had general observations conducted on the television teams currently in Rwanda," the Phoenix Force commander began. "Typical overt intelligence gathering. The point of interest is that the Soviet Union sent a television news crew. Care to guess who's among them?"

"Pasternak?" Manning inquired, his tone suggesting he hoped he was wrong.

"That's right," Carson said, surprised they considered this important news. "Comrade Viktor Pasternak, the darling of Soviet television in person. You've probably seen his guest appearances on some of the American TV shows. He pops up on that one talk show. You know, the one with the ultraliberal host who's always running down American policies?"

"Yeah," McCarter said with a nod. "I recall hearing that same bastard whining about British aggressions in the Falklands and American 'atrocities' in Grenada and Libya, but he never asked his pal Pasternak to discuss the Soviets in Afghanistan or Angola or Nicaragua. I guess that never bothered him."

"You Americans pride yourselves on freedom of speech," Lebrun began as he used a corkscrew to pry loose a cork from a bottle of white wine. "Don't you believe people have a right to ideas that might disagree with your own? We French citizens regard this as a basic liberty."

"I reckon a fella has a right to opinions I don't agree with," McCarter stated. "And I have a right to think he's an arse because of it."

"We must continue—although it pains me to interrupt this discussion of international social issues," Katz said with a sigh. "We need to explain why Pasternak is a special cause for alarm for us. You see, gentlemen, we met Pasternak on a previous mission."

"Then he knows you guys are special agents or commandos or..." Carson began, a puzzled expression slithering across his face. "Hey, what the hell are you guys exactly, anyway?"

"We're in charge—that's all you need to know," Kat replied. "And unfortunately, Pasternak knows we're co nected with covert operations for the U.S. government. H doesn't know about our Oval Office authority, but he aware that we're fairly high up in rank. Pasternak also ha some idea of our methods."

"He's lucky," Kagera muttered, rolling his eyes towar the ceiling. "You've been working with us for the past tw days, and I haven't figured out what your methods are.. aside from killing people, of course."

McCarter snorted angrily as he answered. "Those bloke were trying to kill us, and we didn't have much of a choic under the circumstances."

"The point is that Pasternak may have recognized u yesterday," Katz said, determined to get back to the sul ject. "That explains the microphones we found in the ho tel. They seemed to be KGB-style bugs put in place in hurry. That's exactly what they were."

"Yeah," Manning agreed. The Canadian stared down a his cup of black coffee as if expecting it to show him som answers. "But just how is the KGB involved in this busi ness? Are they trying to find out what's going on or are the responsible for the Lake Kivu incident?"

"That's one of the things we have to find out," Katz re plied. He took out his cigarettes and stuck the pack be tween the hooks of his prosthesis to withdraw a cigarett with his left hand. "We've had enough encounters with th KGB in the past to know there isn't much they're not capa ble of."

"Well," Carson began as he slumped into a seat by th table, "there's a lot of talk about *glasnost*, the new 'open ness' at the Kremlin. Maybe it's true, but I'm not gonna be it extends to the cloak-and-dagger boys in the KGB."

"The Soviet Committee for State Security doesn't alway follow the rules set down by the Politburo," Katz stated "When Lenin set up the Soviet version of Marxism, he di vided the power between the Politburo, the military and th ecret police. When Stalin took over, he gave more power to he secret police to serve as an enforcement arm against political enemies—real and imagined. The organization has changed names several times since then, but it has remained very powerful and sometimes operates without the authority of the Kremlin.''

"The KGB is the largest intelligence network in the world,'' Manning added. "The Soviet GRU, military intelligence, is the second largest. The problem with having spy outfits that are that big and powerful is that they become difficult to control. Even Moscow can't keep track of what these networks are up to all the time.''

"Washington and London aren't always so trustworthy,'' McCarter said and shook his head. "And there ure isn't any reason to believe Moscow is any better.''

"None of my friends are Communists, either,'' Katz reminded the Briton, "but I don't think the Kremlin would authorize any drastic new activities in Africa at this time. It simply doesn't make sense, because the Soviet Union has a ot of domestic problems to deal with and they've already had some serious trouble in Angola and Mozambique.''

Carson was drumming his fingers on the table as he watched Katz blow a smoke ring across the room. "I still don't think we can dismiss the Russians as prime suspects,'' he insisted. "Now, who else would gain by discrediting the United States and the other Western democracies by pulling something like that Lake Kivu business?''

"Massamba still has me bloody curious,'' McCarter announced. The Briton got up from his chair and began pacing the room. "That bloke and some of his mates stopped Giraudeau and Cordero in the street last night and were very interested in their activities. Maybe that's a coincidence, but it still seems odd to me after what happened to us at the lake.''

"Well, we don't have much on file about Massamba,'' Kagera admitted. "He isn't a native Rwandian. Technically, Massamba is still a citizen of Chad. He travels from

country to country throughout Central Africa, and we're
not even sure what he does to make a living. Apparently he
arranges deals—sounds like a go-between for businesses and
potential customers. Probably he has done some work as a
translator. Massamba speaks several languages fluently."

"He's obviously well educated," Katz stated. "Generally
speaking, isn't it true that most Africans who receive a uni-
versity-level education are born to a wealthy family?"

"Here in Rwanda we have the National University of
Butare," Kagera said with a shrug. "I believe there are currently about eight hundred students enrolled, more than ever
before. That should give you an idea of how common university education is in my country. We like to think of ourselves as a progressive little nation. I don't think it's just
nationalistic pride when I say that our standards of living
and education are higher than those of most of our neighbors. However, universities are basically for the upper crust
of our society. I'd say that's even more true for Chad and
most of the other African nations than it is for Rwanda."

"So Massamba is well educated, probably from a wealthy
family, and his politics are sure to be anti-West even if not
pro-Soviet," Katz mused. "I heard him running down
American and Western Europe, and I wonder if he does the
same with Soviet expansion in Africa?"

"Not that I've heard," Kagera answered, "but I've never
heard him actively cheer the Russians and the Cubans in
Angola or Mozambique or point to the People's Republic
of the Congo or Togo as models for African nations. Only
an idiot would say Ethiopia's government is a success."

"Mengistu and his comrades might consider their government in Ethiopia a success," Carson commented. "Of
course, they took over because they literally had a shoot-out
and were still standing when the smoke cleared. Maybe they
don't worry that the same thing could happen to them if
there's another 'Gunfight at the Addis Ababa Corral.'"

Calvin James and Rafael Encizo entered the conference
room. They were a little confused by Carson's remark and

wondered why the hell the CIA agent was rambling on about Ethiopian politics. James shut the door and headed for the coffeepot. Encizo waited for McCarter to pace past him and moved to a chair by the table.

"We checked out the weapons used by the gunmen at Lake Kivu," the Cuban announced. "They were about twenty or thirty years old, maybe older. Soviet-made AK-47 assault rifles, French MAT-49 submachine guns—all but one converted to fire 7.62 mm ammo with an extended barrel. Miller tells me he's seen this sort of thing before in Nam."

"And in Congo," Carson added. "For the same reason, too. Former French colonies with a lot of MAT submachine guns left over, and Communist forces get a hold of them. Makes sense to alter the weapons to handle the same caliber as the Kalashnikov rifles."

"We don't know if these guns came from the Congo or not," Encizo insisted. "Probably leftovers from old conflicts. Gun-runners in Zaire, Chad, Central Republic of Africa or anywhere that used to be controlled by Belgium or France could have gotten a hold of this stuff. These weapons were all pretty scratched up, and they'd seen a lot of wear, but they were still in good working order. A couple of the dead men also had handguns—French MAB and a Browning 1935 Model 9 mm pistol. Hard to tell what the guys who blew up might have been carrying. However, their uniform was a type of jungle camouflage outfit of a French design that is still favored in the Congo. There may be a connection."

"I examined the bodies for tattoos, scars, dental work and other stuff that might help identify the nationalities of the guys who jumped us," James stated as he walked to the table with a cup of coffee. "No tattoos, either the commercial or the tribal ones associated with initiations and rites of manhood. There were scars, of course, but nothing that was much help. One guy had his appendix removed. All of them had been cut up by knives in the past, probably from street fights when they were younger. Two had old bullet scars, apparently from small-caliber weapons.''

"Sounds like former hoodlums hired for the job," Gary Manning commented.

"That might be right," James replied. "The soles of the dead men's feet were not heavily callused, and their hands were fairly soft. They were men accustomed to cities, not farms, and for sure not the product of any of the more remote traditional villages. Another point of interest is none of them carried any type of talisman or good luck piece."

"Well, they didn't carry any driver's licenses, passports, dogtags, wallets, keys or even coins," Lebrun said with a shrug as he poured himself his third glass of wine. "What's so surprising about the fact that they didn't have any good luck charms or religious items?"

"Well, many hoods are surprisingly superstitious," James explained, "and so are a lot of Africans. I'm not saying they all run around with juju bags filled with crocodile teeth and leopard claws, but most wouldn't think of going into a combat situation without some sort of symbol of supernatural protection. It could be a crucifix or prayer beads, and others might carry a piece of bark or a stone that represents the powers of a so-called 'primitive' religion. But these guys didn't have anything like that. Not so much as some hairs from a rabbit's foot."

"Damn Commies are atheists," Carson declared. "If these bastards are Marxists, all they'd have to do would be to quote some crap from *Das Kapital* to reinforce their courage."

"Actually there are thousands of Communists who consider themselves to be devout members of various religions," Katz corrected. "Italy and France have large Communist parties, and most of their members claim to be good Catholics. The lack of amulets, talisman or good luck items doesn't prove the enemy are Marxist or connected with the Soviet KGB. It does suggest they came from an urban background. They probably had little religious upbringing or rejected it in later life.''

"Which leaves us pretty much at square one," Manning said with a frustrated sigh.

A telephone rang. It was an in-house line within the French embassy. Lebrun answered it. His face was grim as he listened to the voice of the caller, then he thanked the caller and hung up.

"I have a feeling this isn't good news," Manning remarked as he watched Lebrun step away from the phone.

"One of my colleagues called to inform me that a radio broadcast from Nigeria carried a rather disturbing news item," the Frenchman began as he reached for the wine bottle once more. "It seems there was a student protest in Lagos—college intellectuals demonstrating against American CIA actions in Africa. Similar to the sort of thing Massamba has been doing here."

"That doesn't seem very unexpected," Carter said. "These things tend to spread pretty fast, and militant groups are bound to hop on the proverbial bandwagon in other countries after the Lake Kivu story got out."

"It's worse than that, my English friend," Lebrun explained. "Someone opened fire with automatic weapons and murdered at least three protesters, and several others have been wounded. The assassins were identified as white men, and the Nigerian authorities already suspect they are probably Americans.''

"Holy shit," James rasped. He shook his head and clenched his fists in impotent anger. "How the hell did they come to that conclusion so quick?"

"I wasn't informed about that detail," Lebrun answered, pouring himself a drink as he spoke. "You fellows have connections with the President of the United States, no? Well, I think maybe you should call and suggest that he tell all Americans currently in Africa on business or plea-

sure to get out as quickly as possible. There is now an excellent chance some of them will be killed if they remain here
much longer.''

11

The American embassy in Lagos was the center of even more activity than the one in Kigali. The crowds that surrounded the embassy were in an ugly mood. A few protest signs waved above the heads of the mob, simple cardboard posters nailed to poles. All bore English demands for the CIA killers to be brought to justice or for America to get out of Africa. Others simply accused the United States of murder.

"I suggest we don't get any closer," Captain Jalingo said in a stern voice. "If they have the slightest suspicion that any of you are Americans, they may attack this vehicle before the soldiers can stop them."

"We've seen enough, Captain," Yakov Katzenelenbogen assured him as he peered between the heads of Jalingo and Kagera to look out the windshield. "In fact, I don't see any reason to be here to begin with."

"I thought you ought to see just how unpopular you Americans are in my country," Jalingo explained. "You may not wish to stay in Nigeria. You're hardly invited here, although my government will agree to assist you if you're serious about helping us find the people responsible for the murders that happened this afternoon."

"Why do you think we're here?" Carson asked. The CIA agent sat in the rear of the small green and white tour bus, along with the five men of Phoenix Force.

"You might intend to try to cover up CIA involvement," the Nigerian officer replied. "Perhaps you've been able to convince my honorable colleague from Rwanda that you Americans weren't responsible for the Lake Kivu incident, but I've seen enough of Westerners meddling in our affairs in the past to be less apt to believe you people. Americans are the most meddlesome of the lot.''

"Shit, man," Calvin James remarked as he peered out the tinted glass of a window to observe the mob at the embassy. "I thought the United States and Nigeria were on pretty good terms. Guess my almanac isn't up to date.''

The mob was much larger than the crowd at Kigali had been, and it seemed to be more unruly. Torches burned as protestors spat out curses and threats. Most spoke English or Hausa, the two official languages of Nigeria, although there were so many angry voices it was difficult to understand anything they said. A smattering of native languages, such as Kanuri and Yoruba, added to the confusion. It sounded like Saturday night at the Tower of Babel.

A very pissed off Saturday night, James thought as he noticed that many demonstrators carried clubs and bricks. It was difficult to guess the size of the crowd in front of the American embassy, but they filled up more than two city blocks. There were at least a thousand, probably closer to twice that number.

Hundreds of soldiers and police formed a barricade between the demonstrators and the embassy. Two tanks and some armored cars also stood by. The grim-faced troops and policemen were armed with bayonets and guns ready and pointed at the mob. A bloody massacre looked ready to erupt if a single person threw a stone. Massamba had controlled the crowd in Kigali. He had preached a lot of propaganda nonsense, but at least he kept the mob from violence. James was surprised to find himself wishing the militant leader was in Lagos that tense, dark night.

"I had doubts about these gentlemen, too, Captain," Kagera began, trying to calm down Jalingo. "However, they were attacked by armed assassins while investigating Lake

Kivu. That convinced me there's a strong possibility the CIA aren't the villains we're after.''

"But you're not totally convinced of that, Kagera," Jalingo replied as he drove the bus onto Balewa Boulevard to avoid the mob. "Although you still helped them with their little deception."

The Nigerian referred to the story Phoenix Force had fabricated before they left Rwanda. Kagera had contacted the Nigerian government and urged them for permission to bring a team of special investigators who had discovered vital information about the Kivu incident that might connect to the Lagos shooting. The Nigerians agreed, with the result that Captain Jalingo had met the team at the airport. He was surprised to discover it consisted of only one Rwandian intelligence officer and six non-Africans—Agent Carson and the five Phoenix Force commandos.

"We didn't deceive your government, Captain," Katz declared. "Mr. Kagera didn't lie. He simply omitted a few details that would have made your people a bit reluctant to permit us to come to Nigeria."

"Don't be too pleased with your little trick," Jalingo replied as he brought the bus to a halt at a traffic light. "You managed to get here, but that doesn't mean you'll be allowed to stay in Nigeria."

"It's bloody wonderful," McCarter muttered angrily. "The blokes on our side don't want to cooperate with us. This isn't going to make our mission any easier. Get in our way enough, you'll make it impossible. Then Nigeria will just have to handle this matter on her own. You keep barking up the wrong palm tree, and you never will solve this mess. Instead, you blokes are playing right into the hands of the enemy."

"We poor little Africans are so ignorant we can't manage to do anything right without the help of the white man," Jalingo said with disgust. "We're getting tired of your patronizing attitude toward black Africa..."

"Shut up, man," James said sharply as he pointed at a white van parked on the corner. "We got eavesdroppers, dammit."

Three white men stood on the sidewalk next to the van. They were dressed in suit trousers with polished dress shoes and white, short-sleeved shirts open at the neck with their ties pulled loose. Their shoulder holsters for pistols were quite openly in view. One of them was shorter than his companions, barely five feet tall, with a round face, baggy eyes and broad, pouty mouth. His face was familiar to television viewers in several countries, although he generally wore a badly made toupee.

"Pasternak," Gary Manning declared when he recognized the Soviet media star.

"Russian television crew," Jalingo said with a shrug. "They arrived here on a plane less than an hour before you arrived. Pasternak's bodyguards have diplomatic immunity and permits to carry firearms. You gentlemen are armed, too, I assume..."

"Careful what you say," Rafael Encizo told him. "They're probably listening to every word."

"We should have checked the bus for bugs," Manning said with a sigh.

"What are you talking about?" Jalingo demanded.

"Pull over," Katz ordered. "Pasternak wants us to see him. He obviously wants something, so let's talk to him."

"This could be a trap," Carson said nervously as he reached into his jacket for a compact .380 Astra Constable under his arm.

"The KGB would arrange something more subtle," Manning assured him. "Besides, Pasternak's a mouthpiece for Moscow, but he isn't KGB. The guys with him probably are, but it's unlikely they'd use such a well-known Soviet citizen for bait to lure us into a clumsy attempt to kill or capture us."

"Cold War paranoia," Jalingo muttered, but he pulled up to the curb and switched off the engine. "I think you're jumping at shadows."

"Right now," James began as he opened the sliding door at the side of the bus, "we don't really give a damn what you think." He stepped from the bus, followed by Katz and Manning.

Pasternak looked at the trio and nodded his head in curt acknowledgement. The KGB bodyguards flanking him stared at the three Phoenix Force commandos with cold dislike. They had a vague idea who these men were and knew they had been responsible in the past for ruining several KGB operations in which numerous Russian agents had lost their lives. Still, the bodyguards kept their hands away from their holstered pistols as Pasternak approached the three Phoenix pros.

"Hello, gentlemen," Pasternak announced as he folded his arms on his chest. "It's been about a year since we met in Belgrade. I knew you were in Africa so I assumed you knew about me, too."

"It's hard to be famous and keep a low profile," Manning replied.

"Ain't it a bitch?" Pasternak said, displaying his knowledge of American slang, one of the abilities that made him such a successful spokesman for the Soviet Union in the U.S. "I decided it would be better to arrange a meeting with you than take the chance you might kidnap me again like you did in Yugoslavia."

"You might recall that your side and our side both benefited from that encounter in Belgrade," Katz remarked, taking out a pack of Camels as he spoke. "How long were you listening in on our conversation on the bus?"

"Since you arrived at the airport," Pasternak admitted. 'You know, I really enjoy American cigarettes. Best in the world. Don't you agree?"

"Here," Katz replied, taking one cigarette from the pack and handing the rest of the Camels to the Russian. "Keep it."

"Thank you," Pasternak said with a nod. "Well, when we learned about the shooting here in Nigeria, we figured this was a hot news story so we headed here as quick as possible. Naturally we figured you'd show up, too."

"And, of course, the KGB operating in Nigeria is certainly aware that Captain Jalingo is a member of army intelligence," Katz remarked. "So, when your people saw him at the airport with a bus, they knew an officer of his status wouldn't be waiting at the wheel of such a vehicle unless he expected someone special to arrive. It was a simple matter to stick a magnetic transmitter on the bus and follow our conversation by radio. Correct?"

"I'm just surprised you didn't think of it," Pasternak said as he leaned forward to get a light for the cigarette between his lips. "Trouble is, you're accustomed to dealing with professionals in intelligence operations. They wouldn't have let their vehicle be bugged so easily. These Nigerians aren't used to this Cold War business. They don't take such things seriously enough. Their main concern is with internal politics. The government is afraid of another coup. They seem to have one every other year in this country, you know."

"Congratulations on being clever," Katz said as he held his Ronson lighter flame to Pasternak's cigarette. "You must have heard something in our conversation to encourage you to stop us for this meeting. What is it?"

"I heard enough to know that you're here to disprove that the CIA was responsible for the shooting here in Lagos," the Russian began, blowing smoke through his nostrils. "You were in Belgrade on a similar mission when we met the last time. You were telling the truth then, and I suspect you're probably telling the truth now."

"Some *glasnost* openness," Manning commented. "How refreshing. I don't suppose you'd tell us if KGB is responsible for the Lake Kivu incident or the assassinations here?"

"Hey, I'm not KGB," Pasternak replied, spreading his arms in a massive gesture. "I don't know everything they're up to. Still, I'm pretty sure they're not involved in this ugly business in Africa. Why would my government do such things?"

"Why are there Soviet advisers and Cuban troops in Angola and Mozambique?" James snorted. "And don't tell me about the USSR liberating the black nations of Africa. We've seen how you guys 'liberated' Eastern Europe and Southeast Asia. What's attractive in Africa for you is control of the natural resources—gold, diamonds, uranium, oil and the rest."

"I don't really care to be called a liar," Pasternak said with a sigh. "I'm just a television newsman. Arguing about politics seems a bit pointless. I believe the CIA isn't responsible for what's happening here, and neither is the KGB."

"All right," Katz began. "Let's go on that assumption for a moment or two. If that's the case, neither side has anything to gain and a lot to lose if we fail to find out who's responsible. Now, do you know anything about Massamba?"

"Interesting character, isn't he?" Pasternak replied with a thin smile. "Very good public speaker. Makes a good impression with the crowds. Nothing like you Americans or the Europeans. Not surprising when you consider his background."

"We don't know much about his background," Manning admitted. "Care to take *glasnost* a bit further and share some more information?"

"Massamba is the son of one of the wealthiest men in Chad," Pasternak began. "At least he was. Big sugar plantation owner who backed Goukhouni Oueddei's provisional government in the early 1980s. Goukhouni was supported by Libya, you might recall. Moammar Khaddafi probably planned to seize control of Chad through Goukhouni. It might have worked if the French hadn't supported Habré's forces in 1983. By 1987, Khaddafi and Goukhouni had a falling out, the Libyans had been driven out of Chad, and Habré was firmly back in power.''

"And what happened to Massamba's family?" Katz inquired.

"They fled from Chad, of course," Pasternak explained. "Massamba and his father went to Libya for sanctuary. Daddy died two years ago, and Massamba has been traveling about from country to country ever since. Naturally he hates France and probably other Europeans and feels CIA probably assisted Habré in the power struggle in his native land."

"Do you think he's behind the recent events in Rwanda and Nigeria?" Katz asked as he tossed a half-smoked Camel to the ground and stepped on it.

"It's possible," Pasternak confirmed. "Massamba would certainly have connections with various would-be rebel groups throughout Africa. Especially any connected to Khadaffi."

"I thought Khaddafi was an ally of the USSR," Manning remarked. "Aren't you betraying your country's interests by telling us this?"

"Not at all," Pasternak insisted. "Khaddafi hasn't been on such good terms with the Soviet Union for a while. He's been sort of a disappointment, you know. Doing things on his own without getting approval from Moscow. If he is behind whatever is going on here, it's another potential embarrassment for my country. We don't need any more hassles right now. Especially since we have such wonderful new friendly relations with the United States."

"You sound a little cynical about *glasnost*," James commented.

"You think *your* side is the only one with doubts about how this so-called 'openness' is going to turn out?" Pasternak replied. "I lived in the United States for several years. Long enough to know you got a lot of crooked, selfish men in politics. I have some strong doubts how much we can trust them. Our Politburo has its share of hard-line gangster types as well. I don't know if either side will keep their word about anything.''

''Anything that keeps us from throwing nuclear missiles at each other can't be all bad,'' Katz remarked. ''Thanks for the information. It's certainly the most useful and enlightening data we've learned so far.''

''Well, you guys certainly suspected that the KGB was involved,'' Pasternak explained. ''This way you won't be coming after Russians for something we didn't do. I know enough about your mystery group to appreciate the fact that, among other things, you're very dangerous. You've killed a lot of my countrymen in the past. One of these days you'll probably pay for that with your lives. KGB has a long memory and they don't forgive.''

''Your friends look like they'd like to settle accounts with us right now,'' Manning remarked, tilting his head toward the two KGB bodyguards.

''They probably do,'' Pasternak admitted, ''but you don't have to worry about them for the time being. You fellas are going to take care of an ugly little mess none of us want to continue, but none of us want to clean up, either.''

''I just hope we turn out to be good janitors this time,'' James remarked.

''Well, good luck and *da svidaniya*,'' Pasternak said with another curt nod that signaled the end of the conversation.

''Until we meet again,'' Katz replied, offering the Russian farewell in the English equivalent.

''May that not be for at least another year,'' James muttered under his breath as they stepped back into the bus.

Captain Jalingo drove the bus three blocks. Everyone in the vehicle remained silent until Katz told him to stop. Manning and Encizo got out, scanned the bus with mike detectors and soon found the Russian bug at the underside of the rear fender. Encizo pried it loose.

''We are ending this broadcast for the night,'' the Cuban said into the small metal disc.

He tossed it into a gutter and watched the disc roll into the opening of a grille lid over a sewer hole. Encizo and Manning climbed into the bus, and Jalingo started the engine.

"Well, does everyone feel stupid or am I the only one?" Manning asked as he slumped into his seat.

"It was careless," Encizo said with a shrug, "but it wasn't really our mistake. We figured Captain Jalingo would know to watch for something like this."

"I don't need this criticism," the Nigerian said sharply as he drove forward. "This Cold War nonsense doesn't involve my country. I might remind you that the United States and the Western nations have tried to meddle in Nigerian politics more than the Soviets."

"What the hell is he complaining about?" James demanded of no one in particular. "Biafra? I wouldn't have thought it was a fond memory. The civil war between the government and Biafra wasn't exactly a shining achievement in Nigerian history."

"Things are pretty odd when we're getting help from the Russians and the people we're trying to help are making our job more difficult," McCarter commented with a frustrated sigh.

"Help from any source is welcome at this point," Katz stated. "Unless Pasternak told us a pack of lies, Massamba is probably the man we want."

"So, do we head back to Rwanda to find him?" Kagera asked. "I suppose we could arrest him on suspicion, but I don't see that we have any proof he's involved."

"We can't arrest him," Katz replied. "That won't solve anything until we have more proof than the word of a Soviet media spokesman who didn't really accuse Massamba of anything except possible connections with Khaddafi in the past. As long as we're here, let's see what Captain Jalingo's people have on the shooting."

"You mean we Nigerians might not be total incompetents?" Jalingo asked sarcastically.

"We wouldn't say anything like that," James replied with
a tone of exaggerated surprise. "After all, you're the only
Nigerian we've met so far, and it wouldn't be fair to judge
them based only on your example."

"Let's try to avoid any more bad blood than we've
achieved so far," Katz urged. "We all have common interests here. We all have the same goals, and arguing is time-
consuming and counterproductive."

"When we arrive at the base, I'll show you what we have
so far," Jalingo assured his passengers. "Hopefully it will
be more useful for you than it has been for us."

"At last," Encizo remarked, "we can agree on something."

12

Massamba smiled as he looked around at the faces of his guests. They were unpleasantly surprised to see one another. None of them knew the names of the other two men but each suspected who the others were—or what they represented. Only Massamba knew exactly who they were and why they were in his tent that night. It was his show, his moment of power and glory.

Jadallah chewed on the long black cigarette holder as he glared at Massamba. The short, waspy Arab wore a white linen suit and a *keffiyeh* headcloth. His outfit labeled him as an Arab, and simple guesswork made it easy for the others to figure he was probably a Libyan.

Colby's fat body was clad in a tight-fitting khaki bush shirt and trousers with canvas boots and a straw hat. He was a white man with a British accent, and the others guessed he was a South African. They were only half-right. Colby was actually a former Rhodesian who had moved to South Africa after the white minority rule in Rhodesia folded in 1980. He seemed uncomfortable seated beside Jadallah and Goubous. Colby no doubt felt that he had been forced to deal with "inferiors." The Rhodesian was accustomed to being part of a white ruling class. To be regarded as an equal with blacks and Arabs offended him.

Goubous, the tall and painfully thin black African seated next to Colby, peered through horn-rimmed glasses at Massamba. He had known the host for many years and appreciated his intelligence and skill as a master manipulator.

oubous also realized Massamba was greedy, ruthless and otentially very dangerous. Although possessed of a brilant mind, Massamba had been warped by past experinces, and his hatreds often clouded his judgment. But oubous knew Massamba was capable of accomplishing hat others might consider impossible.

"I'm so glad you all made it," Massamba began, leaning ack in a folding chair that was barely large enough to acommodate his powerful body. "I apologize for failing to aform you that there would be others present, but I thought ou might be discouraged from coming if you knew this ouldn't be a one-on-one conversation."

"This wasn't part of our agreement, Massamba," Jadllah said in a hard, flat voice. The cigarette holder bobbed p and down as he spoke through clenched teeth. "I don't ke surprises. Not when they concern a business deal such s ours."

"I understood this was a private matter," Colby dered, and fluttered his pudgy fingers in a gesture of frusation. "A covert operation. Now, what sort of game do ou think you're playing?"

"A power game, of course," Massamba replied calmly. You Europeans have been playing power games in Africa r centuries. You ought to recognize one by now."

"I'm not European," Colby said, clearly offended. "I'm s much an African as you are, Massamba."

"Not quite," Massamba answered. "Oh, you can trace ack your ancestors four or five hundred years before you each the ones that arrived on a boat from England. Take a ok at the color of your skin. You'll see my ancestors have een here longer. We were here before the Europeans came 'civilize' us by making us serfs in our land."

He turned to face Jadallah and added, "Even before you rabs came down from the Middle East to shuffle us off to ur slave markets. You put us to work as beasts of burden nd cut off the testicles of infant African boys so they could e trained as proper eunuchs to guard your harems."

"Massamba," Goubous said with a sigh. "Spare us thi lecture about how we Africans have suffered. It may su your needs when you stand before the crowds of ignorar followers who believe you're some sort of political mes siah, but I know you too well. You have the blood of to many Africans on your hands to convince me that yo grieve for their plight, past or present."

"You always were a bit impatient," Massamba mused a he glanced up at some moths that hovered around the ker osene lamp hooked to the bar at the ceiling of the tent. " remember when we met in March, 1979. You were an assis tant to one of the leaders of the rebel groups that planne to put Goukhouni in power in Chad. Ironically that mee ing was in Lagos, Nigeria. All of you know what happene there earlier today?"

"It's hardly a state secret," Colby remarked as he starte to rise from his chair. "I'm impressed by the efficiency c your organization to carry out assassinations, but your fla grant lack of regard for maintaining security has convince me to terminate our arrangement..."

"Sit down, Mr. Colby," Massamba ordered. "You're nc going to terminate anything except your own life if you wal out of this tent now."

Colby stared at him, stunned by the threat. Jadalla nearly bit through the stem of his cigarette holder and at tomatically reached for the Makarov pistol inside his jacket However, the Libyan arrested the action, aware that h would seal his own death warrant if he killed Massamba i the man's own camp. Goubous simply frowned and shoo his head.

"This sort of talk isn't necessary, Massamba," he statec "After all, you brought us here to try to get us to work tc gether on this little scheme. Correct?"

"That's the way I prefer to do it," Massamba co firmed. "If Mr. Colby has lost interest in our arrangemen he may, of course, leave *after* he's heard my offer."

"What if I still refuse after I've heard what you have to say?" Colby demanded. "How do I know you won't kill me?"

"Because I'm not stupid," Massamba replied. "If I kill you, I run the risk of making enemies with your associates in South Africa. I don't know how many former Rhodesian elitists have managed to achieve positions of power in that country, but I don't care to find out. However, if you walk out now you're completely cutting off my chance to make one thousand million CFA francs. That's about ten million dollars in American currency or approximately five million British pounds sterling. Now, I'll kill you if you chop me off from that sort of money without even giving me a chance to explain."

"A thousand million francs?" Goubous repeated with surprise.

"That's how much I need from each of you," Massamba explained. "My own finances are running out. The money you previously invested has already been spent. Most of my men are mercenaries. They're very reliable, highly trained and professional, but they are also expensive. Soldiers expect to be paid, and a mercenary's only loyalty is to his wallet."

"I see," Jadallah began. "These two represent investors, as well. You failed to mention that during our previous meetings."

"Each of you thought you were the only source financing my operation," Massamba admitted. "You think you've been cheated? Not at all. Because you didn't realize how much you were buying into."

"My deal with you," Colby began as he thrust a thick stubby finger at Massamba, "and I assume the same deal you made with the others, was to discredit the United States in countries of Central Africa that do not have Soviet-connected Marxist governments. With the Americans out of favor, the anti-West tide would also turn against trade with the Europeans. Then my associates' businesses in South

Africa would be able to move in and pick up that trade because those countries would be desperate to keep their economy afloat."

"Exactly," Jadallah added with a firm nod.

Massamba, looking very pleased, smiled benignly. "Yes," he replied, "but why settle for a temporary increase of profits in trade when you can have so much more? I didn't lie to you about what to expect if this operation works. The Americans will be driven out, and the European trade will be cut in half, but only for a while. Of course, you can make enormous profits during that time, but you'll have unlimited wealth and power if you take control of these crippled nations when they become ripe for revolution."

"You will recall we attempted revolution in Chad," Goubous commented. "It didn't work out very well for any involved. Do you agree, my mysterious Arab friend?"

"Indeed," Jadallah said grimly. "That attempted coup was a great disappointment to Libya. My country is getting very tired of disappointments."

"Aren't we all?" Massamba replied with a shrug. "However, we have an opportunity to claim full control of nearly one-third of the entire continent of Africa. I'm talking about the majority of the countries of Central Africa— Nigeria, Cameroon, Zaire, Rwanda, the Republic of Central Africa, Uganda, Niger, Mali and, last but not least, Chad."

"That's insane," Colby declared, stunned by the suggestion.

"Nothing insane about it," Massamba insisted. "It is simply a logical progression of events that we've already started. With the Americans and Western Europeans out of the trade, the economies of all these nations will begin to crumble. Then it is easy to turn the people against their government. After that happens, all that's needed is for someone to move in and take control. Someone who can reestablish trade, prop up the economy and keep the ignorant masses from starving to death. By that time they won't even consider asking for more than that."

"Let's get back to reality," Goubous insisted. "You know very well what happened in Chad. The French backed Habré and the rebel forces failed even before Khaddafi pulled out his support."

"But the French aren't strong enough to defend several African governments simultaneously," Massamba insisted. "They certainly won't do it if they've already lost most of their trade with those countries. That was our problem in the past. We didn't strike out at the powers of the West first, then at the economy to make the nation ready to fold."

"What makes you so certain these countries would rather see us in control than the Soviets?" Colby asked. "Or have you forgotten about the damn Communists?"

"Why do you think I've waited so long to carry out this operation?" Massamba replied. "Because I was waiting for the time to be exactly right. The Soviets have spread themselves too thin. They have serious economic and social problems in their own country, and they've had great difficulties in other lands, as well—including here in Africa. They're trying to mend political fences with the West, for now at least, and they're not in any condition to try to take over control of any other African nations."

"In your opinion," Colby snorted. "And, as you say, 'for now.' That situation might change in a few years."

"In a few years we'll make enormous profits," Massamba said with a smile. "Billions in whatever currency you wish to name."

"How generous," Jadallah said dryly. "If this is such a simple matter, why do you need us? Just because you need the money for your mercenaries?"

"I'm representing myself and a small group of individuals who are both greedy and ruthless," Massamba said with a shrug. "But our needs are modest compared to the ambitions of men such as you. Politics in Africa are too risky."

"That seems obvious, or you wouldn't even think of trying to start revolutions in eight African countries," Goubous commented.

"Nine," Massamba corrected. "Politics are unstable in most African countries. You know how many coups and attempted coups have happened in this continent just during the past ten years? I'm not foolish enough to think I can successfully hold control of a single country, let alone several. I don't have your organizations or government connections. I can't get military backing or establish new trade with the West when the time to do so would be advantageous. Someone—rivals from within or conspirators from the outside—would assassinate me. Any of you would do it. So would a thousand others."

"So you just want enough money to retire?" Colby asked suspiciously.

"To retire in luxury," Massamba added. "To be wealthy for the rest of my life. I also want the satisfaction of knowing that the people responsible for destroying what my father built in Chad will no longer be in charge of that country or any other. So I admit revenge has its appeal, especially if I have a fortune big enough to keep me happy and rich while I live out the rest of my life away from this troubled land."

"Then you really do plan to leave Africa?" Goubous inquired, pushing his glasses high on the bridge of his nose. "I never thought you'd fit in anywhere else. The turmoil and intrigue here is exactly the sort of environment men like you thrive in."

"I'm approaching middle age," Massamba explained. "I've been exiled from my homeland and forced to wander about, using people, making dirty deals like this and arranging for murders to be carried out for neo-political reasons. Yet I am still the son of a plantation owner, and that's what I intend to be in the future. I want a home, land and prestige so I can eventually give something to my son whenever I get around to having one. Africa can go to hell as far as I care. You can divide up the countries and decide who rules what in the future. You're welcome to Africa. For me it's a place of bitter loss and shattered dreams.''

"Dividing up nations is absurd, since we don't have them yet," Jadallah remarked. "A great many black Africans would not welcome rule by Libya or South African whites."

"They don't have to know who's in charge," Massamba answered. "Put in black leaders you can control. Take a lesson from the Soviets and the Cubans. Don't worry about the trade. They'll deal with your countries when they see they have no choice if they want to avoid economic ruin. Zimbabwe—after it assumed its new identity following the end of white rule as Rhodesia—severed relations with South Africa because it objected to apartheid. Less than a year later, they faced economic collapse and practically begged South Africa to reestablish relations and trade. The plan will work."

"I believe you might manage it," Goubous stated with a nod, "but my belief doesn't extend to one thousand million francs."

"Then let's say half now and half later?" Massamba suggested.

"Two hundred million now and the rest later," the other former Chad rebel answered.

"Three hundred and fifty," Massamba said firmly.

"Two-fifty," Goubous responded.

"Three," Massamba insisted.

"Two hundred and fifty million," Goubous repeated. 'I'm not going any higher."

"I'll agree to three hundred million CFA francs," Jadallah announced, tapping the edge of his lower teeth with the tip of his cigarette holder. "The money will probably be in Lebanese pound notes."

"That's acceptable," Massamba assured him.

"I don't represent an oil-rich Arab country with a cooperative government," Goubous told him. "My organization is a collective group of rebel leaders and their followers, who are trying to establish a permanent home."

"At least one of your rebel leaders is actually a former dictator forced to flee his country in 1979," Massamba replied. "I understand there's still a price on his head for 'crimes against humanity' committed when he was in charge of his nation. Unless you need him, I suggest you kill the fat bastard and turn him in for the reward. That ought to be good for at least a hundred million francs."

"Too late," Goubous said with a sigh. "He's already dead. Two hundred and fifty million is the best we can do."

"Then you'll have to expect a smaller portion of Africa when the time comes to take over," Massamba stated. "Whoever contributes the most rightly deserves the larger share."

"What's a larger share of daydreams worth?" Colby asked, shaking his head with disgust. "This entire business is absurd."

"Not absurd," Massamba insisted. "Unique, perhaps, but not absurd. Look, I already explained that the times are right for this operation. Another thing in our favor is that no one would suspect something like this. Who would think that three very different forces—based in different countries with no obvious goals in common and no apparent connection with one another—would covertly take over nine countries after they've been plunged into turmoil by events seemingly unrelated to them."

"I can't make a decision on three hundred million francs," Colby confessed. "You know I only represent a group of Rhodesian businessmen and landowners currently living in South Africa. We don't run that country, although we do have some influence with certain politicians. Pretoria would probably kick us out of the country if the government found out what we were doing."

"They'll look the other way when the profits come in," Massamba assured him.

"You'd be astonished if you ever learned people aren't as corrupt as you're convinced they are," Goubous commented.

"With examples such as you three?" Massamba laughed. "The ignorant masses might not be corrupt, but that's only because they have no power. Those who rule and control others are always corrupt. It's the way of the world. You wouldn't be here if it was otherwise."

"I certainly can't make any commitments to financing you on such a large level," Colby said in a weary voice. He was clearly tired of the discussion and in no mood to listen to Massamba's cynical philosophy. "I'll talk to my associates in South Africa and we'll see what we can agree on..."

"If you're not going to participate any longer in this operation," Massamba began as he rose from behind his desk, "you'll be required to deliver one million CFA francs or the equivalent in whatever currency in order for me to keep your role in this matter secret."

Colby glared at Massamba, startled and outraged by the remark. The fat white man hauled himself from his chair in a manner that resembled poorly made heavy machinery.

"Are you threatening me?" he demanded, shaking with anger.

"I'm simply stating a fact," Massamba replied as he pointed to a patch of canvas in the side of the tent. It was slightly lighter than the rest of the canvas, but there were several such patches that could serve as windows in daytime by lifting the canvas folds to expose the screens built into the tent.

"What have you done?" Jadallah asked with alarm as he began to reach inside his pocket.

"Leave the pistol in its holster," Massamba warned. "Draw the gun and you'll be dead before you can use it."

"What's going on here, Massamba?" Goubous inquired, trying to sound more calm than he felt.

"Behind that canvas is a videotape camera," Massamba explained. "It has made a complete record of this conversation. Visual and audio proof of everything we've said tonight."

"You goddamn black savage!" Colby snapped. "You think you can get away with blackmail, you stupid munt bastard..."

"The last pale-faced turd who called me a munt choked to death on his own testicles," Massamba warned. "I tore them off with my bare hands and stuffed them down his throat."

Colby's mouth closed into a hard, pale line as he slowly returned to his seat. He didn't know whether Massamba's claim was true, but he figured the huge black man was physically capable of such an act. Colby had not intended to call Massamba a munt. The term was a Rhodesian colloquialism that meant one was a "thing," less than an animal. In Colby's native country, "munt" was more offensive than "nigger." Obviously Massamba was familiar with the expression.

"There, that's better," Massamba said with a nod. "I'll let it go this time, Mr. Colby. I'm certain it just slipped out because you were understandably alarmed when I told you about the camera."

"He's not the only one," Jadallah said stiffly. "If you think you can blackmail us, you're not as smart as I thought you were. You may rule this camp, Massamba, but I have connections with people who can hunt you down wherever you go. People who solve problems with sniper rifles and plastic explosives. That's among their more civilized methods."

"This isn't blackmail," Massamba assured his guests. "It's insurance. I wouldn't want you gentlemen to decide to send any unpleasant individuals such as you described to try to reclaim your money or dispose of me as a 'loose end.' I believe that's the correct expression. Well, I've already made other video tapes of previous meetings with all of you. Copies of those tapes are currently in bank vaults in other countries. Even I don't know exactly where all of the copies are. That way, having me tortured or drugged won't do you any good. However, when I die, attorneys in charge of my wills—I have five, all in different languages and different countries—will be instructed on reading the wills to send the tapes to certain embassies, Interpol offices, a couple of television news departments ... Well, I'm sure you get the idea.''

"In other words, we'd better make certain you have a long and productive life,'' Goubous commented. "You'd have a hard time blackmailing us without revealing your own role in this conspiracy as well. So I believe you're telling the truth about this unconventional insurance policy.''

"Actually,'' Massamba began, his dark features tinted orange by the glow of the lantern. The big African smiled as he looked at Colby. "The camera is behind me so my face is never on videotape, and my voice can be edited out. Since I made previous tapes when I met only with you, Mr. Colby, I could expose you without jeopardizing anyone else in this operation.''

"Then it is blackmail,'' Colby declared.

"No, no,'' Massamba insisted. "I'm just explaining something that *could* be done. But I'm sure that won't be necessary. Peace of mind is certainly worth one million francs to a man like you, Mr. Colby.''

"You're a treacherous character, Massamba,'' Colby said in a hard, angry voice. "I don't know that I can trust a man like you.''

"Trust me to do what's advantageous to me,'' Massamba answered. "I have nothing to gain by turning over any of these tapes to the authorities. Provided, of course, that we continue with the plan so everyone gets what he wants.''

"Except the people of nine African countries,'' Goubous remarked with a sigh.

"They'll be no worse off than they are now,'' Massamba replied, but it was obvious he didn't care about the fate of his fellow Africans. "The influence of the Europeans and America's relations with Africa will suffer when this is over.

Accomplishing that goal will be worth almost as much as the money.''

Massamba didn't intend to admit that, for him, the revenge was actually more important than the money. The others understood greed and ambition. They trusted the instincts that drove a man to financial goals and new levels of greater power. None of them would appreciate the passions that motivated Massamba.

Soon, he vowed, the whole world would feel the shock waves of his passions. They would feel it at the other side of the world when Americans trembled with fear at the very thought of setting foot in Africa.

13

The television screen showed wild panic as people rushed about, and the chatter of automatic fire mingled with screams and angry shouts. There was a blurring as the scene swung from terrified civilians to four bodies sprawled across a platform.

"The video tape was shot by a National Television Authority news crew," Captain Jalingo explained. "Hand-held video camera. Most of the footage isn't very good. The cameraman's hands shook rather badly. No one had expected anything like this to happen."

"Except whoever opened fire on the demonstrators," Yakov Katzenelenbogen remarked as he puffed on a Camel cigarette and gazed thoughtfully at the television screen. "This was an anti-American protest group? Mostly college students?"

"That's right," the Nigerian officer confirmed. "The main speaker was the head of a social reform group. Politics were left of center, but not really Marxist."

Phoenix Force, Kagera and Carson sat in Jalingo's office at a military base outside Lagos. It was crowded and uncomfortable. Non-smokers had to endure the situation as best they could, as Katz, McCarter, Kagera and Jalingo all indulged their habit. The office was small, the door and windows were closed and there was no air conditioning. The television set was a small black-and-white model hooked up to a VCR. The picture was poor, but clear enough to show the scene of the shooting in reasonably good detail.

The screen continued to reveal confusion and carnage. The cameraman had managed to point his video camera at two figures in the distance. The pair used the side of a building for cover as they fired M-16 assault rifles at the crowd. Little of them was visible on the screen, but both gunmen were white. They wore toque-style wool hats, sunglasses, and their mustaches and beards appeared to be fake. They also wore gloves and dark blue windbreakers.

"Look at those disguises," McCarter remarked with disgust. "They could have worn masks to hide what color they were, but they obviously wanted everybody to see they were Caucasians."

"We've considered that," Jalingo declared. "But we haven't ruled out the possibility that it was done on purpose to show us the assassins were CIA agents as a warning to back off from criticizing the United States. A lesson that even if we know the Americans have murdered Nigerians in broad daylight, we can't touch them."

"Bullshit," Agent Carson complained. "I'm CIA, for Crissake. We're not responsible, and if we did pull a stunt like this, we wouldn't be stupid enough to use American-made weapons and honkie gunmen. No offense to the honkies...uh, white guys, in this room. America isn't popular enough in Africa for us to figure we could get away with this sort of thing."

"Perhaps you think America is feared in Africa," Jalingo replied with a shrug. "You're an arrogant people, accustomed to regarding Africans as backward inferiors..."

"Put a lid on that crap," James complained. "I'm tired of smelling it."

As they all watched, the camera swung back to the crowd. Several uniformed police rushed toward the snipers, pistols in hand. Two of them fell as another salvo of automatic fire racked the streets. The other officers ducked behind parked automobiles for cover as bullets shattered glass and punctured the metal skin of the vehicles.

"One of the policemen died in the hospital half an hour later," Jalingo stated. "The other was still on the critical list last I heard. He may also be dead by now."

"It could have been worse," Encizo remarked as he studied the TV with professional interest. "They're spraying bullets. Firing for effect instead of controlled bursts. The gunmen are obviously trying to keep the police at bay and the crowds panicked."

"They look like they succeeded," Gary Manning said with a frown. The Canadian watched the screen as billows of green fumes poured into the street. "Tear gas?"

"The snipers tossed several grenades loaded with it," Jalingo confirmed. "The killers managed to escape. Their weapons, beards, glasses, hats and jackets were found in an alley."

The gunfire on the television ceased. Most of the crowd were too frightened to move from cover. The slain figures lay in pools of their own blood. Sirens wailed faintly as police cars headed for the scene. A few figures stood and walked unsteadily toward the corpses. However, one individual boldly jumped onto the platform and waved his arms to get the attention of anyone who cared to look in his direction.

"Just look at that," Calvin James rasped when he recognized the man. It was the dashiki robe and the wooden earring that brought true recognition. "That's Juvénal! One of Massamba's buddies."

"The CIA!" Juvénal shouted from the television. "CIA did this just as they murdered Africans in Rwanda! American butchers! American genocide!"

"Son of a bitch set up the hit and even threw in a crier to spout out a phony editorial," Manning commented.

"You're certain he's one of Massamba's men?" Kagera asked, turning to face James.

"Absolutely," Encizo stated. "I was with Giraudeau when we encountered that joker on the street. I don't figure he just happened to be in Lagos when this shooting occurred."

"We've got to find that bastard," McCarter said in a firm voice. "He can tell us about Massamba and what the hell these people are up to."

"We'll need your help, Captain," Katz told Jalingo.

"Of course," the Nigerian officer replied. He looked down at the floor, unwilling to face the others. "I would prefer that the CIA and the Americans aren't responsible for this, you know. Until now, all the evidence seemed overwhelming that this was a CIA operation."

"Uh-huh," Carson muttered, unconvinced by the Nigerian's half-hearted apology.

"How do we find this Juvénal character?" Kagera inquired, chewing on the stem of his pipe. "Nigeria is a large country."

"If he's here to stir up trouble in public, he won't be hard to find," James commented. "Since Lagos has the largest population of any city in Nigeria, I doubt he'll leave right away."

"He may have even taken a commercial flight under his own name," Katz remarked. "More likely he took one of the bush planes and landed at a less public airstrip. He may even have arrived with those white gunmen—whoever they are. Still, you might check with airport security to see if they have any video footage of passengers who arrived in Nigeria from Rwanda or Zaire within the last twenty-four hours."

"All right," Jalingo agreed. "Any other ideas?"

"One thing we've learned from past experience is never let an opportunity for a few hours' sleep slip away," Katz answered. "You never know when you'll get another chance during a mission like this. I suggest we get something to eat and devote some time to rest. We'll start again first thing in the morning."

"The way things have been happening lately, I'm almost afraid to wake up and hear what happened during the night," Carson admitted.

"If something happens, it will happen whether we get some sleep or not," Manning said with a shrug. "But I'd say it's pretty unlikely they'll carry out another sniper attack right away. Not if the enemy is following a pattern."

"I don't see any pattern," Kagera admitted.

"Well, we're still putting it together," Katz replied. "The ruthless slaughter of innocent civilians is the only thing we know for sure. If Massamba is behind it, he or his people may follow up with propaganda speeches condemning the U.S. and the CIA. We'll find out tomorrow if this is a real pattern or simply coincidence."

"So far the strongest evidence against Massamba is based on the word of Pasternak," McCarter said with a growl. "That Moscow flunky isn't the most reliable source I can think of."

"We'll just have to see what happens next," Encizo said philosophically. "Theories are one thing, but facts are what matters."

"Especially when they can get us killed," James added.

PHOENIX FORCE HAD SEEN little of Lagos during their nocturnal trip through the streets. The city looked quite different in the light of day. James stared out the window of the bus as it headed for the heart of the city. Most of the surrounding buildings were only two stories tall and rather shabby in appearance. Lagos reminded James of an African version of Tijuana.

The traffic was heavy, compared to most African cities. Cars, cabs and buses struggled for space on the three-lane streets. The sidewalks were more crowded than the streets. Hundreds of people teemed along the pavement. Many wore Western clothes, while others were dressed in dashikis or white robes with turbans. The latter were probably Mus-

lims, who comprise more than a third of Nigeria's popula
tion.

Population is a major concern in Nigeria as the birthrate
has remained high and attempts at birth control policies
have failed. It is estimated that by the year 2000 Nigeria'
population will exceed five hundred million.

However, Nigeria boasts a long tradition of education and
cultural arts. The bus passed a secondary school with stu
dents on the grounds, many playing cricket under the su
pervision of an adult coach. The school, like the sport in
progress, reflected the influence of British colonialism and
European missionaries. Indeed, Christianity is the mos
common religion in Nigeria, but numerous Koranic school
are also found throughout the country.

A cloud of smog hovered over the city from factory
smokestacks. Nigeria's industries were still growing with
emphasis on textiles, rubber products and petroleum. It was
also one of the leading producers of steel and aluminun
among the central African nations and probably the leader
in automobile manufacturing in that part of the continent
Signs with familiar American corporation logos were a
common sight as the bus continued the journey through the
congested streets.

"There's the rally," Gary Manning announced as he
peered out a window at the crowd assembled at a park.

A large group of people had gathered around a platform
to listen to Massamba. He had arrived in Lagos earlier that
morning. The international press corps had been notified in
advance, so Massamba's arrival in Nigeria was well cov
ered by the media. Massamba was rapidly becoming fa
mous for being a fiery speaker who stood up for the rights
of black Africans. He knew how to influence crowds and
play the press like a skilled violinist. Massamba was exactly
the sort to find overnight celebrity status under the circum
stances.

Of course, he might be responsible for the circum
stances, as well.

The crowd held the now-familiar protest signs with the same mottoes Phoenix Force had seen in Rwanda and during the previous demonstration at the U.S. embassy in Lagos. The crowd was clearly captivated by Massamba. It was less hostile than the mob at the embassy the night before. Massamba kept a lid on them and urged his listeners not to resort to violence. Yet his message was the same as before. Massamba blamed the West in general and the United States in particular for all the ills that befell Africa.

James and Manning didn't pay much attention to Massamba's speech. They had heard it all before. The Phoenix pair were more interested in the crowd. A large group of police and an equal number of soldiers stood by, although the spectators didn't seem apt to riot. Nigeria had endured more than its share of stormy politics in the past. The military and the police tried to keep an eye on any situation that might blow up into a serious, perhaps bloody, incident.

Captain Jalingo parked the bus near the crowd while James and Manning examined the crowd through the lenses of binoculars. They soon spotted the white minivan at the opposite side of the park. Kagera and the other three members of Phoenix Force were in this vehicle. Manning gathered up a two-way radio unit and pressed the tansmit button.

"Hawk One to Hawk Two," the Canadian spoke into the walkie-talkie. "We're in position. Over."

"We see you," Katz's voice replied from the radio. "We've also spotted the associate of Mr. Personality, Hawk One. He's standing by a battered old brown pickup truck. You'll see it parked at the path to the east of your position."

James trained his binoculars on the vehicle Katz had mentioned. Juvénal and two younger tough-looking men stood beside the pickup. They seemed to be simply casual observers of Massamba's rally. Juvénal fingered the handle of his ever-present *panga* in the belt sheath.

"I see him," James told Manning. "The son of a bitch is just hanging around as though he's part of the crowd. Got a couple of men with him."

Carson appeared in the view of James's binoculars as he observed Juvénal and his companions by the truck. The CIA agent wore a light gray business suit, straw hat and dark glasses. A black briefcase swung in his fist as he strolled behind the pickup truck. Carson looked like an African business executive on his way to work who decided to stop by the rally from curiosity. He stood behind the pickup for a moment and stared at Massamba on the platform. One of Juvénal's companions glanced over his shoulder and looked at Carson. The CIA agent smiled, nodded at the man and continued to walk up the sidewalk away from the park as if he had lost interest in the crowd.

"Carson just pasted them," James announced. "I don't think they suspected anything."

"Did he plant the bug on them?" Jalingo asked eagerly, an unlit cigarette dangling from his lip and a burning match clutched in his fingers. He forgot the flame for a moment and yelped in pain as the match burned him.

"I couldn't tell," James answered.

"Hawk Two," Manning spoke into the walkie-talkie once more. "We saw the Company man in the area. Any idea how his luck has been today?"

"Oh, he's been lucky," Katz's voice replied. "Let's hope the rest of us will be lucky, too. Keep your eyes open. Over and out."

Manning switched off the radio. He smiled and showed James a thumbs-up sign to signal success thus far. The Canadian was especially pleased, since the idea of having Carson plant the tracking device had been his. Massamba and his people already suspected the Phoenix Force members were more than visiting journalists, so none of them could get near Juvénal without making the guy suspicious. But Carson was not known to the henchmen and managed to carry out his role unnoticed.

Juvénal and his friends didn't suspect that Carson was CIA or that his briefcase concealed a special CO_2-powered harpoon device with a trigger in the handle. Virtually noiseless, the contraption fired a two-inch dart with a steel point and an electronic homing device in the plastic shaft. The miniature harpoon had been fired from the barrel, concealed at the base of the attaché case, when Carson stood briefly behind the truck. A receiver unit was in the van with Katz, McCarter and Encizo. Obviously, the signal from the tracking device had been picked up by "Hawk Two," which meant Carson had succeeded in firing the harpoon homing transmitter into the rear of the pickup truck.

"So, now all we have to do is wait," Manning declared as he leaned back in his seat.

"Yeah," James agreed. "And hope they don't notice the bug or that we tagged the wrong vehicle. It's gonna be a bitch if they just happen to be hanging around that truck and it doesn't belong to any of them."

"I wish you wouldn't say things like that," the Canadian muttered as he reached for a long aluminum case. He unsnapped the latches and opened it. It contained a disassembled Belgian-made FAL assault rifle with a scope and four fully loaded magazines, along with an additional 200 rounds of 7.62 mm NATO ammunition in a side compartment. He removed the parts and started to assemble the rifle.

"Are you sure you'll need that thing?" Jalingo began as he struck another match and managed to light his cigarette without burning his fingers a second time.

"I'm not sure I won't," Manning replied, still putting his weapon together.

James followed suit, handing the binoculars to Jalingo and retrieving his M-16. He began assembling the weapon while the Nigerian officer assumed surveillance duties. Manning attached a foot-long silencer to the barrel of his FAL and slid a magazine into the well of his weapon.

"You don't intend to kill Juvénal and his comrades, do you?" Jalingo asked, a trace of concern in his voice.

"That depends on him," James answered as he attached the barrel section of his M-16 to the frame and tightened it in place. "But we want the bastard to talk, and corpses aren't very good at conversation. We won't kill anybody unless we have to."

"Sometimes we have to," Manning added with a shrug.

JUVÉNAL AND HIS COMPANIONS climbed into the pickup truck and drove from the park as Massamba completed his rally. Rafael Encizo watched the screen of the tracking receiver unit in the van. A white blip revealed the direction the truck was headed. Kagera was set to go, but Katz gestured for him to wait.

"The tracking device has a range of twenty kilometers," the Israeli explained as he rose from his seat and headed for the back of the van. "Let them get a headstart of at least five kilometers before we start the pursuit. After all, that's the idea of the homing device. This way we don't have to follow close enough to risk being seen by Juvénal and his men."

"I still think we should have done this to Massamba instead," Kagera remarked, drumming his fingers on the steering wheel. "He must rank higher in the conspiracy, and he may even be the leader."

"There are three reasons we're following Juvénal instead," Katz explained in a weary voice. "The first is the simple fact that Massamba's too smart to deal with in this manner. He's not going to lead us to a secret base or stronghold of some sort while he's in Nigeria. He probably just meets with henchmen like Juvénal and has them carry out his orders. Massamba isn't the sort to make many mistakes."

"I know," Kagera said with a sigh. "And we discussed that if the assassins are still in Nigeria, Juvénal is more apt to be in direct contact with them than Massamba. What's the third reason?"

"Pasternak," Katz answered. "The darling of Soviet television gave us much of our information about Massamba. We have to regard that as a questionable source. The Russian bear has its own interests in Africa. Perhaps Massamba's scheme wouldn't be in their favor, and they're simply letting us handle him so they don't have to worry about catching heat if events turn into a political time bomb. It's also possible Pasternak, acting for the KGB, gave us a false lead, or it could be part of an attempt to lure us into a trap."

"That sounds a little paranoid," Kagera commented.

"Paranoia can be a healthy thing at times," Katz replied as he moved into the back of the van. "This is one of those times."

The Phoenix Force commander joined McCarter and Encizo in the boxlike cabin of the van. The Briton was already armed with his KG-99 machine pistol as well as the Browning Hi-Power in shoulder leather. McCarter had also donned an ammo belt with magazine pouches and grenades. A short leather quiver with several bolts hung on his left hip. The feathered shafts jutted from the scabbard.

The bolts were for the weapon McCarter held in his hands. The Barnett Commando crossbow was a modern-day version of an ancient design, with a sturdy skeletal stock and a cocking lever for greater speed in reloading and cocking between shots. A scope was mounted to the frame.

Encizo was studying the tracking screen. He wore his assortment of handguns and knives with the addition of grenades and spare ammo pouches. The Cuban's MP-5 submachine gun was propped against the wall within easy reach. Encizo glanced up at Katz as the Israeli shrugged out of his jacket to reveal a SIG-Sauer P-226 pistol under his right arm.

"Still picking up the signal?" Katz asked.

"Coming through fine," Encizo confirmed. "Juvénal and his buddies are about a quarter of a mile from here and they seem to be moving to the northwest now. Sort of a zigzag pattern. Maybe they're trying to figure out if they're being followed.''

"Carson will be here any second now," Katz stated as he reached for a case that contained an Uzi submachine gun and other gear. "We'll wait until our quarry is approximately two miles from us. If Carson isn't here by then, we go without him."

"Might be better if he didn't come along," McCarter commented. "Bleedin' CIA are better at sneakin' and peekin' than in a firefight."

"We don't know there will be a firefight, David," Katz reminded the Briton.

"Leave me something to hope for, mate," McCarter replied with a wolfish grin.

14

The blip on the tracking screen guided Phoenix Force and their allies as they pursued the pickup truck. Juvénal's vehicle had traveled steadily northwest, toward the center of Nigeria. The van and the bus remained roughly five miles behind the truck.

The farther they traveled from Lagos, the more Phoenix Force saw of traditional Nigeria. The vehicles passed Hausa villages with mud brick houses and thatched rooftops. Barefoot people, clad in bright dashiki robes, watched the bus and van roll by while they herded cattle and labored in the fields. More than half of all Nigerians are still farmers. The villagers were accustomed to traffic on the roads and had little interest in such matters unless the passing vehicles disturbed their livestock.

They also saw a few Fulani tribespeople on the road. Generally found farther north, the Fulani wore multicolored robes and head scarves. Women carried children on their backs, and men carried hardwood walking staves. A couple were leading ox carts filled with millet and sorghum. They were probably headed for the city of Ibadan, one of the major centers of commercial trade in Nigeria.

The Phoenix Force vehicles continued to follow their distant quarry, unseen except in the form of the blip on the tracking screen. The roads were rough and unpaved, little more than dirt paths worn into the ground in the savanna grasslands. Some king vultures perched on the limbs of a rugged baobab tree. The scavengers watched the van and bus, their heads turning to follow the progress of the vehicles.

The climate became steadily warmer as Phoenix Force and their companions moved inland. Lagos's location on the coast, along the Gulf of Guinea, kept temperatures reasonably pleasant for an equatorial region. In the north, the climate became dry and hot, influenced by the desert winds from the Sahara.

The savannas of Nigeria had been the home of numerous species of large animals, but the lion, zebra and wildebeest had been driven out by the growing population that steadily extended across the face of Nigeria. Poachers, as well as legitimate hunters had taken their toll, but the biggest enemy of African wildlife had been—and will continue to be—the escalating population rate and increase of industries and mining operations.

Phoenix Force saw some domesticated cattle herded along, and a pair of camels with Muslim riders. Beyond that they saw no other animal life except a few birds and an occasional lizard or snake that scurried out of the path of the approaching vehicles.

Calvin James was seated next to Jalingo in the front of the bus, almost bored by the journey. The van led the way and stirred up clouds of dust for the pursuing bus. The view from the windshield was monotonous. A dirty fog of flying sand, the shape of the van a hundred feet ahead and a virtually featureless savanna.

Suddenly something hit the windshield. James gasped with surprise and stared at the object pressed against the outside of the glass. It was a hard-shelled beetle, nearly ten inches long—not including its six powerful hook-shaped legs. The insect was about five inches wide, with a comparatively small head for the size of its big armored body.

"Holy cow!" James exclaimed, startled by the enormous beetle. "Look at that thing."

"Yes," Jalingo replied, only mildly surprised. "It's a Goliath beetle. I believe it's the largest insect in the world.

hey're not very common, and you hardly ever see them in
Jigeria. More likely to find the Goliath in Ghana or Mali.
Nothing to be worried about, you know. I admit it's a bit
tartling, but the Goliath doesn't bite or sting. If you tried
o pick him up, he might give you a nasty pinch, but other-
"ise the beetle is harmless.''

"I'm still glad he's on the other side of the glass," James
dmitted.

Insects had never been creatures that James viewed with
reat fondness, yet he watched the giant beetle with interest
s it lumbered along the windshield and hood like a tiny
ank with six legs. The markings on its shell were quite
:riking, black and brown with a cream-colored stripe across
s head and thorax. The beetle's wings opened like armor-
lated flaps, and the insect suddenly hurtled from the
vindshield and flew out of sight.

Aside from the visit by the Goliath beetle, the trip was
neventful until the van came to a halt. Jalingo stopped the
us as well, and David McCarter opened a door at the rear
f the van and emerged, dressed in a camouflage fatigue
niform, sand-colored beret and armed to the teeth. Yakov
atzenelenbogen followed, clad in a similar manner with his
Jzi dangling by his left hip by a shoulder strap.

"Juvénal's truck has come to a stop," Katz announced as
e stepped onto the running board of the bus by the driv-
r's side. "It's about six kilometers away. If we're lucky, he's
:ached a base of operations. Hopefully the two white gun-
nen who opened fire on your people in Lagos will be there."

"Sort of wide open spaces here," Manning remarked as
e appeared behind Jalingo. "If we drive up in these rigs,
ney'll see us a mile away."

"They may see us if we approach on foot," McCarter
ated as he gazed at the terrain ahead. There was little cover
nd only the undulations of the savanna could be consid-
:ed as anything remotely similar to a hill. "They must be
ver those knolls. Just out of view for us and out of view for
em. You can bet they got sentries posted."

"It should be dark in a few hours," James commented "Maybe we should wait."

"And maybe they're planning to pull out tonight or carry out another attack," Katz replied. "We can't allow this chance to pass by. It might take days or even longer to get a similar opportunity."

"Well, we can't jump to conclusions," Jalingo said. "It's possible Juvénal is just visiting family or friends in Nigeria."

"Yeah," McCarter snorted, "and maybe Queen Victoria was really Jack the Ripper."

"The captain has a point," Katz allowed, reaching for the pack of Camels in his shirt pocket. "It's unlikely Juvénal is innocent, but not impossible. We'll know more when we reach wherever he's parked his truck."

"How do we reach it unnoticed?" James asked, wondering what the Phoenix commander had in mind.

"We don't," Katz answered with a shrug. "I'm going to take the bus. It's less suspicious than the van. Frankly I never learned how to drive one, so I'll need someone at the wheel."

"I'll do it," McCarter volunteered.

"All right," the Israeli replied. "The rest of you get your gear and head over to the van."

"Just the two of you are going ahead?" Jalingo asked with surprise. "What if they open fire on the bus?"

"Hopefully they won't start shooting at a tour bus driving by on a dirt road," Katz answered. "If we have any trouble, I'll be in radio contact with the rest of you. Basically we'll just try to get close enough to get a general idea of what we're dealing with. It could be anything from a small camp with a few men to a large bivouac area with a hundred or more men, complete with machinegun nests and surrounded by sandbags."

"We're not equipped to take on something that size," Jalingo said, his eyes wide with astonishment from the mere

ssibility that there could be so many opponents. "Maybe
e should call in reinforcements."

A squad of crack Nigerian paratroopers were on call,
med and ready to be alerted to jump into choppers and
ad for whatever site Captain Jalingo ordered them to.
lingo could radio the squad commander at any time if re-
forcements were needed.

"Let's see what we've got first," Katz urged.

"You know those bastards might have rocket launch-
s," James remarked as he climbed from the bus. "They
ight just blow the hell out of the bus the second they see
"

"Calculated risk," Katz replied simply, firing up a ciga-
tte with his lighter. "That's why I'm going personally. It's
y idea, so I should take the risk. I just wish I didn't need
driver."

"No problem," McCarter assured him.

The British ace was always eager to take on any danger-
s challenge. McCarter lived for the thrill of the ultimate
citement of putting his life on the line. The Briton readily
lmitted to that craving. The awareness of his addiction to
rills prevented him from getting so carried away on a
ission that he was a risk to his partners and the success of
e mission. The fact that he was still alive spoke for Mc-
rter's uncanny skill in combat.

"Maybe I should go along with you," Manning volun-
ered as he stood at the door of the bus. "You might need
hird man for backup."

"You're our best rifle marksman," Katz told the Cana-
an. "You can serve as better backup from a distance in
is situation. Besides, there's no point in putting more of
r group in a high-risk situation than necessary."

"Okay," Manning agreed reluctantly. He canted the FAL
sault rifle across a broad shoulder and headed for the van.
Good luck and don't get yourselves killed."

"Drive carefully," James called back to McCarter as he
gan to follow the Canadian, "for a change."

"I never had an accident in my life," McCarter growled.

"What about the time you crashed that glider into tho
helicopters in the Bahamas?" James inquired.

"They were in my bloody way," the Briton answered.

"I hope there won't be too much in our way on the road,"
Katz commented. "Let's go."

THE BUS ROLLED along the dirt road and headed toward th
minuscule hills of the savanna. McCarter drove the vehicl
He had reluctantly removed his shoulder holster and store
the KG-99 and Barnett crossbow behind the driver's sea
concealed by a canvas tarp. The Briton's Browning pist
was jammed into the cushion of his seat as he sat behind th
wheel.

Katz rode in the middle of the bus. The Israeli sat by
window seat, walkie-talkie in his lap. Unlike McCarter, Ka
still wore his shoulder holster and ammo belt with grenad
and magazine pouches. His Uzi subgun lay on the floor b
his feet, fully loaded with a foot-long silencer attached to th
barrel.

The Israeli stared out the window as the bus approache
a small farmhouse with a grain silo and two tiny shack
About a dozen goats wandered around the farm propert
The crops had been neglected and covered by clusters o
weeds. The brown pickup truck, a large military-style truc
about the size of a U.S. Army deuce-and-a-half and tw
British Land Rovers were parked near the farmhouse.

"Hawk One, this is Hawk Two," Katz spoke into th
walkie-talkie. "We've found the quarry. They're not alon
Judging from the size of their base and number of vehicle
I estimate there are at least twenty, perhaps twice that man
people here."

Katz reported a brief description of the setting. He n
ticed a high knoll near the road. The ridge extended f
more than a mile, positioned less than a hundred yards fro
the farmhouse. It was a strategically useful site that had n
been overlooked by the men at the farmhouse. A tall bla

n, dressed in khaki shorts and bush shirt, stood at the
nmit of the ridge with a Heckler & Koch assault rifle
dled in his arms. A scope was mounted to the steel frame
the weapon, and the man held a walkie-talkie in one
nd.

'They know we're here,'' Katz remarked.

'Yeah,'' McCarter replied from the driver's seat. "I just
pe their radio isn't set on the same frequency as ours.''

'That's a cheerful thought,'' Katz said with a sigh. He
ped the Briton's concerns would prove unfounded as he
ntinued to report the farm setup into his own walkie-
kie.

As the bus drew closer, several figures poured out of the
mhouse. Four men, armed with automatic weapons,
nped into two Land Rovers. Others stood by the door of
farmhouse and watched as the vehicles bolted forward
head straight for the approaching bus.

'They're coming at us,'' Katz spoke into the walkie-
kie. "They don't look friendly, but they aren't shooting
.''

McCarter stopped the bus and waited for the Land Rovers
close in. He tensed as the vehicles rolled to a halt at the
se of the bus. McCarter started to reach for the Brown-
under his seat, but arrested the motion.

Two men stepped out from the vehicles. Young black men
h grim faces and hard eyes, they marched to the door at
passenger's side of the bus. One carried a French MAT-
submachine gun while the other held a Chinese Type 50
gun.

'What's going on?'' McCarter called to the pair. "Is
nething wrong?''

'Open the door!'' the one with the MAT-49 snapped as
rapped the stubby barrel of his French chopper against
glass frame of the bus's window.

'Now, keep calm, mate,'' McCarter urged and reached
the lever to the controls to the door. The doors hissed as
y opened. "I'm just a driver.''

"Raise your hands!" the man with the French weap⟨ ordered as he jumped inside the bus and pointed his MA⟨ 49 at McCarter's head. "Don't move!"

"Have to move a bit to raise my hands," the Briton ⟨ plied, slowly lifting his open hands to shoulder lev⟨ "Look, I admit I got off the route somewhat, but this i⟨ bit extreme..."

"Shut up, you white garbage idiot!" the gunman ⟨ manded, spittle flying from his mouth. His eyes burned wi⟨ hatred, and the skin at his knuckles was white from strai⟨ The man was a muscle twitch away from pulling the tri⟨ ger.

The other gunman entered the bus and shuffled p⟨ McCarter. He pointed his Chinese subgun at the rows ⟨ empty seats in the vehicle. The gunman swung the weap⟨ from row to row, but saw no one. McCarter sat quiet⟨ hand still raised and his eyes fixed on the man with t⟨ MAT-49 aimed at his forehead.

"What happened to your passengers?" the guy with t⟨ T-50 chopper demanded.

"Bunch of tourists," McCarter answered. "Dropp⟨ them off in Kabba."

"That is some distance from here," the gunman co⟨ mented. "How did you manage to get here?"

"Bloody accident," the Briton explained. "I got lost ⟨ my way back. I don't know what's going on here, and ⟨ just as soon not know any details..."

"You're not an African," the creep with the Fren⟨ weapon stated. "Why would you be driving a bus in Ni⟨ ria?"

"I've been living here for nearly ten years," McCar⟨ said. "I thought I knew the country pretty well. Guess I w⟨ wrong."

The other gunman grunted and turned his attention ba⟨ to the empty passenger seats. His comrade kept McCar⟨ covered. The British ace glanced out the windshield at t⟨ Land Rovers. Two armed opponents were still in one of t⟨

vehicles, their attention fixed on the bus. The sentry on the knoll was no doubt keeping an eye on the bus, as were the others still positioned at the farmhouse.

The triggerman armed with the T-50 slowly walked down the aisle in the middle of the bus. He scanned the surrounding seats suspiciously and shifted his weapon from side to side. The gunman continued to move toward the rear of the bus when the sound of an engine and tires thundering on the road reached the group.

The van suddenly raced along the road and came up behind the bus rapidly. The sentry on the ridge raised his H&K rifle to his shoulder and prepared to take aim. Suddenly his head snapped back violently as a 7.62 mm slug smashed between his eyes and burrowed a lethal tunnel through his skull. He literally died on his feet and toppled limply from the knoll.

The gunmen inside the bus didn't hear the muffled report of the silencer-equipped rifle, but they had been distracted by the sound of the van. The man with the T-50 subgun glanced out a window for a fraction of a second. He turned to look at the bus seats once more and saw Yakov Katzenelenbogen rise from behind the backrest of a seat.

The Phoenix Force commander triggered his Uzi submachine gun. The weapon rasped as three 9 mm rounds spat from the silencer. All three parabellums crashed into the African gunman's chest, left of center. The flunky toppled backward, collided with the armrest of a seat and fell gracelessly to the floor. The Chinese T-50 clattered unfired next to the dead man's body.

The gunman with McCarter turned his head toward the shooting and saw his partner begin to fall. Stunned by the unexpected attack, he shifted his attention away from McCarter for a shred of an instant. That was long enough for the British warrior to leap from his seat and grab the gunman's MAT-49 with both hands.

McCarter shoved the French chatter gun downward to force the muzzle to point at the floor. The African pulled the trigger, and the subgun blasted a useless volley of 9 mm slugs into the floorboards. McCarter's head snapped forward to hammer the front of his skull into the center of his opponent's face. The Briton delivered another head-butt and smashed his forehead into the bridge of the African's nose.

The gunman's features danced, blood oozing from his nostrils. McCarter held on to the MAT-49 with one hand and hooked his other fist into the side of his opponent's jaw. The stunned African started to sag. McCarter whipped a knee between the man's legs and quickly grabbed the MAT-49 in both hands to shove the metal stock into his opponent's solar plexus.

The man folded at the middle and started to crumple to the floor. His eyes bulged, his mouth hung open, lips and chin streaked with his own blood. An ugly choking sound rattled from his throat as he began to vomit. McCarter easily wrenched the MAT-49 from the man's feeble grasp.

"Don't make a mess in here," the Briton snarled as he planted a boot in the African's chest and kicked him out the door.

The disarmed and disabled man fell from the vehicle and McCarter quickly popped open the door at the driver's side and slithered out, the confiscated MAT-49 in his fists. The two hoods in one of the Land Rovers began to leap from their vehicle. Another 7.62 mm round scored a deadly bull's-eye in the center of one man's forehead. He abruptly dropped dead beside the Land Rover while his partner ducked behind the other side of the rig for cover.

The man fumbled with the bolt of his Czech-made Skorpion machine pistol as he knelt by the Rover. McCarter poked the barrel of the MAT-49 around the nose of the bus and trained the weapon on the huddled gunman. The Briton triggered the French blaster and nailed the disoriented thug with five 9 mm slugs. The man cried out and collapsed to the ground, his chest chewed open by the multiple high-velocity rounds.

McCarter reached inside the bus to grab his Browning pistol from the seat cushion. He thrust it into his belt and fished the Barnett crossbow from behind the seat. Katz moved to the rear of the bus and opened the emergency exit. The Israeli climbed outside and stepped behind the bus for cover.

But the men at the farmhouse paid little attention to the bus. The van was headed straight for them. Rifles and submachine guns sent salvos at the van, and bullets raked the hood and windshield. Glass shattered and projectiles whined against the metal body of the vehicle.

But the enemy failed to notice two figures that jogged behind the van as it advanced. Calvin James and Rafael Encizo used the vehicle for cover to get closer to the farmhouse. The black commando thrust the barrel of his M-16 around the rear of the van and fired at the figures in front of the house. An enemy gunman fell, a trio of 5.56 mm bullet holes in his chest.

James sprinted to the enemy vehicles parked near the house. He triggered the M-16 as he ran and sprayed the remaining opponents with a long burst of automatic fire. A gunman toppled to the ground, both arms wrapped around his bullet-torn stomach. The others ducked low and awkwardly returned fire without taking time to aim. James felt the rush of hot air as bullets rocketed inches from his running form. The Phoenix pro dashed to the side of the deuce-and-a-half truck parked by the house and ducked behind it for cover.

The van rolled to the front of the house. The two remaining gunmen continued to fire at the vehicle, although the bullets seemed useless against the van. No driver was visible at the windshield. Captain Jalingo was actually behind the wheel, sprawled on the floorboards and steering the van as best he could from the awkward position. A canvas tarp covered the Nigerian officer. He heard broken chunks of glass tinkle as he moved his arm forward. The broken fragments of the windshield covered the tarp. Jalingo's fingers trembled as he grabbed a rock and pressed it on the brake pedal. The van came to a halt.

The two gunmen turned their attention toward James's position at the deuce-and-a-half. The black commando triggered a short burst at the pair. The M-16 rounds missed the hoodlums and tore into the frame of the house above their heads. The gunmen crouched low and opened fire from a kneeling stance, but James had already retreated behind the cover of the truck.

Encizo suddenly appeared from the rear of the van. He pointed his H&K machine pistol at the two gunmen and squeezed the trigger. A trio of 9 mm rounds ripped into the upper torso of an opponent who was still trying to get a clear shot at James. The man fell back against the side of the house with an expression of astonishment plastered across his face. He glanced down at the bullet holes in his chest as he slumped into a sitting position and died.

The other gunman swung his FAL toward Encizo, but the Cuban fired his MP-5 chopper before his adversary could take aim. Two parabellum slugs smashed into the man's face, and a third punched through the hollow of his throat. The gunman dropped his rifle and tumbled onto his back. He twitched slightly and stretched out in the final stillness of death.

Encizo jumped back behind the van a split instant before a volley of automatic fire erupted from the open doorway of the farmhouse. More shots burst from windows, and at least one weapon snarled from the silo. James saw a figure lean around the side of the silo, but the man ducked back before the Phoenix fighter could aim his M-16.

A voice cried out from inside the house. A gunman stationed at a window had been hit in the chest by a 7.62 mm bullet. The man fell backward and dropped to the floor, pink foam issuing from his open mouth. The projectile had punched through a lung. Juvénal saw the man fall and quickly jumped away from the window. He cursed through clenched teeth and peered around the edge of the window frame.

"Where the hell did that shot come from?" he wondered aloud.

GARY MANNING HAD ASSUMED a prone position on the ridge, his FAL rifle braced against a shoulder. The Canadian marksman had approached the site on foot and taken out the sentry who had previously been posted on the knoll. From the elevated vantage point, Manning had used the scoped rifle to blow away one of the opponents by a Land Rover and the gunman at the window.

The silencer attached to the barrel muffled the report of Manning's weapon and helped mask the muzzle-flash. Manning had developed his skill as a sniper when he was assigned to the 5th Special Forces in Vietnam as a special observer. He had "observed" several NVA officers through the telescopic sights of sniper rifles during missions behind enemy lines in Nam. Since he joined Phoenix Force, the Canadian warrior had ample opportunity to hone his skill.

Manning peered through the scope as he scanned the farmhouse and surrounding area. From his position he saw the east side of the house and the silo clearly enough. He also noted movement between the shacks near the silo, and the Canadian got hold of the backpack that lay on the ground beside him.

He pulled open the flap and reached inside. Manning's personal bag of tricks included an assortment of explosives, detonators, timers and other devices of fearsome destructive capability. Manning fished through the items and found two gray plastic discs. He removed one disc. A metal circle in the center included a timing dial. Manning turned the dial to the number three setting and gripped the rim of the disc with his fingertips.

The device was Manning's own invention. It resembled a Frisbee and functioned in much the same manner, except it was lined with several ounces of C-4 plastic explosives. The

U.S. Navy had previously experimented with weapons of similar design, but discontinued such tests because the use for such a weapon seemed too limited to be worthwhile.

Manning himself rarely used the "disc bombs." However, he had found that the discs were more accurate and would travel much farther than a conventional hand grenade. The timing mechanism and detonator in the center of the disc was perfectly balanced to provide a true trajectory. Manning had used the devices in the past, and they had always worked well in the appropriate situations.

He aimed the disc, rose to a kneeling stance and swung his arm in a hard cross-body sweep. The disc hurled from his fingers and sailed across the farm property. Just as it whirled toward the shacks and floated between the small structures, a figure bolted from behind cover and ran for the silo. The disc exploded before the man could get five feet.

The explosion tore the shacks apart, and the fleeing figure suffered a similar fate. He was ripped limb from limb and decapitated by the blast. The mangled remnant of at least one other corpse hurtled into the air. The burning wreckage of the shacks collapsed on the grisly charred chunks of human debris. A single figure was kneeling by the silo, his head covered with his arms. Manning reached for his rifle, but James also spotted the lone opponent and fired his M-16 at the man. He collapsed in a kicking, thrashing heap, three 5.56 mm slugs in his upper body. The man's convulsions were brief, and he soon sprawled lifeless on the ground.

A burst of automatic fire accompanied the sudden spew of dirt from the ridge near Manning's position. The Canadian rolled away from the geyser of flying earth. His heart raced as he grabbed the backpack and pulled it clear of the immediate area where the bullets had struck. Obviously he had been spotted when he hurled the disc bomb.

"So much for keeping a low profile," the Canadian rasped through clenched teeth as he crawled along the ridge, rifle in one hand and the pack in the other.

HENRI GROWLED SOURLY when he realized he had missed the man on the ridge. Like Manning, the Belgian mercenary was armed with a FAL assault rifle, but Henri's weapon didn't have a scope. He retreated from the window as Calvin James fired a salvo of M-16 rounds at him.

"That bastard is one of those CIA scum from Rwanda," Juvénal declared as he took a French MAT-49 subgun from a dead comrade on the floor.

"Congratulations," Henri sneered, and cast an angry gaze at the African. "You must have led them here."

"You have no proof of that!" Juvénal snapped, tempted to use the MAT-49 on the mercenary.

"Stop arguing!" Francois, a French mercenary and ex-Foreign Legion, told them. "We have enough to worry about outside without fighting each other in here!"

The farmhouse wasn't very large and was currently crowded with twenty members of Massamba's private army. Most were black Africans of various nationalities. Only four were white mercenaries from France and Belgium. The few small rooms had been converted into makeshift barracks with cots and duffel bags stuffed with clothing and other gear set up for the men. All were well armed with weapons of various types, but they had been caught off guard and were still disoriented by the unexpected attack on the base.

Abdul Saidu was especially upset. The Nigerian Muslim was a secret supporter of Khaddafi and the Libyan-backed effort to overthrow the government of Chad in the early 1980s. He had sent his wife and children away in order to let Massamba's forces use his unsuccessful little farm as a base of operations. Now he wished he had joined his family instead of staying on his property. Saidu had not expected to see his farm turned into a battlefield.

He wasn't much of a farmer, but he was an even worse excuse for a fighting man. Short and fat, extremely nearsighted and suffering from bronchial infections, Saidu was in no physical condition to take on any trained opponent. Whoever launched the attack on the farm were obviously

top-notch warriors. So far they had taken out more than
dozen of Massamba's so-called soldiers. Saidu sat in a co
ner, a pump-action gun in his fists. The weapon gave him
little comfort, but he clung to it desperately as he alte
nated between watching the others scramble about the roo
and praying to Allah for mercy and salvation.

Juvénal poked the barrel of his MAT out a window an
triggered the subgun in a wild spray of 9 mm rounds. H
exhausted the magazine and looked around for spare amm
Henri glanced at the African and clucked his tongue wit
disgust. Juvénal might be an accomplished fighter with
panga, but he didn't know how to handle firearms worth
damn. In their present situation, Henri reckoned Saidu wa
more useful than Juvénal. At least the farmer had enoug
sense to keep out of the way of the others and he was no
burning up ammunition like an idiot.

"They've got explosives, Henri," Francois warned th
Belgian merc. "It won't be long before they blow this hous
to bits just as they took out our men by the silo."

"Oui," Henri agreed grimly. "This place will become
big communal coffin if they decide to blast us."

"We've got grenades," Juvénal stated. "Let's use them
dammit! Blow them up before they can do it to us!"

"Merde alors!" Henri snapped in reply. "We can't stan
directly in front of the windows or doors without gettin
shot. All we can do is stand back and lob grenades out th
windows. I wouldn't count on that being very successful."

"It will be much easier for them to do it to us," Franco
added, "but we have to do something."

"We can't stay boxed in," Henri stated. "So far the a
tacks have come from the front of the house and the ea
wing. They may not have the rest of the house covered
We'll toss grenades through windows on those sides an
hope the explosions distract them long enough to allow u
to escape out the other exits."

"What if you're wrong and we're surrounded?" Juvénal asked as he squatted beside a corpse and relieved it of a magazine for the MAT subgun from an ammo pouch.

"We still have better odds in the open," the Belgian insisted. "And why don't you give that gun to someone who knows how to use it?"

"Why don't you stick a bayonet you-know-where," Juvénal replied with venom in his tone.

"Tell me about it later," Henri told him. "Let's get those grenades."

PHOENIX FORCE HAD a different plan of action. Calvin James aimed his M-16 at the house, with the barrel canted high. Attached to the underside of the barrel was an M-203 grenade launcher. He triggered the sturdy launcher and felt the familiar kick ride through the frame of the assault rifle, driving the buttstock forcibly against his hip.

A 40 mm projectile hurtled from the big muzzle of the M-203. It rose in a high arc and plunged down on the roof of the farmhouse like a malevolent meteor. The grenade exploded on impact, and the roof burst apart in a shower of broken tiles and chunks of mud brick. Flames rose from one of the upstairs rooms. Glass shattered and fire crackled along the sills and window frames.

"That's it!" Rafael Encizo shouted at the men inside the van. "Move out! Hurry!"

Captain Jalingo pushed open the door by the driver's side and crawled from the van, the tarp still draped across his back. Broken bits of the windshield fell from the canvas as he tumbled onto the ground. The van blocked him from the enemy as he rose unsteadily to his feet. Jalingo was trembling, nerves still shaken by the experience while huddled under the steering wheel.

Encizo fired his MP-5 at the front of the house as Kagera and Agent Carson jumped from the rear of the van. Both men carried Beretta M-12 submachine guns that hung from shoulder straps within easy reach. Each man also carried

three SAS "flash-bang" grenades. They yanked the pins
from one grenade each and hurled the blasters at the nearest window. Encizo supplied cover fire to discourage the
enemy from trying to fire at them long enough for Carson
and Kagera to throw the grenades and duck behind the van
for cover.

The Cuban also jumped behind the van and removed the
spent magazine from his H&K subgun. Grenades exploded
inside the house as he slid a fresh magazine into his weapon.
More glass shattered from downstairs windows and the front
door burst open. Jalingo opened fire with a British Sten
from the nose of the van and raked the doorway with a salvo
of 9 mm parabellum rounds.

A figure stumbled across the threshold. One of the white
mercenaries had been stunned by the concussion blast of the
"flash-bang" grenades and had staggered into the path of
Jalingo's burst of bullets. The merc tumbled from the
doorway and fell to the ground, his shirtfront stained with
fresh blood.

Encizo opened fire at the windows with his MP-5 in one
fist, its stock braced on a hip. He hurled another concussion grenade with his other hand and tossed it through the
doorway. The grenade exploded, and the entire house
seemed to tremble from the blast. A battered and bloodied
figure sailed across the threshold and fell beside the corpse
of the European mercenary.

Henri, Francois and Juvénal had seen the grenades fly
into the house and had bolted into other rooms before the
concussion blasts occurred. The trio joined several other
Massamba flunkies who had managed to escape the full effects of the violent shock wave. All suffered from throb-
bing pain in their heads and were half-deaf from the ringing
in their ears. It was obvious they couldn't hold out much
longer, and one more batch of grenades could render them
all dead or unconscious. The front room was already littered with senseless and lifeless figures.

They smashed the glass of back windows and jumped outside at the west side of the house, hoping that the house wasn't surrounded, while others bolted out the back door and tried to run. The silo and the shattered remnants of the shacks offered little protection, but it seemed the only alternative to staying in the house.

"Man, this is like a penny arcade," James rasped as he aimed his rifle at the fleeing figures at the rear of the house.

He led the shots by aiming ahead of the targets and firing as they closed in. The enemy literally ran into the path of his bullets. Two opponents fell to the ground, and the others swung their weapons toward James's position. A well-placed trio of 7.62 mm rounds drilled into the chest of one gunman. The man felt his heart explode and wailed in mortal agony and terror, aware that he was doomed before his brain switched off forever.

The other gunman realized the shots had come from a different direction from James's position. He raised his head and stared at the ridge in time to see Gary Manning point the FAL assault rifle. The Canadian marksman squeezed the trigger, and three 7.62 mm slugs smashed through the other man's face. The bullets exploded through the back of his skull in a gory shower of brains and blood.

FRANCOIS JUMPED OUT of a window at the west side of the house, an American-made M-10 Ingram machine pistol in his fists. Two black African thugs followed him through the window. They glanced about, weapons ready, but there was no sign of danger. The fields overrun by weeds seemed deserted, and no opponents were visible at either end of the house.

Henri climbed over the windowsill to join the others, his FAL rifle in one fist. The Belgian merc sighed with relief. Apparently their unknown opponents were not as professional as they seemed. They had failed to cover all the exits.

Suddenly a terrible sharp pain exploded in Henri's left thigh, just above the kneecap. He screamed and fell sideways, clutching the FAL in both fists. The pain in his leg locked the muscles and branched out through his groin and abdomen, riding the nervous system like an electrical current. He glanced down to see the cause of his agony. The feathered end of a crossbow bolt jutted from his thigh. The steel-tipped point protruded from the back of his thigh.

Francois and the two Africans swung their weapons toward the weeds. The marksman with the crossbow must have been hidden somewhere among the neglected fields, yet the silence and lack of muzzle-flash of the weapon made it impossible to locate the archer. Based on the direction the bolt had come from, they had a vague idea where the unseen opponent might be hidden. The men with Francois opened fire in a desperate attempt to hit the invisible assailant. The French merc held his fire and moved behind the two Africans, using them for a shield.

Bullets shredded the weeds and half-grown stalks in the field, but nobody lurched into view, and there were no cries of pain. Henri awkwardly shifted his rifle about and tried to cover the space with sweeping motions, although he had no better idea where their quarry might be.

Suddenly a salvo of automatic fire erupted from the front of the house. An African gunman was knocked off his feet and hurled backward into Francois. The French mercenary lost his balance and fell with the twitching body sprawled across his chest. Blood splashed Francois's shirt and face, blood from the bullet-torn flesh of the man on top of him. Francois used his machine pistol to push the dying man aside and low-crawled toward the rear of the house.

Yakov Katzenelenbogen stood at the front of the house and triggered his Uzi once more before he retreated around the corner. He glimpsed the violent convulsion of the second African gunman as he ducked for cover. Katz knew he had hit the man in the upper torso with at least one 9 mm slug and had probably lodged in him the entire 3-round burst. However, he stayed behind cover, and the chatter of Henri's FAL rifle revealed that this decision had been a wise one. Bullets chewed at the corner of the house, scant inches from Katz's position.

"Determined little bastard," David McCarter whispered as he crawled under the tangled weeds with the Barnett Commando crossbow cradled across the crooks of his elbows.

The British ace worked the cocking lever of the Barnett to position the bowstring. He loaded another bolt, careful to use a quarrel marked with blue feathers. The red feathers labeled bolts with cyanide in the fiberglass shafts for instantaneous death when needed. McCarter aimed carefully and peered through the scope of his crossbow. The cross hairs centered on the head and shoulders of the Belgian mercenary.

McCarter squeezed the trigger. The bowstring sang a short, shrill tune, and the bolt shot from the weapon. The missile streaked from the weeds and struck Henri in the right biceps. The Belgian shrieked as the rifle fell from trembling fingers. Henri grabbed his wounded arm with his left hand. The crossbow bolt had pierced his upper arm, puncturing the muscle and bone.

Francois cursed as he saw the other European mercenary thrash about helplessly on the ground. The Frenchman pointed his M-10 at McCarter's position—or where he guessed it to be—and opened fire. A volley of 9 mm rounds raked the fields and blasted apart more foliage. He swung the Ingram toward Katz's position and triggered another salvo. The Israeli drew back from the corner of the house as bullets tore chips of mud brick from the building.

The French merc's M-10 chopper suddenly stopped spitting parabellums. Francois glanced down at the cocking knob and bolt to discover a spent cartridge casing jammed in the breech. He slapped the cocking knob and shoved it back to clear the breech. Another 9 mm round slid from the magazine into the breech, and Francois prepared to fire at McCarter's position once more.

Katz appeared at the front of the house. He moved around the corner in a low, kneeling position. The mercenary saw the motion, turned and swung his Ingram toward Katz. But he aimed too high, unprepared for Katz's low stance. Francois tried to adjust his aim. Katz fired first.

Three 9 mm slugs punched into Francois's solar plexus and rib cage. Bullets blasted his heart and ripped through his right lung. The force threw Francois off balance, and he triggered his M-10 as he fell backward. A long burst of parabellums rattled from the weapon with a streak of flame blazing from the stubby barrel, then the mercenary crashed to the ground.

RAFAEL ENCIZO RUSHED to the open front door and slapped his back against the wall next to the doorway. Captain Jalingo charged forward and headed straight for the threshold. Encizo gestured for the Nigerian to stay back, but Jalingo had already stepped in front of the doorway.

Automatic fire erupted from the room within. Jalingo cried out and toppled backward, struck by at least two high-velocity bullets. The Nigerian officer landed on his back, his shirt stained with blood. The Sten subgun slipped from his fingers as he instinctively reached for the wounds in his chest. Jalingo raised his head slightly, tried to speak and coughed up a crimson glob that dripped across his chin and neck.

Encizo saw Jalingo fall, but there was nothing he could do for the African at that moment. He thrust the barrel of his MP-5 through the doorway and opened fire. Glancing inside the house, he saw several figures sprawled across the floor, bloodied and battered, unconscious or dead. Another African gunman staggered into a wall, his chest ripped open by a column of bullet holes.

Yet another opponent ducked down in a low huddle behind the end of a bullet-riddled couch. Encizo gestured for

Carson and Kagera to cover him. The pair nodded and the Cuban warrior dove across the threshold and fired his H&K chopper as he entered the room, spraying the walls with 9 mm rounds and exhausting the magazine. He hit the floor and went into a shoulder roll, then discarded the empty MP-5 as he came up in a kneeling stance.

The figure behind the sofa rose from cover, a Skorpion machine pistol in his fists. Encizo yanked the H&K P9S pistol from leather as the enemy gunman took aim. The Cuban snap-aimed and fired. Carson also triggered his Beretta chopper at the same instant. Five parabellum missiles slammed into the enemy gunman. The man's Skorpion virtually jumped from his hands as he spun about and collapsed across the armrest of the sofa. He landed on the cushions and tumbled onto the floor, out of the game for good.

"Hey, we got that one!" Carson called out, surprised by his own actions. Then he noticed the other bodies that lay sprawled across the floor. "Jesus wept!"

"I think that's mentioned somewhere in the Bible," Encizo replied, sounding more relaxed than he felt. "Get Kagera and make sure none of these jokers are playing possum. Stay alert. I'm going to check the next room."

The Cuban gripped his H&K pistol in a Weaver's combat grip as he approached the kitchen. It was a small room with a table, some chairs, a wood-burning stove and a chunky white icebox. A man stood at the back door and stared out at the bodies that lay outside. He turned to see Encizo at the doorway.

"Hope you understand some English, Juvénal," the Cuban announced as he pointed the P9S at his opponent's chest. "Do you understand 'parabellum'?"

"You!" Juvénal exclaimed, his fearful eyes indicating that he wasn't happy about renewing his acquaintance with the man he had last seen on the streets of Kigali.

"Drop the gun and raise your hands," Encizo instructed. "There's nowhere to run, anyway. You can surrender or you can die. Either one is okay with me."

Juvénal held the MAT-49 submachine gun by the barrel in one hand. His other hand rose to shoulder level as he extended the French chopper as if to offer it butt-first to Encizo. The Cuban kept his pistol trained on the man's chest and slowly shuffled through the archway into the kitchen. Juvénal still wore the big *panga* jungle knife in a belt sheath, but he didn't appear to carry a sidearm.

"Here," Juvénal said, holding the MAT-49 by the barrel and canting the buttstock toward Encizo. "Take it."

"Drop it," Encizo insisted, suspecting a trick. "I won't tell you again."

"Very well," the African replied with a shrug.

He suddenly tossed the subgun at Encizo's face. The Cuban instinctively dodged and clubbed the weapon aside with a forearm. Juvénal's machete suddenly hissed from its sheath and the African swung the heavy blade in a vicious sideways stroke. Encizo felt the machete strike the barrel and frame of his H&K pistol. The force tore the gun from his hand, and the pistol clattered onto the floor. Encizo was startled, but relieved that he still had all his fingers.

Juvénal swung his *panga* in an overhead cut, both hands fisted around the hilt. Encizo reached for the Cold Steel Tanto knife on his belt. The six-inch blade seemed like a toothpick compared to the big machete. The Cuban shuffled away from the flashing jungle knife and collided with the table. Juvénal's second stroke missed the agile Cuban, but the African smiled with sadistic confidence as he raised his *panga* once more.

"I think maybe I'll chop off an arm," he chuckled, weaving the blade of his machete to and fro. "Then a leg and maybe something else. Then I'll watch you bleed to death."

He thrust the machete forward in a short stabbing motion, but suddenly altered the stroke and swung a roundhouse cut at Encizo's head and neck. The Cuban had not been fooled by the feint. The machete was designed for chopping and slashing, not thrusts and stabs. Encizo figured his opponent was a skilled knife fighter who developed a style of using the *panga* that suited the strong points of the weapon. The Cuban held his Tanto knife in one hand and grabbed a chair, hoisting it high to block his opponent's attack.

The machete struck the chair hard, splintering the seat. A leg popped off and fell to the floor, but the chair still effectively blocked the *panga* attack. Encizo struck out with his blade. The Tanto stabbed into soft flesh under Juvénal's rib cage and sliced a deep gouge in his abdomen. The slanted tip snagged on bone and Encizo turned the knife to yank it free.

Juvénal gasped in agony as blood poured from the wound. However, the attack had failed to cause any real damage to any internal organs. The African was hurt, but he wasn't in mortal danger from the injury. Juvénal could not effectively wield his machete, because Encizo had closed in on him. The thug realized he had underestimated Encizo. The Cuban was clearly a veteran knife fighter who had appreciated that Juvénal's *panga* had a greater reach, so he had cut the distance between them to reduce the African's advantage.

Juvénal yanked his machete free of the chair and jumped back before Encizo could launch another attack. He swung the *panga* as hard as he could, and Encizo again blocked the attack. The heavy blade chopped into the chair's backrest, less than an inch from Encizo's fingers. Half the chair snapped free of the portion the Cuban held. Splintered wreckage fell to the floor, and Juvénal lashed out with the machete in a short cross-body stroke.

The unsharpened spine of the blade struck Encizo across the chest. The blow sent the Cuban hurtling backward into the archway. Juvénal raised his machete and prepared to charge. Encizo's arm snapped forward like a catapult and released the Tanto. The knife wasn't designed for throw-

ing, but Encizo was an expert with a blade and could hur
the Tanto with remarkable accuracy and force at short dis
tances.

The Tanto struck Juvénal under the solar plexus. The tij
pierced skin and muscle to cut into the top of his stomach
The African cried out in surprise and pain. He glance
down at the Cold Steel knife jammed in his flesh. Two an
a half inches of sharp metal was buried in Juvénal's belly
The Tanto wobbled slightly as the African stepped for
ward. He glared at Encizo with raw hatred and raised th
panga high.

Juvénal charged, determined to destroy the Cuban. En
cizo hopped back through the doorway on one foot as h
lifted his other leg to reach for the Gerber Mark 1 in an an
kle sheath. Juvénal closed in swiftly and swung his *panga* i
a vicious overhead stroke. The heavy blade struck the to
arch of the doorway and lodged firmly in the top beam.

"Your last chance," Encizo commented as he stared int
Juvénal's astonished face. "You blew it."

Encizo thrust the Gerber under his opponent's chin. Th
point of the double-edged blade punctured the hollow o
Juvénal's throat. The Cuban twisted the dagger and cu
across the side of his opponent's neck to slice the jugula
and carotid.

Juvénal released his *panga* and stumbled backward, blooc
gushing from the terrible wound in his neck. He clawed a
his throat as his knees buckled and he wilted to the floor
After a few minutes Encizo reached down and grabbed th
hilt of his Tanto knife to pull it free. Then Encizo shook hi
head and stepped over the body to search for his fallen H&K
pistol.

"Oh, my God," Carson rasped. The CIA agent stood a
the doorway and stared down at the bloodied remains o
Juvénal. "I think I might be sick."

"Then don't look at it," Encizo suggested. He returnec
the Cold Steel Tanto to its sheath and examined the pistol tc
be certain it had not been damaged when it fell. "Shootin;

seems to have stopped. I think the fighting's over. We have any prisoners out there?''

"Some of them are alive," the Company man answered. "One of them claims he owns this farm. Says the others took over the place and forced him to let them use it for a base. Figure he's telling the truth?"

"It's possible," the Cuban replied with a shrug. "I doubt it 'cause these hombres probably would have killed him if he wasn't one of their bunch. We'll question him with the rest."

"I think Jalingo's dead," Carson said grimly.

"I saw him go down," Encizo stated. "That's another score we have to settle before this mission is over."

15

Colonel Wukari frowned as he sat behind his desk and ex
amined photographs of the corpses strewn across the farm
property and inside the wreckage of the house. He looked
up from the photos and glared at Yakov Katzenelenbogen
Kagera and Carson. The three men sat across from the desk
and waited for Wukari to speak.

"This is a rather incredible story," Wukari commented as
he drummed his fingers next to the collection of photo
graphs on the desktop. "You say that this carnage wa
caused by just you three and five other men?"

"You make it sound as if we slaughtered an innocen
farming village," Kagera said stiffly. "The farm belonged
to Abdul Saidu. He had allowed more than thirty armed
terrorists or mercenaries or whatever you choose to cal
them to use his property as a base of operations here in Ni
geria."

"They had automatic weapons," Carson added. "Look
at the pictures, dammit. We had a big gun battle with those
bastards. Captain Jalingo was killed..."

"I am painfully aware of that," the colonel assured him
"The captain was one of my best men. I am distressed by his
death, and I'm even more alarmed by this story you've told
me about some sort of insane conspiracy involving the man
called Massamba. You know, he's been gathering quite a
large following since that terrible business in Rwanda."

"I'm with the security services in Rwanda, Colonel,"
Kagera reminded Wukari. "Mr. Carson and I have been

working with Bidault and his team since they arrived in Africa. Believe me, everything we've told you is true."

"Captain Jalingo apparently thought so," Wukari replied, interlacing his ebony fingers on top of his desk. "I've read his last report before he left with your group this morning. The captain had been very skeptical of your claims when you first arrived, but he seemed convinced you were telling the truth when he wrote the final report. Needless to say, it would be more advantageous to my government if Massamba and his people are responsible for our recent troubles instead of the United States and the CIA."

"My partners are questioning the prisoners now," Katz explained. "Mr. Giraudeau is an expert at administering scopolamine and other truth serums."

"I understand such drugs can be dangerous," the colonel said grimly. "I hope your friend doesn't kill the prisoners during interrogation. We'd like them to stand trial so we can have the pleasure of executing them ourselves."

"Your government certainly has a claim on the captives," Katz agreed. "You're welcome to do whatever you want with them after we learn more about Massamba's plans. Other African countries and the interests of the United States are in jeopardy as well as your country, Colonel. We all have good reasons to put an end to this nightmare."

"Of course," Colonel Wukari replied with a nod. "Nigeria values its relations with the United States and Rwanda. My country and Rwanda are both members of the Organization of African Unity and the Nonaligned Movement."

Katz resisted the urge to comment about the two organizations Wukari mentioned. Nearly all African countries belonged to either one or both organizations. Nations as different as Egypt and Botswana were members of the OAU and countries with as little in common as South Africa and Ethiopia belonged to the Nonaligned Movement. Membership in these organizations did not prove Nigeria and Rwanda had any common interests or friendship. Nations

of every political system are found in the United Nations—
including bitter enemies that despise each other.

The colonel was just trying to express his willingness to
cooperate with Phoenix Force and its allies. Katz was not
going to embarrass the man or risk alienating Wukari. They
still needed the help of the Nigerian government in general
and military intelligence in particular. If Colonel Wukari
wanted to pretend the OAU was a brotherhood of bosom
buddies and the Nonaligned Movement meant more than its
innocuous title suggested, that was fine with Katz as long as
he continued to assist them in their mission.

Calvin James joined them a few minutes later. The hard-
ass from Chicago seemed tired as he sunk into a chair next
to Katz. Colonel Wukari was aware the tall black American
was one of "Bidault's" teammates, but he wasn't sure which
one.

"Mr. Gird-oo?" the colonel asked hopefully.

"Huh?" James replied. He reminded himself that he had
a cover name that he still wasn't used to responding to.
"Giraudeau, Colonel."

"You were the one in charge of administering truth serum
to the prisoners?" Wukari inquired.

"Yeah," James confirmed. "Used scopolamine on those
in reasonably good physical condition. One guy has a broken back. A beam from the ceiling fell on him. The farmer,
Saidu, has a number of health problems, including very high
blood pressure and a bleeding ulcer. Too risky to use such
powerful drugs on either of them."

"What about that honkie bastard?" Carson asked. He bit
his lip and sheepishly said, "I mean the white gunman?"

"Well, I think he was in better shape before he got two
crossbow bolts in him, but he was still fit enough to inter-
rogate with scopolamine," James explained. "His name is
Henri Liége. He's a mercenary, originally born in Zaire
when it was still the Belgian Congo back in the mid-fifties.
The dude's been free-lancing as a merc for quite a few years.
Apolitical and amoral, he doesn't have any loyalties except

whoever pays him. Massamba was paying him a lot and romised a hell of a lot more when this operation is finhed."

"Operation?" Wukari asked.

"Apparently, ever since Massamba's family screwed up Chad and lost the ol' plantation," James said with a ock Southern accent, "Massamba has been trying to come p with a way to get even with everybody he figures screwed ver his daddy and make himself rich in the process. Acually he's pissed off at France for backing Habré during the ttempted coup by Goukouni in Chad, but he also thinks CIA was involved, so Uncle Sam is on his shit list, too. Massamba seems to think if he can force the U.S. out of frica, the influence of all the Western European countries ill subside, as well."

"But what does he hope to accomplish?" Kagera asked, early confused.

"Okay," James continued. "Massamba figures most of he countries of Central Africa are run by bootlickers conolled by the West. Pretty distorted viewpoint, but I guess he guy's a little twisted. He figures if the powers of the West re washed up, the economies of these countries will fall part, and the people will be ready for revolution."

"The man's insane!" Wukari exclaimed. "He thinks he an carry out revolutions in four or five countries at the ame time?"

"Nine countries total," James explained. "And he oesn't intend to do it by himself. He's got sponsors who've een helping to bankroll this venture. Massamba managed o establish contacts with radical factions in Libya, some ower-hungry white supremacist types in South Africa and n outfit that seems to be comprised of black African dicators and their followers who got kicked out of power over he years. Nice to see integration in action, huh?"

"Now it begins to make sense," Katz said with a nod.

Carson looked around at the men, looking more conused than before. "It does?" he asked.

"Three factions that appear—on the surface—to ha[v]
nothing in common have the opportunity to seize control [o]
nine African nations with failing economies," Katz e[x]
plained. "None of these groups actually represent any go[v]
ernment, so finding proof of a conspiracy would be ve[ry]
difficult. They divide up the pie, probably using pupp[et]
governments and giving lip service to criticizing each oth[-]
ers' regimes. If they can only hold on to power for one yea[r]
they'll make an enormous profit by the trade in Africa['s]
great natural resources. Gold, oil, coffee, uranium, the li[st]
goes on and on."

"And what about our people?" Colonel Wukari aske[d]
"What happens to them?"

"These guys don't care about people," James answere[d]
"Look at what Massamba's done. He's had close to tw[o]
hundred people murdered in less than a week. By the wa[y]
Henri Liége was one of the guys who shot down those pe[o]
ple in Lagos. He and a French mercenary pulled the tri[g]
gers, but Massamba gave the orders."

"Bastards," Wukari hissed, shaking his head in disma[y]
"I will personally direct the firing squad for these scum. I[n]
fact I want to be one of the men with a rifle when we p[ut]
them to the wall."

"Well, I think you have enough to put the prisoners o[n]
trial," James declared. "Saidu is ready to testify again[st]
them in order to save his own neck. Massamba is anoth[er]
story."

"Why?" Kagera inquired. "The Belgian's confessio[n]
links Massamba to this mess. He's obviously the maste[r]
mind. As soon as we can find him, we'll have the butch[er]
arrested."

"Not yet," Katz urged. "Massamba has become a leade[r]
of a strong anti-West movement in Africa. He's been a ver[y]
effective spokesman, and his rallies have received wide[-]
spread media coverage. The man's almost a television c[e]
lebrity. An international figure, thanks to all the pre[ss]

overage he's gotten since this business began. Before you
arrest him, you'll need more proof than you have now.''

"Yeah,'' James agreed. "Liége's confession won't stand
up in court. He's got two maimed limbs and he made the
confession under the influence of drugs. The other pris-
ners are all battered and busted up to some degree from
being in the same room with concussion grenades when they
exploded. It'll look like these guys had been forced to talk.''

"Who cares how it looks?'' Wukari snapped. "The mur-
derous pig is guilty. If he doesn't stand trial, maybe we'll
take care of him in a more direct and economic manner.''

"You'd better care how it looks,'' Katz warned. "Unless
we can prove Massamba is responsible, thousands of people will claim he was set up by the governments of Rwanda,
Nigeria and the United States because we were afraid of
what he was saying. They'll say the confessions were beaten
out of prisoners, and you'll see demonstrations and riots by
his followers.''

"If you assassinate him, it'll be even worse,'' James
added. "This is one clever son of a bitch, and we have to be
even more clever if we're gonna nail him.''

"Any idea how we can do that?'' Carson asked, rolling
his eyes toward the ceiling. "Every time we seem to be about
ready to solve this thing, something else goes wrong.''

"We've made considerable progress,'' Katz reminded the
CIA agent. "Massamba won't get away.''

"A couple things came up in interrogation that might
help,'' James stated. He shifted his shoulders to stretch the
muscles in his upper back and neck as he spoke. "Liége
mentioned that Massamba made videotapes of his meetings with each of his sponsors. He said he and some of the
other European mercenaries sometimes took copies of these
tapes when they went back to Europe. Tapes were stored in
security deposit vaults in Switzerland. Liége thinks other
copies were put in banks in Jordan and Saudi Arabia, as
well. Insurance to make sure none of his sponsors would
decide to have him killed.''

"It'll take some time," Carson said, his expression suddenly brighter, "but we can find out about those banks. CIA, NSA, Interpol and whoever else we need can get on this as soon as we make a few phone calls."

"By all means," Katz agreed. "I'll contact our chief of operations in the States. He can get White House authority to put the request on top priority level. Of course, I'm sure Massamba has these accounts under false identities. He wouldn't use his own name or the name of any of his men. Even with the cooperation of all these agencies, it might take weeks to locate the deposit boxes."

"We may not have to wait that long," James declared. "Liége also said Massamba was planning to meet with all three representatives and tell them about one another. Apparently none of them knew others were involved, and Massamba needed to get financial assistance from all three. He'd also decided it was time to let them know certain details. I guess even the sponsors didn't realize how big this operation really is. Anyway, Massamba was supposed to be at the special meeting while Juvénal and Liége handled the hit in Nigeria. That way Massamba could take care of business and have an alibi that he wasn't in Nigeria when the phony CIA hit team gunned down people in the streets of Lagos."

"Massamba arrived at the Lagos International Airport on a commercial airliner," Katz remarked. "We need to find out where that plane came from."

"Miller and Cordero are already taking care of that," James assured him. "They contacted the colonel's communications section and they should have a computer interface with the airport by now. Getting the schedule won't be hard, and we'll know where Massamba was before he flew to Nigeria."

Silence fell over the group as they looked at Katz, who was thoughtfully tapping the steel hooks of his prosthesis along the metal armrest of his chair. "Very good," he said. "It won't take Massamba long to realize something hap

ened to his people here in Nigeria. He may already know
what's happened. The man has clearly formed an intelli-
ence-gathering network in several African nations, and we
an only guess how efficient that outfit might be. Let's as-
ume it is very efficient and Massamba is already aware his
peration here has gone sour and we know quite a bit about
is scheme. How will he react?''

"If I was in his position, I'd get the hell out of Central
frica in a hurry," Carson stated. "I'd go as fast as I could
s far as I could manage. Wouldn't surprise me if he was
etting ready to fly to Paris tonight."

"He might take that option," Katz replied with a nod.
he Israeli's brow wrinkled in thought. "But I'm not con-
inced we can count on that. Massamba has obviously
lanned the whole operation for a long time. He must have
vested virtually all his time, energy and finances into this
ffort. He's also fallen in with some very dangerous peo-
le. His organization appears to be comprised of mercen-
ries, criminals, possibly political zealots of one extreme or
ie other. Folding up and running might be out of the
uestion. He's put too much into it, and his own people
ight kill him if he tries."

"He won't run," James said, his voice sounding con-
nced of his statement. "That bastard isn't about to leave
ow. I've met him. Talked to him briefly and gathered more
formation about him from seeing him at these rallies and
terrogating the prisoners today. Massamba figures he's
narter than anybody who might try to stop him. He likes
ie game he's playing, because he likes using people and
aking others look foolish. That dude is not going to back
ff because of one setback."

"So, what do you think he'll do?" Kagera inquired.

"We have sort of a covert war going here," the black
merican replied. "Massamba's cat-and-mouse game has
rned into a shooting contest more than once now. If I read
m right, he'll retaliate the best way he can. From his point
view, an offensive would be another attack that's de-

signed to look like part of this phony CIA plot he's tryin
to sell to the public.''

''I think you might be right,'' Katz agreed. ''If so, Ma
samba will probably put his next hit into operation as soo
as possible. I doubt he'd order another shooting and try
make it look like CIA gunmen. Not after what's happene
in Nigeria.''

David McCarter knocked on the door and entered wit
out waiting for anyone to tell him to come. The British a
appeared eager to report to the others. A Player's cigaret
hung from his lips, unlit and bobbing up and down as h
spoke.

''Got the information from the airport,'' he announce
''Massamba arrived on a flight from Cameroon.''

''Cameroon,'' James said, his eyes widening as the di
turbing thoughts formed inside his head. ''Lake Nios
Massamba's going to repeat the 1986 tragedy in Came
oon.''

''My God,'' Carson whispered.

''Now, you can't be sure of that . . .'' Colonel Wukari b
gan.

''No,'' Katz admitted. ''But there's a very good chanc
my friend guessed correctly. We don't have time to deba
this. If he's wrong, we'll find out when we get to Lake Nios
Colonel, we need a plane to Cameroon as quickly as you ca
arrange it.''

Colonel Wukari reached for his telephone and said, ''G
your gear ready and be out on the runway in five minute
Your plane will be waiting for you.''

16

oenix Force arrived at the international airport at Dou-
a. The largest and most densely populated city in Camer-
n, Douala was also a center for trade, businesses and
nsportation. Hotels and office buildings towered above
ops and fish markets. A variety of motor vehicles and bi-
clists traversed the paved roads as the five-man com-
ando team and their companions rode in the back of a
ench-made military transport truck.

Seated on hard wooden benches, the men were concealed
the canvas covering and back flaps tied down to the tail-
te. It was humid and uncomfortable in the back of the
ck. Kagera and Carson had accompanied Phoenix Force
Cameroon. The other man in the back of the vehicle had
roduced himself as Major Amban when they deplaned at
e airport.

Amban was a muscular black African with a stern face
d a shaved bullet-shaped head, displayed when he slipped
f his cap. The major wore a jungle fatigue uniform that
med to suit his personality. He was a career military man
o had served in Cameroon's armed forces since 1963,
en he was a seventeen-year-old soldier helping to put
wn the Communist rebels of the Cameroon People's
ion. Forty-three years old, Amban was a field-grade of-
er with the Ministry of Domestic Security.

"I speak both English and French," Amban stated with
hrug. He didn't bother to add that he also spoke Foulbé,

Ewondo and smatterings of three other tribal language
"What do you prefer?"

"English would be better," Katz replied. "However, mo
of us understand French, so if you feel more comfortab
explaining something in that language, that won't be
problem."

"Both are official languages in Cameroon," Amba
stated. "I'm from the west, near the Nigerian border. E
glish is the primary language of that region. Parts of it we
once under British rule, of course, and we're also quite clos
to Nigeria and do a great deal of trade with them. Local r
dio stations in Douala and Buea broadcast many progran
in English, and naturally, we get English broadcasts fro
Nigeria, as well. However, I'm telling you more than yo
probably care to hear. Past experience has taught me mo
Americans know very little about African countries and a
most nothing about Cameroon. I have a tendency to sl
into improvised edification at times."

"You can talk about whatever you like, as long as we'
setting out for Lake Nios," Rafael assured him.

"Don't worry," the Cameroon officer replied. "That
where we're headed. The message we received from Col
nel Wukari was very alarming. To be honest, there are ce
tain things I do not understand. If someone is trying to carr
out some sort of sinister plot that could take the lives
hundreds of Cameroonians, I would think we should ser
at least an entire company of soldiers to Lake Nios. I
stead, I was told by the minister that we were requested
simply post a small observation unit in the area and keep th
troops out unless individuals involved in sabotage near th
lake were spotted before you gentlemen arrived."

"If you send in dozens of armed soldiers, you'll scare th
enemy off or even clash with them and kill them all in ba
tle," Katz explained. "We want to take some alive, if po
sible. Besides, there won't be a large number of opponen
to deal with. We don't need a hundred guns, but we cou
use a hundred eyes to help spot the enemy."

"Would I be jumping to too many conclusions to assume this involves activity similar to what happened in Rwanda at Lake Kivu recently?" Amban inquired.

"Very perceptive, Major," Gary Manning remarked with a nod of approval.

"Not a difficult deduction," Amban insisted. "After all, none of us are apt to forget what happened at Lake Nios in 1986, and the similarity of that incident and what happened in Rwanda certainly hasn't escaped us. We're also aware of the claim that the American CIA is responsible. Sheer rubbish."

"You dismissed the possibility quite soundly," Kagera said, recalling that he had not been so quick to assume the CIA was not involved when the mission began.

"Rwanda doesn't know the damn Communists the way we do in Cameroon," the major answered. "We've had trouble with those bastards for nearly thirty years. The last big incident was an attempted coup in 1984. The Americans aren't apt to do things like what happened in Rwanda, but the Communists certainly are."

"The men we're after aren't Communists," Carson told him.

"Really?" Amban seemed surprised. "Who are they then?"

"We'll explain on the way," Katz promised. "Do you have radio contact with the observation group?"

"With the unit commander," Amban replied. "The observation teams are in touch with him, of course. Covering the area near Lake Nios required more then one team. I was told that my men should concentrate on observing the rivers and streams that flow into or out of the lake. That's not many, I understand. Lake Nios is a crater lake, you know."

"They might use underground streams," Calvin James stated. "If the bastards are there, they'll have to be close to pull it off. Probably within half a kilometer or less."

"Incredible," Amban said. "Now you said *if* they are there? You mean it is possible this alert is needless? There may not be a conspiracy to sabotage the lake?"

"Odds are about fifty-fifty," David McCarter replied as he opened an aluminum case to get out his KG-99 submachine gun. The Briton screwed a foot-long silencer on to the barrel of the weapon. "Maybe better than that if we're lucky."

"Lucky?" the major said, narrow eyebrows raised.

"We're hoping to get some of the men who are connected to a bigger conspiracy," Manning explained. "It's a long story, Major."

"It will take a while for us to reach Lake Nios," Amban said with a sigh. "I'll be interested in hearing this story, gentlemen."

The truck soon pulled off the paved streets and drove onto a dirt road. The surroundings became darker. It was past midnight, but the darkness was due more to the absence of street lights and the headlights of passing traffic than to the hour. The road led through forests of bamboo and ebony trees. Gradually the terrain turned into tropical rain forest. The passengers saw little of the scenery from the back of the truck, but the cries of night birds and chattering monkeys told them of the abundant wildlife around them.

Without warning, the truck came to a halt. Phoenix Force reacted immediately. Calvin James and David McCarter swung over the tailgate, through the canvas flap and landed nimbly outside the rear of the vehicle. Back to back, they held weapons ready and peered into the forest of oil palms that flanked both sides of the dirt road.

Inside the truck, Encizo drew his Tanto knife, switched it to his left hand and seized the pistol grip of his MP-5 subgun with the right. He held the knife ready to slash the canvas to create an opening for his H&K chopper. Manning moved to the rear of the vehicle, FAL rifle in his fists. Katz had gathered up his Uzi and tore back the flap at the cab to see whether the driver was all right.

Major Amban was astonished by how quickly and efficiently the five foreigners responded to the possibility of danger. Carson and Kagera had seen Phoenix Force in action, yet they were also impressed by the swift and perfectly coordinated actions of the fighting unit. The driver glanced over his shoulder and stared at Katz's face at the back window.

"What happened?" the Israeli inquired, his voice even and a calm and clear inflection in the tone.

"Gorillas," the driver replied.

"Guerrillas?" Encizo inquired with surprise, misunderstanding the driver's explanation.

"They're in the middle of the road," the driver said, wondering why the others seemed alarmed. "They'll be out of the way in a moment. Nothing to be concerned about."

Calvin James glanced round the corner of the truck and saw a large figure move across the beam of the headlights. The Chicago-bred commando was startled by the sight, but held his M-16 pointed toward the sky. The huge hairy creature walked on all fours, knuckles on the ground, partly propelled by powerful arms and massive shoulders.

"Hey, man," James whispered to McCarter. "You gotta see this. It's really somethin'. Don't scare 'em."

McCarter joined his partner at the edge of the truck and watched the gorilla shuffle across the road. The beast turned its head and looked at the men. Small dark eyes peered from beneath the thick ridge of the ape's heavy brow. It stopped for a moment and observed the pair, unsure if they were a threat. Another large gorilla appeared beside the first, followed by two smaller and younger apes and one baby that clung to the back of an older sibling.

"By God," McCarter whispered, his voice containing a rare trace of awe and fascination. "Aren't they magnificent?"

"Yeah," James agreed with a grin. He was careful not to show his teeth when he smiled, aware that many primates regard that as a sign of aggression. "Gorillas are on the en-

dangered species list. You don't get to see them living i
their native environment much, anymore.''

The apes observed the men with curiosity, but they ha
obviously seen people before and sensed they were in n
danger. James knew that the popular image of gorillas a
dangerous killer brutes is a product of pure fiction. Th
large primates are vegetarians that feed mostly on bamboc
plants. Shy and gentle by nature, the gorilla has never beer
a threat to man. Indeed, the opposite is true. The great ape
have been hunted and slaughtered by men that ranged fron
pygmies armed with spears to modern poachers with high
powered rifles. The gorillas' habitat had been torn apart b
lumber projects and expanding civilization.

The gorillas crossed the road and headed into the fores
at the other side. James and McCarter climbed into the bacl
of the truck, and the driver put the rig in drive. The vehicl
continued on its journey. Phoenix Force relaxed, but lef
their weapons within easy reach.

"You know, this is my third trip to Africa," James com
mented, "but I never saw anything like that before.''

"We have some gorillas in Rwanda, too," Kagera stated
"Most are at the national park. They're protected by law
but poachers still manage to kill about a dozen or so eacl
year. The park rangers find the dead gorillas with the head
and hands chopped off. Poachers generally leave the rest.''

"Jesus," Manning clucked his tongue with disgust. "I'v
been a hunter all my life. When I shoot a dear, I eat him.''

"I seem to recall you stocked our headquarters mess hal
with about half a ton of venison a couple years ago,'
McCarter remarked. "Everybody was eating that deer fo
about a month.''

"You liked it well enough," the Canadian snorted, awar
the Briton always had to find something to complain abou
between battlefields. "My point is, a real hunter doesn't kil
for trophies. Life is too valuable to take it for that reason
Why the hell would these poachers want the heads anc
hands of gorillas, anyway?''

"They sell them," Kagera answered. "Mostly in markets n Hong Kong, where people pay large amounts of money or a gorilla skull table lamp or ashtrays in the palm of a enuine gorilla hand."

James shook his head in disbelief. "That's sick."

"Odd that people use the term inhumane or bestial in re-ards to behavior no animal would resort to," Katz re-narked as he took a pack of Camels from his pocket. "No nimal can match the horrors committed by mankind, vhether these acts are against the beasts or against his fel-ow human beings."

"Yeah," Encizo agreed. "That's the reason we have to do nissions like this. I guess we'll keep doing this sort of thing ntil the nature of mankind itself changes."

"Then I don't figure we'll ever be out of work," James eplied.

HILLIP BOKORO tapped the heavy lead-filled handle of the ullwhip against the palm of his hand as he paced next to ne radio operator inside one of several tents of a tempo-ry bivouac. The whip was Bokoro's favorite weapon. It vas made of twisted rhinoceros hide and mahogany. Bo-oro had used such a whip many times in the past to disci-line workers when he was a foreman at Massamba's lantation. Occasionally he had used the whip against op-onents with weapons. Bokoro was usually able to disarm n enemy with a single lash and then enjoy flogging him into bloody pulp.

Although he would never admit it, Bokoro was sick of orking for the Massamba family. He had virtually been red to serfdom on the plantation, the son of a Massamba ervant. It was a harsh life, and he learned it was better to e the one with the whip than the person under the lash. hillip Bokoro grew to be a hard and bitter man.

He was also illiterate. Eighty percent of the population of had cannot read or write, and Bokoro wasn't among the rivileged few. The only skills he knew were those acquired

in the service of the Massamba family. The only educatio
he had was what they had taught him. When the Massan
bas got involved in the attempted coup against Habré's rule
Bokoro had hoped things would change. If he became
hero of the revolution, he might be rewarded with a high
ranking position in the military or internal security. The
they would have to teach him how to read and write. The
he would no longer be an ignorant flunky, used and manip
ulated by those with education and knowledge.

However, nothing had really changed for Bokoro. Th
revolution had failed, and the old man was dead, but Bc
koro was still his son's property. The younger Massamb
was even more ruthless and cunning than his father. He ha
placed Bokoro in charge of other men because he knew h
could trust a man who was so ignorant and totally cond
tioned to serving the Massambas. Bokoro was loyal be
cause he had no other choice. At the age of twenty-seven, h
was unfit for anything except following Massamba's order
and making others do likewise.

Bokoro realized that was the reason Massamba had pu
him in charge of the operation in Cameroon. No doubt Ju
vénal or Henri or Paul Dalashi would have been given thi
duty instead of Bokoro if they were available. However
something had happened to the base in Nigeria. Juvénal and
Henri had not reported to Massamba, and he had to as
sume they were either dead or the authorities had arreste
them. Dalashi had remained in Rwanda and had to sta
there to gather up-to-date information on what was goin
on, since several of Massamba's people had been killed nea
Lake Kivu. So the task fell to Bokoro, because he was th
only one left to handle it.

"Shouldn't they be there by now?" Bokoro asked the ra
dio operator, hoping the man would not realize he wore .
wristwatch that didn't work because he didn't know how t
tell time, anyway.

"It might take a while longer, sir," the radio man replie
as he slipped the headset onto his neck in order to hear Bo

koro more clearly. "This operation was put together in a hurry, and we didn't have some of the people who were originally supposed to handle this job. The men who were scheduled to guide the others to Lake Nios never returned from Nigeria. We were forced to send men who really didn't know the area very well..."

"I'm aware of that, dammit!" Bokoro snapped. He felt that the radio man was talking down to him and acting superior. "We have a mission and I don't care what excuses these men have—they'd better not fail."

"I'm sure they won't, sir," the communications technician assured him, and slipped the headset back over his ears.

Bokoro saw a glimmer of fear in the other man's eyes, and it pleased him. The radio operator might be better educated than Bokoro, and he could read and write and work with fancy machines. Nonetheless, Bokoro was bigger and stronger than the thin young man who sat in front of the field radio. Nearly six feet tall and built like a keg of nails with heavily muscled limbs, Bokoro was a formidable figure. Unsure of his mental capabilities, he was inclined to rely on his physical powers to compensate, and violence was something he enjoyed.

He secretly hoped something would go wrong with the mission. So far it was fairly dull. Bokoro had thirty-two men under his command at the Cameroon base. Only six had headed for Lake Nios on foot. The majority remained at the bivouac area in case something happened to the team sent to sabotage the lake.

Bokoro glanced about the camp. Several men sat in a circle on the ground, playing some sort of game. Others were asleep inside tents or in the trailer sections of trucks. Two chatted together as they cleaned and oiled their weapons. Bokoro wasn't sure where the rest were or what they were doing to pass the time during what seemed to be a very boring assignment.

"I just got the signal!" the radio operator announced, glad to have something to report to Bokoro, whom he considered to be an unbalanced savage. "Two short beeps. Tha means they reached the lake, and they're about to set up the portable shack, pipes and tanks. They'll repeat the signal a soon as they're finished. That'll mean they're on their wa back to the base. Looks like everything is going smoothly sir."

"I suppose so," Bokoro said with a shrug, disappointe that they wouldn't see any action that night.

"Oh, no!" the radio man exclaimed, an expression o alarm on his face. He pressed the fingers of one hand to th headset by his right ear as if hoping to change what h heard. "The distress signal just came through! One long beep. Something has happened to them, and whatever it is they aren't able to transmit a verbal message. Sounds lik trouble, sir. Serious trouble."

"All right," Bokoro declared, unable to repress a smile "All you damn loafers, listen to me! We're pulling out im mediately and going to help our comrades! Get your asse in the trucks and wake up those lazy louts inside. Looks like you'll have to earn your wages after all. Now, move!"

17

The area surrounding Lake Nios was similar to Lake Kivu in Rwanda. Rugged volcanic rock cradled the tranquil waters. The peaceful beauty of Lake Nios did not hint at the terrible tragedy that claimed the lives of seventeen hundred villagers in 1986. The soil near the lake was very fertile, and abundant vegetation thrived in the immediate region. Despite the catastrophe, farms and villages still remained in the Nios area.

The headlights of the truck scanned the hilly area beyond the dirt road. The vehicle could not travel up the steep terrain, and the driver stopped the truck. Phoenix Force, Tagera, Carson and Major Amban emerged from the rig and headed up the hill on foot. All eight men were armed, but Amban carried only a sidearm and a two-way radio as they climbed the rugged surface.

The Cameroonian officer in command of the observation teams had contacted Amban via radio to report that his men had not only spotted six suspicious characters near Lake Nios, but they had captured the intruders, as well. Major Amban was delighted by the news, because it meant the threat to the villagers near Lake Nios was over and his soldiers had dealt with the situation. The special five-man unit of foreigners would only have to collect the would-be saboteurs, thanks to the efficiency of Amban's Cameroonian troops.

They scaled the hill with relative ease. Columns of oil palm and rubber trees lined the hill, and ferns three feet high

formed a network of natural hedges. Insects and tree fr
ceased their night songs as the men approached. A b
rustled near Carson's feet, and the CIA case officer sw
his Beretta toward the sound and nearly squeezed the tr
ger. Gary Manning clapped a hand on Carson's shoulde

"What are you doing?" the Canadian cautioned i
harsh whisper.

"I think there might be a snake in there," the CIA g
answered tensely, still reluctant to redirect the aim of
Beretta.

"No poisonous snake is big enough to swallow a p
son," Manning told him. "They can't eat people, so
only time they bite a human being is if they're scared."

"*I'm* scared," Carson admitted.

"Keep going," Manning instructed. "If there is a sna
in the bushes, hanging around here will just make it m
nervous."

"What if there are more snakes up ahead?" the Co
pany man asked nervously.

"I'll keep an eye out for them," Manning promis
"Just keep moving. Okay?"

They continued up the hill and eventually reached a p
near a narrow stream. Four Cameroonian soldiers poin
rifles at six figures dressed in Bamileke garments. T
Bamileke tribe—native to western Cameroon—is noted
ornate embroidery and multicolored beads in unusual
signs. The brightly colored robes with imaginative d
mond-shaped patterns and beadwork of intric
craftsmanship certainly did not make the six captives
pear to be terrorists. However, a tarp had been pulled av
from their wooden cart to reveal a set of aluminum v
panels, two large metal tanks, a motorized pump and d
ens of sections of plastic tubes.

Several weapons lay at the feet of the prisoners. T
canvas packs and a walkie-talkie radio unit had also be
taken from them. A soldier with twin bars on his col
smiled at Major Amban as he led Phoenix Force to the si

"Good work, Captain," Amban announced with a ᴄeerful nod. "I see their disguise didn't fool you."

"The villages in this area are mostly Fulani tribes," the ᴄptain explained. "It seemed suspicious that half a dozen ᴬamileke would just happen to be in the area at this time. ʰhen we noticed they all carried military rifles and subma- ᴄine guns. Still, we waited until they removed the cover ᴼom that cart. When we saw the contents, there was no ʳom for doubt."

Calvin James walked to the cart and examined the con- ᴺts. He grunted with satisfaction that the gear was vir- ᵃally identical to the deadly equipment used near Lake ⁱivu. Rafael Encizo glanced down at the weapons on the ᴼound. Three Soviet-made rifles, two French subguns and ᵃ American M-10. The Cuban nodded.

"Same sort of international combination of weaponry ᵉ've encountered with Massamba's people in the past," he ᵃnounced. Encizo turned to face James. "You guessed ᵍht, amigo."

"Everybody gets lucky once in a while," the black com- ᵃando replied with a grin.

"The radio," Yakov Katzenelenbogen declared, point- ᵍ at the walkie-talkie with the steel hooks of his pros- ᵉsis. "They had it, as well?"

"Yes," the Cameroonian captain confirmed, "but they ᵈn't get a chance to use it."

"There's a signal key on that radio to transmit Morse ᵉde or whatever sort of non-verbal communications they ⁱght use," Gary Manning stated. "One of these guys could ᵃve sent a signal to their base by just grabbing the radio ᵈd jabbing a thumb on the key button."

"That's a short-range unit," McCarter added. "The sig- ᵃl wouldn't carry on a frequency more than two miles. ᵉy must have a bleedin' base not far from here."

"We can make them talk," the captain offered. "Of ᴼurse, they'll scream a lot first."

"Hey," Carson began, placing a hand on his stomach. "
don't want any part of something like this . . ."

"No one is going to be tortured for any reason as long
we're with this operation," Katz declared in a firm voice.

"I don't approve of such tactics either, Bidault," Kage
said. The Rwandian intel officer shrugged as he added, "B
we may not have a choice, under the circumstances."

"Torture is not only morally objectionable," Katz a
swered. "It's time-consuming and less reliable than yo
might think. If you hurt someone enough, he'll tell you ju
about anything to make the pain stop. That doesn't nece
sarily mean he'll tell the truth. To do it in a manner th
would efficiently break down an individual's resistance tak
hours. With very tough characters it might take days, ar
with total fanatics it won't work at all."

"We might do something very nasty," the Cameroonia
captain suggested. "Make an example of one, and the otl
ers will talk."

"I said no and I mean it," Katz insisted. "If they ma
aged to send a signal to their base, it probably means the re
of the group have already pulled out by now, anyway. Eve
if they didn't, they'll realize something went wrong whe
these six fail to report back to the base."

"How long do you reckon it would take for six blokes
set up the junk to pump their nasty chemical compoun
into the lake?" McCarter inquired, asking the question
large in case anyone cared to venture an opinion.

"The flimsy little shack just snaps together," Encizo a
swered, "but I'd say setting up the pipes and operating tl
pump with the tanks would take at least two hours."

"Yeah," James agreed. "Sounds about right to me, to
Maybe we got enough time to catch them if we hustle. M
jor, you figure you can get your men in the field and try
block off possible escape routes within about a ten-kilomet
radius?"

"I suppose it is worth a try," Amban replied. "We caught ese scum. Perhaps we'll be lucky enough to take the rest them before daybreak."

Amban had just finished speaking when a mighty explo-on startled all the men on the hill. The sound came from low, somewhere along the road. A yellow glow of flames tween tree trunks hinted at the destruction at the foot of e hill. Manning darted to the nearest thick tree trunk and ised his FAL to shoulder level. The Canadian marksman aced the barrel of his rifle along the trunk and peered rough the Starlite scope. Designed to magnify reflected ght by special optic fibres, the Starlite scope allowed anning to observe bright light without the risk of being inded by the glare.

"It's the truck," the Canadian told the others. "The one e came in."

Shades of yellow and green were visible through the lens the Starlite. Manning saw the flames dance about the ushed and burned hull of the truck, then spotted the arred corpse of the driver lying sprawled on the road near e wreckage. He altered the aim of the FAL and scanned e forest through the scope. Figures lurked among the trees d the tall ferns. The advancing shapes carried rifles and bmachine guns. One man fumbled with a large tubelike ject and fitted a torpedo-type missile into the muzzle.

"We got company," Manning announced. "At least a zen. Probably more. They're well armed. At least one PG or similar weapon."

"RPG?" Carson asked nervously, unsure what it was, but rtain he would not like the answer.

"Soviet rocket launcher," James explained. "Kind'a like azooka. Probably what they used on the truck."

"Jesus," the CIA man rasped, clutching his Beretta opper for security.

"You said we'd only have to worry about five or six n," Major Amban reminded Katzenelenbogen.

"Massamba threw something at us that we didn't fore see," the Phoenix commander admitted. "He didn't us backup groups before on a hit, and we didn't expect him t do it this time. We should have considered the possibility but we didn't."

"Worst mistake you can make is to underestimate th enemy," McCarter hissed through clenched teeth. "And w did it."

"What should we do, Major," the Cameroonian captai inquired, clearly desperate for advice.

"Get to the trees and find cover," Katz ordered. H glanced up and down the footpath as he spoke, Uzi brace across his artificial arm. "Tie the prisoners' hands behin their backs and—"

Several automatic rifles snarled from the tree line at th opposite side of the stream. One of the Cameroon soldier cried out and fell backward, blood squirting from bull holes in his torso and upper arm. The rifle hurtled from h fingers as the man hit the ground in a twitching heap. Th other two troopers dove to the ground. Bullets tore at th earth near them. One soldier screamed when a slug sha tered his elbow.

"Sons of bitches!" James exclaimed and swung his M-1 toward the muzzle-flash of the enemy weapons across th stream.

The warrior from the Windy City opened fire. H glimpsed the dark silhouette of a head and shoulders abov the glare of an opponent's weapon. The figure recoiled v olently as a trio of M-16 rounds slammed home.

Manning trained his FAL on the enemies coming up th hill. He saw a head clearly in the lens of the Starlite. Th cross hairs marked the skull near the temple. Mannin squeezed the trigger and saw the bullet hole appear exact where he planned it. The familiar recoil of the FAL rif rode into his shoulder, and the report bellowed into th night.

His target was already dead. Manning didn't have to
·eck on the man's body to be sure of that. The Canadian
·mediately searched for another opponent. He spotted a
·rrorist gunman who was about to duck behind a tree
·unk. Manning again centered the cross hairs and fired an-
·her 7.62 mm missile. The man's body jerked from the
·rce of the high-velocity slug and spun about into view.
·anning blasted a round into the center of the terrorist's
·rehead. The man's face disappeared under a crimson flow
· he dropped to the ground.

Manning continued his search for more aggressors but
·as distracted by a burst of submachine gun rounds plow-
·g into the ground near his feet. The Canadian sucked air
·rough clenched teeth. One of the enemy had spotted him,
·t the man's subgun lacked the necessary range and accu-
·cy. If the gunman had a rifle, Manning thought he prob-
·ly would be thrashing about on the ground with one or
·ore bullets in him.

Manning switched his FAL to full auto and returned fire
· the general direction of the enemy triggerman. A shape
·ped among the shadows and dove for shelter among a
·uster of ferns. The Canadian quickly yanked the pin from
· fragmentation grenade and tossed the explosive egg at the
·nts. The M-26 blaster rolled downhill and exploded when
· eached the ferns. The mangled corpse of the terrorist flew
·om the blast and tumbled down to the road at the foot of
· hill.

The Canadian warrior hurried to another clump of trees
·out two hundred feet from the one he had been using for
·ver. No enemy fire chased him, which meant they prob-
·ly had not seen him move. Manning pressed himself
·ainst the trunk and reached inside his backpack. It was
·kward, but he managed to locate two packets of C-4
·astic explosives. He knelt by the base of the sturdy ebony
·e and placed the first charge at the roots. Then he took a
·ecial blasting cap and tiny radio detonator from his
·ckets and set them in the soft white packet.

Manning switched on the radio receiver unit. It was ▮
bigger than a cigarette filter, but it would pick up the rig▮
low frequency signal from a quarter mile away. The Can▮
dian took a deep breath and moved on as automatic fi▮
erupted from the gunmen on the side of the hill. Manni▮
dove for cover and rolled back to the tree trunk. His hea▮
raced as he shifted the FAL into a prone position. Then ▮
realized none of the shots had come close to his position.

"I'm going to feel really stupid if I have a heart attack ▮
the middle of a gun battle," Manning muttered as ▮
planted the second C-4 packet at the base of the tree.

THREE OF THE CAPTIVES took advantage of the situatic▮
and grabbed the weapons they had been forced to disca▮
when the soldiers captured them. One scooped up an AK-▮
and started to swing it toward James's position.

Katz saw the gunman and quickly trained his Uzi on t▮
treacherous opponent. The Israeli triggered a 3-round bur▮
and stopped the gunman with the trio of 9 mm parab▮
lums. The beautifully made Bamileke robe was torn a▮
smeared with fresh blood as its owner toppled backward.

Another man dressed in tribal finery grabbed up a MA▮
49 subgun and swung it toward Katz. The Uzi fired firs▮
and a column of bullets ripped a diagonal line of gory hol▮
across the man's face. His skull burst apart like a balloo▮
full of blood and gray matter. The man folded up lifeless▮
next to another of his comrades who had managed to sei▮
an Ingram machine pistol.

A soldier, lying prone less than ten feet away, fired his ▮
fle. A 7.62 mm slug punched through the gunman's right e▮
and plowed into the socket to burrow a lethal trail in ▮
brain. Another ex-captive produced a .25-caliber pist▮
hidden somewhere in his robe and triggered three shots rap▮
fire into the face of the trooper who had killed his co▮
rade.

Katz fired the Uzi again and raked the pistolman's tor▮
with a volley of parabellums. Major Amban also saw t▮

terrorist gun down one of his soldiers and quickly aimed his French MAB pistol at the man. The Cameroonian officer pumped two 9 mm slugs into the enemy's chest before the man could hit the ground.

Suddenly a large projectile sizzled overhead and descended on the defenders, a cometlike tail of smoke trailing behind it. Phoenix Force and their companions ducked low, and the RPG rocket plunged to earth. It exploded on impact. A brilliant white glare burst from the crater at the blast point. Shrapnel pelted the Cameroonian captain who failed to find cover in time. The officer was tossed into the air in a bloodied inanimate lump. Another prisoner had raised his head at the wrong moment, and flying metal sheared off the top of his skull.

Calvin James aimed his M-16 at the opposite side of the stream and triggered the M-203 grenade launcher. The 40 mm shell rose high and swooped down on the enemy position. Screams responded to the fragmentation blast when the grenade exploded. James bolted for the gunmen's lair, followed by Rafael Encizo and Kagera. Dazed opponents were staggering about among the trees. One man howled in agony as he clutched what was left of his right arm. It had been abruptly amputated at the elbow by the explosion.

The two Phoenix Force commandos and Kagera trained their weapons on those who were still armed. James's M-16 snarled and drilled a gunman through the heart with three 5.56 mm rounds. A Massamba killer popped up from behind a boulder with a Skorpion machine pistol. Encizo promptly sprayed him with a burst of H&K parabellums. The man yelled and slumped behind the rock.

Kagera got another with a salvo of 9 mm Beretta slugs, and James swung his rifle toward a terrorist, but held his fire when the man quickly threw down his weapon and raised both hands in surrender.

Another opponent was less obliging. Although both his eardrums had been ruptured by the explosion, the determined Massamba flunky reached for a Spanish Star pistol on his hip. Encizo pointed his MP-5 at the man, but the half-crazed opponent continued to draw his sidearm. The Cuban lowered his aim and triggered a burst of 9 mm rounds.

Bullets raked the lower limbs of the enemy gunman, destroying bones and kneecaps. The man shrieked and dropped on his back. His pistol forgotten, the wounded terrorist clawed at his shattered legs and howled for help.

"No more!" a terrorist exclaimed as he stuck his empty hands into the air, his eyes wide and his body shaken by fear as he stared at the crippled comrade on the ground.

"That's up to you, shithead," James informed him.

BOKORO HELD his rhino whip in one fist and a .45-caliber Colt pistol in the other as he led half a dozen men up the hill. The terrorist commander wasn't certain how the battle had gone. He had tried to attack in a U-shaped formation, similar to the "buffalo horn" method traditionally used by the Zulu warriors. Bokoro had vaguely remembered Massamba talking about the Zulu as great warriors and praising their battle tactics. He figured a modern version of this method would be the best way to attack the people who captured his hit team.

The trucks remained parked on the dirt road, several men still stationed with the vehicles. They had been instructed to stay alert in case other opponents appeared on the road. The truck they had discovered and destroyed had been a military rig, which meant the Cameroonian army was probably involved.

Massamba was not so bright after all, Bokoro thought with a certain degree of satisfaction, although he realized the situation was very critical. The highly educated, pompous son of a wealthy plantation owner had been more worried about a team of special agents or commando warriors from the United States. Damn Americans were reputed to be gutless cowards with a lot of money. Even Bokoro knew that because he had heard it often enough. Massamba had said t himself on many occasions in the past, but the five mysterious experts from America had worried him more than all he military and intelligence personnel put together. Now it eemed the Cameroonian military threatened the success of heir operation.

How did they suspect anyone would try to sabotage the ake and why had they seized the men who were well disguised as innocent Bamileke tribesmen? Bokoro figured the answers to such questions would have to wait. The gunfire and explosions at the site suggested their opponents had put up a better fight than Bokoro had expected. He wondered now many soldiers were at the site and whether it was possible that they outnumbered Bokoro's forces.

About ten of Bokoro's men were already on the hill, afraid to venture forward, because a sniper kept at bay any who tried to get closer, and two submachine guns chopped down anyone who succeeded. *Bastard cowards,* Bokoro judged with disgust. They would either fight, or he would kill them himself....

Without warning, four explosions erupted simultaneously. Men near the blasts were blown apart, their limbs ripped out of the sockets and bodies split open. Others shrieked as splintered wood became flying shrapnel, vicious projectiles that pierced flesh like darts from dozens of blowguns. Bokoro saw his men stagger and fall, bloodied from a hundred wounds.

Gary Manning had detonated the C-4 plastic explosives at the bases of trees by simply pressing the button of a radio transmitter. The signal triggered the detonator and set off the charges. The trees burst apart at the roots, and the sheared-off trunks crashed down on the advancing terrorist troops. Two were killed when heavy ebony and oil palm trunks smashed into their heads and necks. Giant logs rolled down toward the surviving members of Bokoro's command.

The Canadian watched the enemy flee from the long wooden juggernauts. Three men failed to get clear of the

logs. They cried out as the trees knocked them down and
rolled over their prone bodies. One log got stuck and came
to a halt, but the others rolled downhill and chased the
remnants of the attack force.

Katz and McCarter also saw the enemy retreat and located the enemy trucks on the road below. Both men lobbed
grenades at the vehicles. Fragmentation and concussion explosions blasted the trucks and sent bodies sailing across the
road. Gas tanks exploded and burning fuel sprayed a trio of
unlucky terrorists who ventured too close to the rigs at the
wrong time. Enveloped in flames, they staggered about like
creatures from hell, fiery demons from another world.

A horrified gunman triggered his MAT-49 chopper and
hosed the burning figures with 9 mm slugs. The blazing
bodies dropped to the ground and lay still. The stench of
burnt flesh rose into the wind and contributed to the fear
that plagued Bokoro's handful of followers.

Bokoro himself had been bowled over by the explosions.
Dazed, he lay on the road. The .45 pistol had been lost when
he tumbled down the hill, but he still held the whip in his
other fist. Three half-stunned terrorists huddled around
their unit commander and started to help him to his feet.
The twin chatter of Katz's Uzi and McCarter's KG-99 announced the pair were chopping down other survivors still
located along the hill.

"What do we do now?" one of the thugs asked in panic,
but Bokoro had no answer. He glanced around hopelessly.
The burning debris of trucks continued to cast a ghastly
yellow light across the road. Slain followers lay scattered on
the hill, on the road and sprawled in mangled heaps among
the grass. Then a lone figure slowly descended the hill, a
large white man with a rifle braced on a hip. A sniper scope
was mounted to the frame of the man's weapon.

One of Bokoro's companions saw the figure and raised
his subgun. Gary Manning fired his FAL from the hip, and
the gunman's head snapped back, then the terrorist wilted
to the ground. The others dropped their weapons and raised

heir hands. Bokoro still held his whip and kept his arms
ow.

"Keep your hands in plain view and step away from those
₃uns," Manning ordered. He repeated the command in
‾rench to make certain they understood. "I'm talking to *all*
᠋f you. Get those hands up or you're dead."

Bokoro was surprised by the calm, even tone of the
tranger's voice. The white man was clearly very serious,
ınd Bokoro had already seen evidence of Manning's
ᴨarksmanship. However, the Canadian continued to step
·loser and stood roughly eight feet away, within range of
ℬokoro's whip.

"Hey, if that guy in the middle doesn't understand,"
Ⅿanning said, switching to French once more, "you two
ɪad better make it clear to him I'm a fraction of a second
ɪway from blowing his head off if he doesn't raise those
ɪands."

Bokoro suddenly thrust a palm into the back of his clos-
st comrade and shoved the startled man at Manning. The
ᵖhoenix pro nearly squeezed the trigger, but realized the
igure hurtling toward him didn't present an actual attack.
Ɪe raised the barrel sharply and swung the buttstock in a
ast, hard stroke to the side of the terrorists's jaw. Bone
racked, and the stooge moaned softly as he dropped un-
onscious at Manning's feet.

The rhino hide whip suddenly snapped forward with a
rack similar to the report of a small-caliber pistol. The lash
truck the frame of Manning's FAL rifle between his fists
ɪnd curled around the gun. Bokoro smiled as he yanked the
vhip and adroitly pulled the FAL from Manning's grasp.

"Hell," the Canadian groaned as the remaining flunky
harged forward and threw a wild kick aimed at Manning's
₃roin.

Manning guarded himself with a swift twist of his leg, and
ɪe kick caught him on the thick muscle of the thigh in-
tead. Manning managed to jab a short punch to his oppo-
ɪent's breastbone. The man groaned and weaved slightly

from the blow. The Canadian deftly caught a wrist in one
hand and yanked the African closer to drive a solid upper
cut to his solar plexus. The thug started to double up from
the squeezing pain in his chest, but Manning hit him with a
left hook that spun him around.

The crack of Bokoro's whip exploded again, and the lash
struck out at Manning, but the terrorist got in the way. The
twisted hide slapped the man's skull and wrapped around his
face like a black boa constrictor. The whip curled at his
throat and snaked around the nape of his neck. A half
choked wail escaped from the man's lips as blood trickled
from the split skin.

Bokoro gasped with surprise and tried to pull his whip
free. Manning quickly seized the end of the lash, which was
still coiled around its victim. Bokoro glared at Manning and
yanked the whip harder. The Canadian did not resist the pull
but moved with it. He suddenly charged straight for the
African and lashed a kick to the man's stomach.

The whip slipped free of the unfortunate terrorist's head,
and the man fell to all fours, face and neck marked crim
son by the lash. Bokoro grunted and folded from Man
ning's kick, but quickly jabbed the hard wood handle of his
whip into the Canadian's stomach. Manning gasped from
the sharp pain as Bokoro's free hand reached for his throat.

The Phoenix commando raised his right forearm to knock
Bokoro's arm aside. The African swung the whip handle at
Manning's head, but the Canadian blocked the attack with
a raised shoulder. The blow stung and numbed his left arm
slightly, but Manning immediately managed to unleash a
hard left jab to his opponent's nose, aware that the arm
might stiffen or cramp if he didn't use it quickly. Bokoro's
head bounced from the punch and blood trickled from his
nostril.

Manning followed with a heel-of-the-palm stroke under
the breastbone. The blow staggered Bokoro and sent him
stumbling three steps backward. Bokoro swung the whip in
a wild roundhouse lash. The tough lash struck Manning

across the small of the back, but they were too close and the lash did little more than sting. Manning retaliated with another jab and clipped his opponent on the point of the chin. Bokoro's head rocked and bobbed forward to receive an overhead right to his already broken nose.

The African howled with pain as Manning grabbed his wrist to try to disarm him. Bokoro pumped a knee to the Canadian's abdomen and grabbed a sleeve. Manning groaned from the blow and felt the sharp tug at his arm. Bokoro was trying to spin him about and attack from behind. If the African succeeded, he could use the whip as a garrote to strangle Manning.

The Canadian held on to Bokoro's wrist above the whip and snaked out his hand to grab the man's neck. He quickly hooked an arm around the African's head and jammed a hip into Bokoro's gut. The Phoenix fighter turned sharply and pulled. Bokoro hurtled over the Canadian's hip and crashed to the ground hard.

The whip got tangled with Manning's legs, and Bokoro tried to pull his opponent off balance. The Canadian suddenly dropped forward to land on one knee in the center of Bokoro's chest, all his weight behind the blow. The African gasped breathlessly as air exploded from his lungs. Manning's fist swung like a hammer and pounded Bokoro in the bloodied piece of gristle that had formerly been the African's nose.

Bokoro howled and thrashed on the ground wildly. He bucked Manning off his chest, and the Canadian rolled away and jumped to his feet. Bokoro got up more slowly, his eyes wide and filled with tears, his nose mashed into crimson pulp and his mouth open to try to gasp air into his tortured lungs. Manning was surprised the man could get to his feet. He was tough and he sure was no quitter, the Phoenix pro noticed. He appreciated a man's strengths—especially those of an enemy.

Bokoro still held the whip handle in his fist and drew back his arm to attempt another stroke. The lash went taut and refused to move as if fastened to the ground. Bokoro was half-blind from tears and pain in his crushed nose, and he didn't see Manning's boot stamp on the lash to pin it down. The African was confused. He thought that Americans were weaklings. His whip had suddenly failed him for the first time in his life, and nothing was going as it should...

Manning nailed him between the eyes with a hard right. The knuckles crashed just above the shattered bridge of Bokoro's nose. The African felt a blinding hot glare of brief pain and dropped unconscious to the ground. Manning reached down and relieved the man of the whip.

"Had a little donnybrook with this bloke?" McCarter inquired as he strolled toward Manning. Smoke curled from the barrel of the Briton's KG-99.

"Yeah," the Canadian said, breathing hard from the battle. "He's a tough stinker, but I don't think he'll smell any better now."

"What?" McCarter was puzzled and glanced down at Bokoro's face. The smashed nose explained Manning's remark. "Oh, I get it now. He won't smell so good. That's almost a joke, mate."

"Not very good, but I don't feel too funny right now," Manning stated. "Battle must be over, huh? How'd we do?"

"A lot better than the other side, Gary," McCarter answered, taking a pack of Player's from his jacket. "A number of Amban's soldiers are dead and one is wounded. Carson caught a bullet in the leg. I think the rest of our team are all right. Best as we can determine, none of the enemy got away. Most of them are dead, of course, but we've got a lot of living subjects to question now. Including this bloke here."

"Yeah," Manning glanced down at Bokoro. "I'd like to find out what he knows."

"What he nose?" McCarter chuckled and puffed some cigarette smoke toward the sky. "Another joke, eh?"

"Never mind," the Canadian said with a sigh.

18

Massamba swept the crowd with the kind of look that seemed to ask each man to declare his loyalty and take account of himself. Massamba then squared his shoulders in the manner of a man who has to deliver painful news. "I have just returned from Nigeria, where the CIA efforts of genocide of black Africans continued to unfold even during my visit," Massamba intoned as he stood on a platform by a street corner near the American embassy in Kigali, Rwanda. "White assassins with American weapons gunned down brave Nigerian youths who dared to criticize the atrocities that occurred in your country less than a week ago. I also heard that a farmhouse, owned by a black farmer who had a family reunion at the time, was attacked by CIA killers and destroyed by these butchers."

The voices of the crowd stirred into an angry growl as Massamba allowed his words to strike home. The group was larger than at his last rally in Rwanda. He resisted a smile of pleasure. The army was growing, and the seeds of revolution were ready to be planted.

"Perhaps," Massamba continued, raising his voice and performing a wide sweeping gesture with his arms to get the crowd's attention, "perhaps the most disturbing thing about this rumor—and I caution you all to remember that it is a rumor—is the claim that members of the Nigerian military actually assisted the CIA in this genocide. They may, in fact, even be putting together a combination of fabricated infor-

mation to try to cover up the crime and even make th
farmer and his family appear to be terrorists.''

Gasps of astonishment were heard. Massamba shook h
head with mock despair and slowly turned to face the tel
vision cameras. There were not as many of them at the ral
that morning as Massamba had hoped. One American T
network was represented, and the Rwandian press was ther
And the British, of course, were present. BBC covered nev
events in Africa better than any news service of the West.

Massamba was surprised to see the Soviet news tean
Viktor Pasternak himself stood next to his cameraman ar
a sound technician armed with a boom microphone. Tw
other cameramen with CCP on their shirts covered the ral
from different positions. Odd, Massamba thought. He ha
expected the Russians to be gone by now and certainly didn
suspect this sort of escalated interest in the rally.

''We cannot allow the United States to use our countri
for biochemical warfare tests and let American gangsters
the CIA murder our people,'' Massamba continued. ''No
can we sit by while officials in our own governments co
spire with these assassins to pursue their own selfish goa
without regard for the lives of black Africans.''

Applause erupted from the crowd, and voices cheere
''Massamba! Massamba!'' Their guru lowered his head
if embarrassed by such approval, but Massamba loved th
sound of the crowd and the cheers. He felt like a god deli
ering the ultimate truth to his loyal followers.

''Excuse me, Mr. Massamba!'' Pasternak suddenly calle
out as he stepped forward. The Russian newsman glance
about to be certain all the cameras had turned toward hir
One Soviet cameraman kept his lens trained on Massamb
but that was all right. They wanted his reaction, as well. '
realize this is not a conference meeting, but I really need
ask you a question, please.''

The crowd fell silent as all eyes turned toward the Ru
sian and the news teams from other nations wondered wh
was going on.

Massamba was angered by Pasternak's unexpected request. The Moscow pig was stealing his moment of glory, and he didn't like it. "It is an honor to be addressed by the famous and world-renowned Viktor Pasternak of the Soviet Union," Massamba began. "However, I must decline to answer any questions at this time. I'm sure you understand. If I granted you permission, the other gentlemen of the press would certainly demand equal time... That's what you call it, yes?"

"Well, you may not be aware of the fact several persons have already been arrested and charged with the murders in Nigeria," Pasternak stated. "The farmer you referred to—Mr. Saidu—and a Belgian mercenary named Henri Liége are among those being charged with murder."

"Where did you get the information?" Massamba asked while a cold chill traveled up his spine.

"If you'll answer my question, I'll be happy to answer yours," Pasternak invited with a cheerful smile.

The crowd remained silent except for a few scattered murmurs. The press corps glanced at one another with wonder, hoping to find some clue to what Pasternak was talking about.

"My question can wait a moment," the Russian announced, clearly enjoying himself. "So your question deserves to be answered first. My source of information has just arrived, Mr. Massamba."

Two long black limousines pulled alongside the curb. The crowd parted, confused and disoriented. The vehicles were obviously government cars. The back door of one vehicle opened, and Kagera emerged with the U.S. ambassador while Massamba stared at them with amazement. Kagera met his gaze without flinching. The ambassador walked to Pasternak and shook hands with the Russian for the benefit of the cameras.

"What is this?" Massamba demanded. "The American ambassador is just a spokesman for his imperialistic government that runs the CIA..."

"Shut up, Massamba!" Kagera ordered. "I spent the la few days in Nigeria and Cameroon before we returned ea lier this morning. I've been shot at by your men, and I'v seen brave men die because of you. Don't make me an more angry than I already am."

"Mr. Kagera and his friends—friends, I am pleased say, associated with my government—had quite a story tell," the U.S. ambassador announced. "And they broug me ample proof their story is true."

"These are lies!" Massamba snapped.

"Our friends are present, but they need to keep the identity secret for security reasons," the ambassador state "Please, do not be alarmed by their appearance."

The back door of the second limo opened. Katz ar McCarter stepped from the car. They wore blue suits, the jackets unbuttoned and the shirts open at the throat. Ka wore a five-finger prosthesis with a glove over the artifici hand. Both wore gray ski masks. Ironically the masks we similar to those often used by terrorists. A collective ga rose from the onlookers.

"Gangsters who hide behind masks like the American K Klux Klan!" Massamba cried. "We are supposed to take th word of such men?"

"Not at all, Mr. Masamba," Pasternak assured him as h gestured for his cameraman to hand him a small plastic cas "You need only answer this question."

The Soviet newsman popped open the case and remov a VHS videocassette tape. He held it high so all could s what he had. Pasternak smiled at the astonishment c Massamba's face.

"This is a very interesting tape," Pasternak stated as h tapped the cassette in the palm of a hand. "I saw it earlie Now, for my question. How can we get in touch with Colb Jadallah and Goubous?"

Massamba suddenly turned and leaped off the platfor to the sidewalk. A police officer stepped in his path, b Massamba slammed a forearm into his chest and knocke

n into the crowd. Massamba ran to a sedan parked near
e platform while his two bodyguards suddenly produced
achine pistols from their coats.

David McCarter's Browning pistol was already in his fist
fore the first bodyguard could point his weapon. The
iton fired a single shot, and a 9 mm 115-grain bullet
ashed into the gunman's forehead. The other saw his
rtner fall and glanced to see Katz aim his SIG-Sauer pis-
.

"Merde!" the gunman exclaimed, and dropped his
apon.

"Massamba!" the ambassador called out, worried that
man would get away.

"Don't worry and everybody stay put," Kagera assured
e dumbfounded crowd. "Everything is under control."

Massamba was reaching for the door of the sedan as the
ver started the engine. Two men appeared in front of the
r. A tall black one and a muscular white one, both in
nouflage fatigue uniforms and gray ski masks. The black
n pointed a Beretta 92-F at the windshield while his
mpanion aimed a Walther P-5 pistol. Both fired a single
ot.

Two parabellums pierced the windshield, and the driv-
s head snapped back across the backrest of his seat. His
e and skull dripped crimson from the exit wounds of two
mm high-velocity slugs. Massamba recoiled from the
rpse and pressed his body against the door.

"Make your move, Massamba," Calvin James said, his
retta pointed at the African kingpin.

"Giraudeau?" Massamba said, recognizing James's
ice. "So it's the little nigger from Martinique. Your spic
end Cordero couldn't make it?"

"He's covering another exit route we figured you might
," James stated. He glanced at the crowd that stood back
d watched with a mixture of fascination, astonishment
d fear. "You want to stand trial or go for your gun and
to shoot it out?"

"I don't carry a gun," Massamba replied as he shrugg
out of his jacket to reveal bulging biceps and a muscul
chest that strained the fabric of his cotton shirt. "See, I'
not armed. You gonna kill an unarmed black man? Th
brainwash you that good, nigger boy?"

"Hell," James remarked as he handed his pistol to Ga
Manning. "There are too many witnesses here for me
shoot you, asshole."

"You think you can handle me without a gun?" the k
African chuckled and balled his hands into fists. "You bla
boys in Martinique must be really stupid. I'm going to bre
you in two, Giraudeau."

"My name's not Giraudeau and I'm not from Mar
nique," James stated as he stepped closer. "I'm an Ame
can. Red-blooded with black skin, and I'm gonna kick yo
ass."

James assumed a karate T-*dachi* stance, his hands pois
at chest and hip level. Massamba snorted with contempt ar
moved closer, parting his massive arms and looking like
grizzly bear on its hind legs. Massamba always looked bi
but James thought the guy resembled an active volcano
black muscle as he prepared to take him on in hand-to-ha
combat.

"Are you sure your friend knows what he's doing?" t
ambassador whispered to Katz.

"I certainly hope so," the Israeli replied as calmly
possible as he watched James square off with Massamba

James made the first move. He raised his hands in a qui
feint and let loose with a snap-kick. His boot seemed
bounce off a solid wall of muscle without effect. Jam
swung a karate chop to Massamba's right forearm to try
make him drop his guard and swung a left hook to the si
of the big man's skull. His hands felt as if he had tried
beat up a marble statue.

Massamba bellowed like a wild animal and seized Jam
by the shirt front and belt. He effortlessly hauled the Pho
nix pro off his feet and tossed him head-over-heels onto t

od of the sedan. James slammed down on the metal sur-
e hard and glanced up to see Massamba raising his ham-
:d fist.

The tough gun from Chicago shoved himself off the car,
1 the fist smashed into the hood, leaving a dent that
uld have done justice to a vandal with a sledgehammer.
ssamba hurried around the nose of the car. Manning—
nding by—was tempted to hit him from behind, but he
:w James wanted to handle the fight alone.

Actually, at that moment Calvin James would not have
ected to some help. Massamba seemed to be Africa's
sion of a killing machine. James was a former top con-
der for Golden Gloves boxing and a black belt in tae
on do, but felt as if he was trying to take out a tank on
s with his bare hand.

Massamba smiled as James backed away. The big man
:ed his fingers with anticipation and moved in. James
denly launched a short kick at Massamba's groin. The
emoth dropped his hands for protection, but James's
ve was only a feint. His other leg quickly shot out in a
h straight-kick. The heel of his paratrooper boot hit
ssamba under the jaw. The giant's head recoiled, and he
ggered back two steps. The Phoenix warrior knew that a
mal man would be out cold or possibly suffer a broken
k from the kick, but Massamba didn't even go down.

ames rushed in and drove a karate ram's-head punch to
opponent's solar plexus, following by a fast left hook to
jaw and another *seiken* punch to the point of his chin.
es suspected he hurt his knuckles more than he hurt
ssamba. The African rammed a big fist into James's
lsection. It felt as if he had been hit by a baseball bat.
e American doubled up with a groan, and Massamba
pped a powerful arm around James's neck in a front-
dlock.

'I'll break your neck and tear your head off," Mas-
ıba menaced through clenched teeth as he started to
eeze.

James felt as though his neck was in a trash compact
His head throbbed, his oxygen supply was cut off, and
bones were ready to crack within seconds. He just had to
and take advantage of the one drawback to a headlock:
other guy still has both arms free. James drove an upper
between Massamba's legs. His knuckles burrowed into so
vulnerable flesh. The African wheezed painfully, and Jan
rammed another uppercut into his opponent.

Massamba swung James by his head and neck and hurl
him aside like a bag of dirty laundry. The Phoenix co
mando sailed into the side of a tour bus parked on the stre
He slumped to the pavement, dazed and battered. Bli
ing, he glanced at the crowd watching the battle. It was
school days, he thought. You meet some bully in
schoolyard after classes and he beats the shit out of y
while everybody watches.

The difference was, he thought ruefully, that he had ne
come across a schoolyard bully who could literally tear h
limb from limb before. Massamba waddled forward,
hand still cradling his bruised body parts. The African's fa
was filled with rage and a lesser degree of pain. At least th
smug smile was gone, James thought as he got to his f
and prepared to take on the monster again.

"Give him a head-butt!" McCarter's voice called
from the crowd. A product of East London, he advoca
his favorite close-quarters fighting tactic.

"Hell," James muttered. "I'll split my skull on this gu
head."

Massamba charged and swung a right cross at Jame
face. The African was enormous and incredibly strong,
he lacked experience in genuine combat. The big man
telegraphed his attack, and James dodged the malletlike
in time. He chopped both hands across the tree-trunk a
above the fist and hooked a knee into his opponent's lo
abdomen.

James stepped behind Massamba and drove an elb
smash into the larger man's right kidney and unleashed

arm like a catapult to chop his hand across the left kidney. Massamba groaned, which was music to James's ears under the circumstances. The American whirled and swung a left hook into the small of Massamba's back.

Suddenly Massamba lashed a backfist at James's head. The blow lifted him off his feet and dropped him on his back. The Phoenix warrior's head ached, his jaw felt as if it could be broken and lights burst painfully behind his eyes. The vengeful shape of his opponent towered over him as the giant approached the fallen American.

Massamba raised a size-fourteen foot and prepared to stomp James into oblivion. The Phoenix pro braced himself on the small of his back and thrust out a kick to drive his boot heel between Massamba's legs. The huge African gasped in agony and toppled backward, then dropped on his knees.

James got to his feet first, and Massamba struggled up once more. The Phoenix fighter swung a left hook to his opponent's jaw. This time Massamba spun about from the punch. Encouraged that his enemy might finally be weakening, James threw a kick to the gut and provoked an uncontrolled coughing gasp. The American raised an arm high and prepared to bring an elbow down on the nape of Massamba's neck.

But a rock-hard fist slammed into his chest and knocked him back five feet. He groaned from the punch, but it lacked the mule-kick force of Massamba's previous blows. The African glared at him, but the eyes were finally a bit glassy and watery. Blood trickled from his mouth, and he swayed unsteadily as he raised his mighty arms once more.

James waited for his opponent to make the next move. Massamba obliged with a clumsy attack, arms extended and hands aimed at James's throat. He was running out of steam and attacked on instinct without thought. James jumped forward to close the distance and lashed out a boot in a flying jump-kick. The heel crashed into Massamba's mouth.

The Phoenix veteran landed poorly and tumbled sideways onto the pavement. He glanced up to see Massamba trying to maintain his balance on rubbery legs, then the big African sank to his knees and crashed down face-first. James looked at Massamba for at least three seconds, expecting him to get up again. Slowly James realized the battle was over and he had really beaten the mountain of muscle.

"I still say you should have given that bloke a head-butt," McCarter declared as he helped James to his feet.

"Only if I could have used your head, man," the black commando replied, glad to discover his jaw was not broken after all.

James breathed deeply and tried to catch his breath. The ski mask didn't help. A red stain appeared on the gray cloth. James was aware he was bleeding at the mouth, but it was a small concern at the moment. The crowd stared at him as if he had walked on water without flotation devices.

Pasternak strolled forward with a wide grin on his broad features. The Soviet newsman nodded at James as he joined Katz, Manning and McCarter.

"One hell of a fight," the Russian stated. "I just hope they have a prison strong enough in this country to hold that brute. Thanks for the exclusive story. You were right. This was great."

"We owed you one for the tip you gave us in Nigeria," Katz informed him. "We wrapped up our mission, and you get greater media stardom. Fair deal as far as we're concerned.

"Who knows," Pasternak said with a shrug. "Maybe we can help each other again if *glasnost* holds out long enough."

A young American reporter and an older BBC newsman crowded around the group and stuck microphones in Pasternak's face. The Russian smiled into a camera and adjusted his ratty toupee.

"When will we get to see the contents of that videotape, Comrade Pasternak?" the American guy asked.

"You a Communist?" Pasternak inquired.

"No," the reporter replied, surprised by the question. "Why do you ask?"

"You don't address me as 'comrade' unless you're a Party member," Pasternak explained. "As for the tape, you can see if it you want to. It's a documentary on Soviet farming methods from Stalin to the present. Quite educational."

"But . . ." The American reporter seemed stunned.

"The tape doesn't have anything to do with Massamba?" the BBC newsman inquired, more intrigued than surprised.

"I didn't say it did," the Russian said with a smile. "Massamba believed the tape concerned his meeting with the three fellows I mentioned. That's because such a tape exists. Our masked friends found out about the videotapes Massamba kept of his meetings with Colby, Goubous and Jadallah. They learned the names by interrogating prisoners, but Massamba didn't know they hadn't found the tape. In short, we bluffed him and made him blow his cool. Columbo used to do it all the time on TV."

"Do you know where the real videotape is or who these three characters might be?" the BBC man asked.

"I can't say at this time, gentlemen," Pasternak replied.

Pasternak couldn't say because he didn't know. Phoenix Force had a pretty good idea who Massamba's sponsors had been. The CIA and its connections would eventually find the videotapes in the bank vaults of different countries, and the three coconspirators would be brought to justice one way or the other.

As for the videotape of the trio meeting with Massamba, Bokoro had talked under the influence of scopolamine and said that he believed one of Massamba's lieutenants, Paul Dalashi, probably had the tape. The Rwandian authorities were already hunting for Dalashi. Whether the tape was found or lost forever was a moot point. Massamba and his organization were finished, and others could take care of the few loose ends. Phoenix Force had successfully completed its mission.

"How come you guys aren't talking to us?" the American reporter demanded, trying to push a microphone in Katz's face.

"Voiceprints," Pasternak explained. "They can't talk because it might give people some way of identifying them if you recorded their voices."

"God, that's paranoid," the reporter snorted.

Just then Rafael Encizo drove up in a Land Rover from an alley and parked near his partners. Like the other Phoenix Force members, the Cuban wore a gray ski mask. He gestured for the others to get in. James was eager to sit down and climbed into the seat next to Encizo. Manning hopped in the back and waited for Katz and McCarter to join them.

But the American newsman wasn't yet satisfied. "Hey," he called as he moved between the Israeli and McCarter to block their path to the Land Rover. "You guys work for the American government, but you gave the exclusive on this story to a Soviet newsman instead of us. That's not very patriotic... I demand—"

Somehow a couple of elbows found their way against his side and shoved him. He clutched wildly at the air in a futile attempt to stay upright, then landed heavily on his behind. He sat looking perplexed while McCarter and Katz climbed into the Rover. Encizo started the engine, and the five men of Phoenix Force headed for the airport.

"I didn't hear what that reporter said," Manning remarked. "Why'd you throw him?"

"Oh," Katz replied with a sigh, "I guess he was just the jerk of the day."

Crime doesn't pay...
especially for the Mob

DON PENDLETON's

MACK BOLAN.

Knockdown

The Mob is muscling in on New York's building trade and the law seems powerless to stop it, but when three union members are murdered . . . Mack takes over. There's a million-dollar bounty on Mack's head and the Capos are eager to pay it. To the Feds, it's the price to pay to end the chaos, even if it means sacrificing the Executioner.

U.S. Army Special Forces battle the Viet Cong in a bloody fight for stolen territory.

VIETNAM:GROUND ZERO™

EMPIRE

ERIC HELM

U.S. Army Special Forces Captain Mack Gerber and his team drive the NVA troops out of Binh Long Province and determine to push their advantage by taking the war to the enemy's doorstep. That's where they teach the VC the first lesson in how to win a war... move in, take ground and when you can, hit the enemy. Hit them hard.

The past blew out in 2001.
Welcome to the future.

JAMES AXLER

DEATH LANDS

Northstar Rising

A generation after a global nuclear war, Minnesota is a steamy tropical paradise of lush plants and horrifically mutated insects. In this jungle, Ryan Cawdor and his band of post-holocaust warriors uncover yet another freakish legacy of a world gone hideously wrong: Vikings.

DL10-R